Praise for *The Walls Are Closing In On Us*

"Mournful, epic, revelatory: *The Walls Are Closing in On Us* tells the life of one man scaled against a world and time more richly drawn than any I've read in years. Brown writes with uncommon grace, weaving a tapestry of memory and regret so real you can feel it in your bones. This has the wonder and sorrow of Denis Johnson's *Train Dreams* and the raw power of classic Southern fiction. A sweeping evocation of a lost time and a forgotten life."

—Kent Wascom, author of the *Washington Post*'s and NPR's best book of the year, *The Blood of Heaven*

"With traces of Paul Harding's *Tinkers* and Denis Johnson's *Train Dreams*, *The Walls Are Closing In On Us* is a moving novel about racial tensions, segregation, and coming of age in a rapidly changing America. This is a book that examines not only the soul of a man but—perhaps—the soul of a nation."

—Austin Ross, author of *Gloria Patri*

"Joshua Trent Brown delivers something special with his debut novel, *The Walls Are Closing In On Us*. Part Donna Tartt, part Thomas Wolfe, wrapped in a *Stoner*-esque search for purpose . . . This remarkable novel grips you and makes you hope for another page waiting with every turn. Without doubt, the best book we've read this year."

—Dan Russell, author of *Poor Birds* & editor of *Grit Quarterly*

The Walls Are Closing In On Us

The Walls Are Closing In On Us

A novel

Joshua Trent Brown

For Branson.

"History is little else than a long succession of useless cruelties."

—Voltaire

PART ONE

1

HE WISHED THEY'D TRIED TO KILL HIM on a spring night. Or even a summer night. But now it was late fall, nearly winter, and the bank of the Log River was damned cold. The wind blew off it like nothing had ever blown before. His wisdom would have said that the trees would keep the wind off of him. But they were of no help in his moment of greatest need, seeming to step aside.

The bite on his ankle hurt like nobody's business. It throbbed like a second heartbeat. Every so often it pounded so hard it felt like maybe there was even a third. He lay there on the dead leaves, the snake beside him, dead too. "Deader'n hell," he thought then. It was something his pawpaw used to use. "That thing is deader'n hell." He chuckled at the thought of saying that out loud in this moment. So he did.

"That thing is deader'n hell," George said as he rolled over and looked at the headless copperhead. Somewhere in the struggle and the machete hacking, the head had plopped off and been thrown somewhere that he couldn't see. But the moon made sure to illuminate what he could see, and that was the snake's body glistening there to his right. After he rolled, he heard a bird fly off overhead. Probably scared off by the sound of the leaves under the weight of his rolling.

"I'm deader'n hell," he said out loud. He said it like a realization that you can't do much with other than live with the truth of it. Like a shrug.

He lay back down, wincing, and looked up at the stars. The moon sure was bright, he thought. And then he thought, why not just say it? No one is around to hear and think it odd.

"The moon might be brighter than I remember it being. But now I just thought that about the wind," he said to himself and the dead snake.

His ankle pounded on. He felt the urge to get up and get help. But he was in the woods, deep in the woods off the river. And, even if he was right about the roundabout direction the boys had taken him and then whatever direction he'd later chosen to run off towards, there was no one around to help. Nobody lived up in the swampy pine barrens. It just wouldn't make any sense. There were no roads in there, regardless. So, he figured that getting up and walking or running in a direction with his bum ankle and his otherwise tired body just wouldn't do any good. The direction of Sandy Creek was only one of his four, or more, options. He'd most likely just end up somewhere out further in the woods and tired. He figured he ought to just rest a while. He could die rested. If he imagined it well enough, he could die in his recliner back home.

There would be Mary Beth. She would be tending to CJ and Nora or making biscuits. George would be tired from a long day of being bent over rifles and revolvers, his hands would be cramped and his back tight. But he'd be happy to be resting to the sound of her washing potatoes or singing a lullaby to CJ or peeling potatoes and throwing them in the pot of water as she went. He could hear it now, the plop of the potatoes in the water. He didn't know if this was his imagination or just a frog hopping in the river somewhere close by. His ankle throbbed and he became aware of the blood coursing through his veins.

It nearly pounded hard enough for him to forget the stab wounds in his shoulder and side. Those boys had gotten greedy with him. Hanging was not enough. They got a taste for torture, with him bound up and standing on the bed of the truck, the rope around his neck. Nolan had a little Case pocketknife. The other boys kept telling him to help tie this old man up so they could get on with it. But he kept saying he wouldn't feel satisfied if this fucking injun just died quickly. The rope was basically painless, he said. He wanted to make sure this motherfucker felt pain. That is what he said, right in front of the motherfucker in question. When Nolan flipped open the little knife, the gold inlay on the handle sparkled in the twilight. For a second, George saw that the boy had carved his initials into the wood above the gold. He wondered, in that second, if the boy did that with all of his knives. Then the other boys saw Nolan walking towards him with the knife and they said all sorts of *What in the hell are you doings* but he just marched on up to George, the rope loose around his neck and tight around his wrists and ankles, and pulled back George's coat and stabbed him right through the shirt in his shoulder. George let out a howl and the boy slapped him with his free hand. The knife was still in his shoulder. Then George howled back at him and laughed. The other boys were quiet. When no one told him to stop, he yanked the knife out and gouged it into his left side, not deep enough to cause too much internal damage but deep enough to make any man crumple. But when his body gave way, the rope caught round his neck and he had to straighten back up so as to not asphyxiate. "What do you think about that, you piece of shit?" the boy said to him as he pulled the Case out of his side and stepped down off the truck. He stood there and stared at him from below, as if looking proudly on a trophy. One of the other boys came up from behind him and snatched the knife away. They argued for a minute but being evil is hard on anyone and they decided to get the job done.

But all of that was gone now. There were holes in him. And the snake had only made more. He was going to die on this dirt and he didn't want to think about those boys anymore. But still, he wasn't dead yet. He could just tell it wasn't happening this instant. And there was Mary Beth in his mind. In a Sunday dress. Leaving for church like always. Sometimes they had sex before she left with the kids. With their clothes on and everything. Before everything went wrong. He could smell her hair right now. He could see the way she would have tended to him right about now. The look of concern on her face. The look of love.

And at the thought of love, he remembered his mammy too. And he thought he might as well invite her into his thoughts first. Because she was there first and she was gone first and she took up so many of his thoughts on a normal day anyway.

"Come on in," he said out loud before he could realize what he was doing. A bullfrog croaked nearby. His ankle throbbed and his shoulder throbbed and his side throbbed and then he was back home as a boy again and all of this was gone.

2

"Georgie," his mammy would call him. She called him that for just about everything. *Dinner is ready, Georgie. Do your chores, Georgie. Don't play too hard and break something, Georgie. Good job on your memorizing of scripture, Georgie.*

In this particular moment, he was naught but six years old.

"Georgie, why don't you go play with the Allen boys?" she asked him. She was standing in their little kitchen, lighting the stove. Her hands were covered with wet flour from the fried chicken she was making. It was Sunday. She always made fried chicken for dinner on Sunday. With biscuits. It would have been his favorite day of the week if not for the fact that he had to get up for school the next day. One time he asked mammy if she could change fried chicken Sundays over to fried chicken Saturdays and she asked why and he didn't know how to explain to her that he wanted to be able to enjoy the full day for what it was without the threat of school the next day so he just said "cause it would be good" and she laughed at him. She had a laugh that could make flowers come back to life. That's what a neighborhood man said to her one time, when George was eavesdropping from his room when she thought he was outside playing. He said "Miss K, you have a laugh that could make flowers come back to life. I ought to go find a dead one and try it out. I bet we could make a killing off of selling flowers with new life, don't you think?" And his mom smiled and laughed again at this. Her name was Katherine. Or at least that was the name she was given for white folk. And then it kind of just stuck and she went by it. Her Choctaw name was Sokkot. Nary people called her that anymore, including other Choctaw people on the reservation. The man that made the joke about her laugh, his name that he went by was Bill. Young George never asked the man what his real name was but they weren't around each other much for long. Really the only thing he had to offer in George's memory was that one comment. They never made a killing off flowers come back to life.

So she asked him to go play with the Allen boys. There were two of them, Chito and Koi. They had white last names but that was only for the census, it was purely made up. The boys' father was real deep in Choctaw culture and history and George's mom talked about how he pitched a fit when the idea was thrown around of giving the two boys white names for school purposes. Like George had. And he'd held firm in that. Chito and Koi were to remain Chito and Koi.

They were alright boys in George's eyes. One was eleven and one was seven and they both thought George was their subordinate. They'd let him play games with him like anybody else but the rules were always different for him. They liked to make things a little harder for him than for themselves and then laugh a little bit when he failed at whatever the point of the game was. But sometimes they were alright. The other rumor about their dad was that he was an angry drunk and he hit their mammy and sometimes he hit them if they didn't disappear when it would start up. Usually, if the two boys were acting mean to him, George's mammy told him that the night before hadn't been too good for them and that he should let them off the hook for whatever emotion they'd decided on. He agreed. He didn't have a pa who hit him, or a pa at all. All the men who would come calling on his mammy were pretty nice to him, all things considered. That was the best part about having no pa, he thought. There weren't many good parts, so it had to be the best.

"Hey whitey," Chito said as George came in sight of them walking down the dirt path to their house.

Chito was sitting in a tire swing attached to a long, dirt-brown rope hanging from the biggest branch in the white oak in their yard. The tree was a beauty, a lot of folks on the reservation were openly jealous about it, and it had taken quite a bit of convincing Chito and Koi's mother to put a tire swing up in it. Mainly for two reasons: it was ugly, and they'd need one hell of a ladder. But she was only right in her assumptions about one of those things. It was ugly, but young boys will find a way to do just about anything if they set their minds to it.

As George walked up the path to their house, Chito yelled out "Hey whitey!" Because that's what they called him. It wasn't hard to guess why. He threw up his middle finger on his left hand at them. This was something he'd learned from them that he'd never use anywhere else, especially not around his mammy, but it was a sort of code with his two best friends. They threw their middle fingers back up at him, after taking quick glances back to their house to make sure no one was watching them.

"Want a ride? We've been out here for an hour already. 'Bout tired of swingin', if I had to be honest with you," Chito said, standing up as George got closer. He obliged and sat down in the tire. It smelled of hot rubber and mildew on account of the summer heat and the thunderstorm that had swooped over the area the night before. The boys had tried tipping it over but they hadn't succeeded in clearing all the water out and it was already stinking with the rest of the water they hadn't gotten out from past storms.

"We got to figure out a way to drain water from this 'fore too long, or we'll have a mosquito nest," George said.

"How do you know where mosquitoes come from?" Koi laughed and nudged his brother as he walked behind George to give him some swing shoves. "He thinks he knows where skeeters come from. Smarty pants over here."

"I read it in a book for class. Y'all were s'posed to read it too, you know."

"Listen, George, I don't give a dang where they come from. I care about where I can send 'em when they start biting me."

"Well that will be the problem if we don't drain this water out."

Koi kept pushing him back and forth. The wind was stale but his swinging created a light enough gust to make his sweat-beaten brow feel a little bit better. The shade of the oak could only do so much. Chito stood in front of him so some of this boy-made wind would get on him too. They did this in silence for a couple of minutes until Koi spoke up again.

"Well how do you figure we do that?"

"Do what?" George asked, his child brain already forgetting what they talked about a few minutes earlier.

"Drain this water out? I don't want no more skeeters than we already got from the ditches."

"Yeah, and pa might be real mad at us if we don't," Chito interjected.

"Right," Koi said, cutting his brother off.

George sat there thinking for a moment and put his feet back on the ground to stop the tire from swinging any longer.

"Y'all got a knife on you?"

"Pa won't let us keep them anymore, on account of the screen door."

George would have asked about the screen door and what had happened to it that was so bad that the boys had seen their pocketknives confiscated, something that could cause any young man at the time to basically give up and just sleep all day since there wasn't much you could do in the great outdoors that could be done without a pocketknife, but George already knew why his two buddies didn't have pocketknives anymore.

It was a rumor that spread through church first. Their ma had told another church lady and it had spread down until within a couple of days the rumor was flying on little notes at the schoolhouse. You couldn't have spread a more important message any faster to a group of people than this. The story went that Chito and Koi had just sharpened their knives up real good on their pa's old whetstone and they'd gone inside for a glass of milk. While inside and chugging that cold milk down to cool off their overheated bodies, they looked back up at the screen door and saw a spider. Now, Koi said it was as big as his hand and Chito said it was as big as his head, but the thing about dead spiders is the size never really matters all too much afterwards. They're just dead spiders then. Might as well be pieces of paper. So, Chito has the brave idea to go kill the thing. And they both figure that it will make their mammy happy. They grab their knives and charge over to the door. Now, Chito says Koi did it and Koi says Chito did it but, just like the size of the dead spider, this is something that doesn't matter to the story either. For the sake of the point, they both stabbed at it. And missed. And there was a big ol' gaping hole in their parents' screen door. They watched as the spider, as quick as lightning, crawled off and sped away across the floor and under a cabinet to a place where it could not be seen and stabbed at again. And their mammy rushed in to see them standing there, knives in hand, staring at the slashed screen door. But they didn't see her because they were trying to figure out how the hell they'd missed and what the hell they were supposed to do. And she got closer to them. And then she screamed at them, *What in Sam Hell are you two doing? What have you done?* And then it happened. Koi or Chito, following our logic from earlier here, spun around with his knife in hand and there was his ma's hand right there and the darn thing gashed her too. Just like the screen door. Right across her palm.

These were the kinds of things that got mentioned at church and school, and while the story might stay the same across these two places and bodies of people, the reactions could not be more different. But, regardless, here they were without pocketknives.

So George just nodded when they said they didn't have a knife on them because he didn't want to hurt their feelings by saying he already knew and he didn't want to make them relive it by asking them what happened. His ma said this was something that was very mature about him. And he said he'd head on back over to his house real quick and grab his. They nodded and he headed off.

Sauntering up to the house and sweating out of every pore on his whole body, he saw there was a car in the driveway. It looked like a Studebaker. Nice car, looked like it was clean before it had to drive up the dirt road and get mud on its tires. It was black with silver trim. George liked nice cars, even if he'd never been in one. His mammy only had an old truck that half the time had to be pulled to start and had rust in just about every spot you could imagine. And it had no windows left in it so they had to lay a bed sheet over it every time it rained. They cut a hole in the passenger side floorboard too, to drain any water that might pool in it. It's where he got the idea for the tire swing.

As he walked in the front door, he saw into the kitchen and, unless it was a trick of the light, there was a tall white man standing there with his hands on his hips and turned towards the side of the kitchen that was cut off by a wall. He could hear his mammy saying something to the man, in a whisper.

George tried to ease the door shut behind him so they wouldn't notice he'd come in, but it was too late and the man had already noticed him coming in. Probably caught the light change in his peripheral, a word that his school teacher used and that he'd caught on to because he thought it was beautiful and hard to say. His ma told him he used it too much, so much that maybe he didn't know what it meant, but she was only just playing.

The man turned to George and his ma stopped talking. The man raised an eyebrow and didn't step forward or move or anything. George didn't either. After a moment he turned back to look at his mammy and said, "Is that him?"

George's eyes had finally adjusted to the dimness of the house then and he could see the man. He was wearing a suit. George had never seen a man in a suit at his house before. He had probably only seen a couple of men in suits his whole life, and usually it was the pastor. His hair was short and swooped over to the right and his jaw was sharp. He looked like one of them movie stars George had seen a few times at the movies when his mammy's salary permitted.

His ma walked around the corner and looked at George. Her face was more concerned than he expected. But not concerned like George had done something wrong or like he was in danger or something. Like she was sad that he was there at that moment.

"Yes," she said, sighing. "Hey baby, what are you doing home so soon?"

"I just," George looked back and forth between her and the man. "I just needed to get my knife."

"What for?" she asked, cocking her head to the side. The man smiled beside her.

"We're working on the tire swing."

"It'll need more than that."

"It's got water in it. On account of the storms. So I thought we could put a drain hole in the bottom of it."

"He's pretty smart, ain't he? And pretty white too, if I must say." The man walked towards George and knelt down to look at him. When he was up close, there was something very familiar about his face and the way it was structured and his eyes and his teeth as he smiled but there was also something that made George want to get the knife and leave, as long as he knew his mammy was okay. "Son, er, George, is that your name?"

"Yessir."

"Good manners. You'll do alright. Especially if that complexion works out the way it is. You'll do alright."

He stood up and turned back to George's ma.

"Is he pretty smart?"

"Yessir, I am," George answered him directly. The man turned back to him.

"Yessir, you are," he said, nodding and rubbing his clean-shaven chin.

"Alright, well, I better get going. You know the deal; this stays between us. And I already gave you the money." He patted his coat pockets absentmindedly. "Yes, I already gave you the money. Let me get out of here then."

As he walked out the door, George turned to him and asked, "You didn't tell me your name."

The man turned around and replied, "That don't much matter, son. Not necessary." And he was out the door and to his car. George turned back around to the kitchen and his mammy was already back around the corner. He could hear her doing something, maybe scrubbing a pot. He walked in the room where she was.

"Who was that man?"

She didn't turn around after a few moments and he shifted uncomfortably with his hands in his pockets.

"Ma, who was that man?"

She turned around finally and her face was red. Her eyes were squinted and running with tears.

"You didn't hear what he said? It don't matter. How about you get your knife and go on back to playing, honey? Dinner will be ready same time as always."

He said okay and retrieved the knife, practically running to his room and out the house and up the path. When he got back to his two friends, they asked him if he'd seen that car go by, that real nice black one. He just nodded.

"It sure was nice," Chito said. "Anyway, you get that knife?"

3

Breath.

George's mammy used to say that we should thank God for the breath in our lungs. We should thank God for breathing as soon as we wake up. Breathing and our heart beating and the sun rising and our eyes opening. All that and more.

But George couldn't always breathe that well. When he was young enough that he could not remember anything he did, his mammy said that he had the first episode. He was sitting there on the floor, a crude wooden train between his legs, in the middle of the kitchen while she cleaned up after dinner. It was winter, so she told him. She said that he had been talking up a storm and making all kinds of noises that might have come from a locomotive with the "choo choo." And then he wasn't making any more noises. She didn't think it odd until a couple minutes later when she turned around to give him a quick motherly glance and he was drawing in a breath as hard as he could. Just sucking on the atmosphere. Trying to pull in everything in the room, if he could, but if he couldn't, just enough oxygen to fill up the size of his two little boy lungs. She cocked an eyebrow up at him but didn't do anything. She thought he was joking. Learning a new funny trick. But she watched as he kept inhaling harder and harder. His face grew redder and redder. And then he just sat there still, like he couldn't inhale no more but nothing had come in so he might as well wait to see if something happens at the top of the incline before coming down. With a woosh and a great heave, he let every little bit of air he had out, seeming to grow tired of the straining.

"Georgie," she screamed.

He looked up at her. He took a tiny breath. One that didn't require voluntary action. He asked her, "What?" His little voice was hoarse.

"Are you okay, baby?"

"Yeah." He coughed and took another breath that sounded like a crackled whistle instead of a small gust of wind. "Why?"

She stared down at him with a look of concern on her face that his little head couldn't understand until he drew in another breath that just didn't seem to want to go all the way inside of his chest, like somebody had tied some twine around him and the air could only go so far down his throat before whooshing back out, like someone had a hold of his lungs and was squeezing the dickens out of them, like he'd squeezed that frog one night when it was getting dark and he was out past his normal time but Chito wanted to go catch a frog by the creek, *bokushi* was what Chito would say, because he was proud of the Choctaw he'd learned from his pa, *let's go to the bokushi and catch a couple frogs*, and George would look at him and say *what are we going to do with the chukpʋlantak when we catch it*, wanting to impress Chito with the couple of words his mammy had taught him when he was complaining that no one taught anything but English to their children but that was only sometimes, most of the time she said she was glad that he could be in a white man's school and he would ask her why and she wouldn't have a real answer, most times she would even say that she knew she was wrong for thinking that but it's just what she thought, really.

Chito would say *what does it matter what we do with them once we catch them.*

George would say *I don't want to hurt them.*

Chito would say *it ain't nothing but a chukpʋlantak, fraidy cat. Just a little ol' frog, George. Can't feel nothing no way.*

And then they'd catch one and it was usually Chito who caught one and he'd poke it and laugh at it when it ribbeted in his hand and he'd squeeze it in his hand until the thing's eyes were about to pop out of its head and then he'd push his hand out in front of George to take it. George hated how slimy they were but he had to admit they were funny. George would hold it and squeeze it gently until he felt bad enough that he acted like it jumped right out of his hand and back into the creek.

That is how he realized that he felt then. Like he was that toad in his hands, his lungs squeezed tight, only exhaling. His eyes bugging out of his head. If he wasn't suddenly so afraid of what was causing this to happen to him, he might have ribbeted.

His mammy must have noticed the quick change of fear on his face because her face of light concern turned into a face of such heavy concern and consequence that only a mother's face can show. George would never know what the concern of a father's face might look like, even when he was much older—they do not put a mirror in front of your face when your child does something terrifying. She reached down and picked him up. But he was already nearly too heavy for her to pick him up and she had to strain so hard that her face became as red as his by the time she was able to get him up and onto her hip.

"Georgie, are you having trouble breathing?"

He tried once more to breathe. It just wouldn't work. He wheezed and his mouth let out a tiny train whistle. At the same time, they felt the rumble of the railroad through town. In another instance, this might have been a moment for shared laughter.

"I think so," he replied. When he spoke and he heard out his own ears for the first time how weak his voice was, it only made him more afraid. And he started to cry.

These episodes—that's what mammy started to call them, his episodes—would come and go. Most were short lived, no matter how frightening they were for him and her. But they became a bigger issue when they started happening outside of the house and the comfort of his ma.

Once, three years after that man had come to his house, when George was nine, he was with a whole group of boys from around town. He and his two brother friends decided to go for a walk down to the baseball diamond—the first time he'd ever been—where the older boys often were on summer days. The older boys that weren't old enough to be working, at least. What they found when they got there was not a baseball game though, but a load of young fellas running back and forth and doing what only could be described, from George's point of view, as what his mom had called "hoopin and hollerin." It had rained recently and they all seemed to be muddy enough to make any mother angry. White shirts were browner than deer hide and, for any of the boys that had them, shoes were no longer shoes of cloth material but things that looked as if they'd been formed straight from the very earth to walk around in. As legs pounded and pumped and the group of boys played, the whole world seemed to George like it had shrunk. There was only this—this coalescence of young boys. He had never seen a group so big, all together. All having what looked to be fun. He couldn't help but smile at it.

"What are y'all doing?" Koi asked one of them as they walked up on the crowd of Choctaw, and a few white, boys. At the present moment, two of them were lined up side by side and most of the flock was yelling at them. Yelling short phrases and single words like "Go!" and "Run fast!" and "Beat him!"

"We're racing," the older boy said, in between chews of what couldn't have been gum because they knew he was too poor to afford gum. He didn't turn towards them, still watching as the two boys prepared side-by-side for whatever it is they were doing.

"For what?"

"Huh?" the boy said, spitting a wad of dark stuff on the ground and turning towards them.

"Well obviously I can tell y'all are racing," Koi said. "But why are y'all racing?"

"We're gambling," the boy said, looking down at George and squinting his eyes. "Say, are you the boy with just a mama?"

"Yeah."

"I heard you had a white daddy."

Koi stepped in between them as George looked in disbelief.

"What are y'all betting on?" Koi asked. "Who wins and who loses?"

"That's about it," the boy said, averting his gaze back to Koi.

"What are you betting with?"

"I'll be damned if it ain't nothing but questions from you boys."

George had never heard one of his peers say a curse word before. He would never disrespect his mammy by talking like that and he knew that neither Chito nor Koi cursed on account of the butt whooping they would receive if their pa ever found out about it, and he couldn't hide his confusion with this boy who kept saying things that just didn't make any sense.

"What's your name?" George asked him.

The boy grinned. He had more teeth missing than he had teeth present.

"If I didn't believe you weren't messing with me. My name is Abi. What's yours?" He stuck out his hand and George reached back out to him, wide-eyed.

"It's George."

The older boy laughed, a big hearty laugh like he was a fat old man and not a skinny native boy.

"You got brown skin, and you go by George. Alright. Want to race? George?"

"You don't have to, Georgie," Chito whispered beside him, just loud enough for his ears.

Behind Abi, they heard another race begin. The hoopin' and hollerin' got louder as young feet pounded hard clay.

"How far do you have to run?"

Abi's face lit up into a grin.

"Oh, not too far. Hundred yards."

"How they measure that?" Koi asked, one hand on his hip and the other shading his eyes from the sun.

"We had one of the white boys bring a yard stick."

"Oh."

"No, you dummy, we just guessing. What do all our pas say? Eyeballed it. Yeah, we eyeballed it."

Koi chuckled like he was in on the joke.

"So, what do you say, George? You look like you might be pretty quick, what with you being skinny and pretty tall. For your age at least."

"Who will I race?"

"Hm," Abi turned back around and surveyed the crowd of boys, one hand rubbing his jaw like he was really contemplating it, the way they'd all seen an adult do at some point, especially the men with beards to rub while they thought something over.

"How about me?"

"What? You're way too old and big to race him," Koi interjected.

"Hey, man, slow down. Hold your horses. *Hokli chim issuba.* You know that? You speak the language?"

"Yeah, 'course," Koi replied.

"Right, of course you do. Well *katanlichit hokli.*"

When he said this, he looked back over at George and Chito.

"Hold tightly," he said, with that same grin. "Okay, so I say we race, me and you, George. But before anybody else says something about it, I think we can do it fair and square. I will run backwards the whole way and you can run as fast as you can the normal way. What do you think, pal? Does that sound fair?"

Before Koi or Chito could say anything else, George said: "Sure. But you never said what we're betting with."

"You don't got no money, George?" Abi asked him. The grin never left its perch on his face, just below the tiny hairs under his nose that he heard his mammy call peach fuzz one time. Before George could reply to him that no, he didn't have no money because he almost never had even held any money in his hands except for the times that his ma had given him the money to pay for groceries every once in a blue moon, that was another thing he'd heard her say one time, in a blue moon, and even if he did have money of his own he wouldn't bring it down here with all these boys he didn't know and didn't trust who might be liable to take it from him or at least beat him in a game like running and then rightfully have it. He would have said that his mammy told him to never take money anything but seriously because there never was enough of it, even if you had a whole bunch. That was something she had said not a week before this. He would have said that the question made him mad because his mammy also told him that you're never supposed to ask somebody if they got money on them unless they owe you some and you absolutely, and then she repeated the word there, absolutely, have to get it from them. But the boy spoke again before George could say any of that.

"I'm just messing with you, George."

"Okay," was all George replied to that.

"We ain't betting anything but the right to brag that we won at school and everywhere else we might want to brag about it."

"What's there to brag about beating a boy that's littler than you in a race?"

"You ever won a race running backwards?"

"No, but I'd like to. And I think anybody ought to brag about it if they do."

With that, he turned and walked towards the front of the group of boys where the makeshift starting line for the races was. All the other kids stared at them as they walked in the open space and Abi shouted out that he and his new friend George were going to race. And before anyone could say anything or ask any of the questions he'd already been asked, he added the main point. That he was going to run backwards. All the boys gasped and laughed and hooped at this. One came up and grabbed George by the shoulders and put him in his starting mark while Abi got himself set and looked over his shoulder towards the finish line, a boy standing at what was supposed to be one hundred yards out.

"Kil itti bailli," Abi turned and shouted at George over the shouting around them.

"What?" George shouted back.

"Let's run this race. White boy."

Before George could understand why he said this to him, the same boy who had put him in place yelled out to them.

"Ready. Atuchina, Atukla, Tikba. Ishtia!"

George jumped out, moving his legs forward as fast as he could. To tell the truth, running was one of his favorite things to do. Sometimes he'd run all the way to Chito and Koi's place just because, or run all the way back home even when he was too tired to do it. He loved the feeling of the wind rushing around you while you put everything you had into going faster. He loved watching cars go by fast. He wished he could be one. He didn't want to own one. He just wanted to run as fast as one. So this race was no different.

The sounds were suddenly gone from his ears. Even though he knew they were still there, he could no longer hear anything. It was just him and the boy one hundred yards away. And the boy was getting closer and closer, while George's heartbeat pounded and soon became the only sound he could register over the wind around him. He breathed hard, sucking in the air to give his legs every chance they could have.

He looked to his left once, to check where the older boy was. He wasn't in front of him. He turned his head a little more. He wasn't right beside him either. He finally glanced far enough back behind him to see that the boy had fallen down, flat on his back.

George stopped, no more than ten feet from the finish line, skidding on the clay as he tried to turn his body back to Abi. He didn't notice immediately that his chest was starting to hurt him like it did sometimes. He sprinted, just as hard as he had been going the other direction, towards his opponent. The boy marking the finish line yelled out "Hey what are you doing?" And to be rightly honest with you, George wasn't totally sure of the answer to that.

As he approached the boy, coming up on the top of his head laying there in the dirt, George asked him if he was alright.

"Yeah," Abi said. His chest lifted and sank back into the ground over and over again as he breathed in. "Just tripped."

"You want some help up?"

"Yeah."

George walked around to where the boy's feet were and reached out a hand. The boy used one hand to start lifting himself up and reached out his left hand to grab George's.

"Can you move just a little closer?" he asked.

George leaned in, his head out past his toes.

The boy grabbed George's hand and pulled him down to the clay in one swift motion. He did it so fast that George didn't even blink. He just saw sky and trees and then dirt in his eyes. He hit the ground headfirst, right on his ear. The boy jumped up and, like nothing had happened, starting running backwards towards the finish line again. He didn't even run fast, he was barely doing more than walking. And all the while, he and every other boy there that wasn't Chito or Koi was laughing.

George stood up. The boy was still a good twenty yards away from the finish line. He dusted himself off and saw that Chito and Koi were coming. But he shook his head at them and started running too, chasing down that awful boy.

His breaths got harder and harder to pull in. He felt his chest tightening but he just thought it to be from how angry he was. He caught up with Abi quickly. And the boy's eyes widened in surprise.

George didn't even notice then that he had crossed the finish line, or the boy that marked it who had a look of sheer shock on his face like he couldn't believe the turn of events that had just taken place before his very eyes, like the hounds of hell had just appeared before him or like an Olympic runner had just walked up and offered free lessons or like God had come down and told him that he was doing a good work being the finish line boy. George's head was down every bit of the last five yards to the finish line, after he'd passed Abi, and the extra ten yards he ran before the finish line boy yelled *Hey dummy, stop running, you won.*

George looked up. There was no one in front of him. He turned around and Abi was standing beside the boy, huffing. His face was as red as an apple.

But George couldn't celebrate this because, when he went to smile, he realized that he couldn't get in a breath at all. He put his hand on his chest and lifted his head a little bit and opened his mouth wide and sucked in air as hard as he could. But it stopped at the bottom of his throat. He tried again and again and again.

Pretty soon, a swarm of boys was around him. They were all cheering and patting him on the back. Chito and Koi were right there in the mix. Bragging rights had been won. But none of them noticed that he hadn't caught his breath in well over a minute. And then he collapsed, right there in the middle of them.

All the young boys got quiet and looked down at him. Half of them ran away, wanting nothing to do with what looked to be the killing of a boy. And a boy who was rumored to be half white, at that. Most of the other half just stood there, staring down at him, his eyes closed and his nose running. Abi was nowhere to be seen. He had walked off into the trees to cry, where he could be alone in it. Koi jumped down on the ground beside him and asked if he was okay. Then the two brothers lifted him up and ran him home together, sprinting faster than any racer had that day.

4

A SNAKEBITE. As George lay there on the riverbank, the throbbing in his leg still reverberating with venom-laced blood, the pounding of his heart beating all the way down from his chest to his ankle, the growing palpitations drum, drum, drumming throughout more and more of his body until pretty soon he figured he would cease to be a man but instead just an echo of poison, he remembered a snakebite from days gone by.

It wasn't his leg, then, that found itself with two puncture marks from a slithering demon. But he remembers it all the same. Or, the rumblings and repercussions of it, that would tug at him on down the line.

His mammy. He thought for a second that he saw her then.

5

"Shit," Chito screamed out as he ran home with a limp and unconscious George in his arms. He nearly threw his friend on the ground and his brother had to hop over and grab the boy, holding the body up in his arms like a hero with a damsel. "Shit, shit, shit."

"What?" Koi yelled.

"Snake."

"What?"

"A snake. It bit me."

When it rains, it pours. That's another thing his mammy used to say to him.

But what about when it's sprinkling? he'd asked her more than once.

Baby, we're not talking about real rain, she'd reply.

Then what are you talking about, ma?

There's a word for it. I've heard the white pastor talk about it. What is it? She'd look at the ground and squint her eyes like her brain was straining and pulling out every box on every shelf to find the word.

Proverbial. That's it. It's proverbial rain, Georgie.

What's that mean?

It means it ain't really about rain. Rain is just standing in place of whatever other bad thing is going on. And in this case, the saying is pointing out that when one bad thing happens, it just keeps on coming. More and more bad things. Until it breaks, eventually, and the sun shines again. But while it's raining, it's pouring down. Big thundercloud. Lightning and rain drops the size of cotton balls.

George would look at her and then look back to whatever he was doing, playing with a toy or fiddling with the radio or something, and then he'd look back up at her. And he'd say, I just don't think I get it, ma.

What is it that you don't get, baby?

Why talk about rain when you could just talk about what's going on?

And she'd laugh. And she'd tell him that he always did cut right to the chase, didn't he? And he wouldn't understand what that saying meant either but at that point he didn't care to go down another rabbit hole of misunderstandings.

"Where did it bite you?"

"My ankle. Shit, shit. My ankle."

"Do you see the snake anymore?"

Both of the boys moved their eyes around the dirt. If they weren't scared shitless before, they were then. They scanned every patch of clay and every patch of grass they could see. There was no snake around. At least not any longer.

"You say you got bit by a snake?" Koi asked, still looking around at the ground.

"Yes," Chito cried.

"Show me."

"You don't believe me?"

"Just show me where he bit you."

Koi sat George down on the ground and Chito lifted his pant leg up just enough that you could see his ankle over his shoes. Koi bent down over their still passed-out friend and peered at his brother's ankle. Sure enough, as tangible as a pinch of salt is between two fingers, he saw there were two little bite marks.

"Son of a bitch."

"What do we do?" Chito's voice trembled and he started to cry.

"We gotta get you and George on back home to pa and mama."

Koi stood back up and patted his brother on the shoulder. He hoped that this gesture would do something, anything, to cheer him up enough to get back to their house.

"What kind of snake was it? Any idea?" he asked before reaching down to grab George.

"It was a—"

Just then, Koi stared at Chito's feet, where George lay. Chito followed his gaze. And there it was again; the snake had slithered up the dirt to their unconscious friend. Adrenaline rushed through them and time slowed down like molasses and Koi just followed along with whatever his brain told him to do. He jumped over George's body and stomped as hard as he could on the head of the snake. He didn't even look at it. He just brought his body weight down on it. He jumped off and looked back down. The body of the reptile was still there writhing on the ground but its head was flattened out like a flapjack and no longer moved.

"What is it?" Chito asked his brother, never having moved.

"A cottonmouth."

Chito began to cry again, harder this time. Koi looked down and George had woken up but he wasn't moving. His breathing was still shallow and letting out hoarse whispers.

THEY PRACTICALLY busted the entire screen door off its hinges flying into their house, their mom speechless as she saw Koi carrying most of the weight of their friend and sweat soaking his shirt and pouring down his head like it had just rained on a cloudless Mississippi day, Chito out of breath and dragging his left leg around like he was an undead rising out of his grave or a zombie or whatever they called them in one of those picture shows, George with his eyes barely open and his mouth cracked just enough to let in the little bit of air that he could while his chest caved in and expanded every half minute or so. She turned around and stared at them like she didn't know what she was looking at. This little legion of horribles, this band of adolescent wanderers that seemed to just come in from a cattle drive across the west, their clothes tattered and dirty and their faces and arms dustier than their clothes. They didn't look like the little fellas that left that morning. Koi sat George down on the kitchen table in front of her and looked up at her, expecting his mama to do something that he couldn't do or say something that he couldn't say.

All she said was, "What happened, KK?"

"George raced this older boy and the boy tricked him and tripped George and then he got up and chased the boy down and beat him and then everybody was cheering and—"

"Koi, baby, slow down."

Behind the boys, the screen door swung open again. They turned around to see their father. His hands were covered in grease.

"Truck wasn't running."

"Koi, keep going."

"What's that boy doing on my kitchen table?" their father asked.

"He won the race and we was all cheering for him and then me and Chito looked down and he was laying there on the ground. He wasn't breathing. And everybody just stood there and stared at him."

"Is he breathing now?" their father spoke up again, moving between the boys to check George's pulse, two fingers to his small neck.

"Yeah, he woke up a little bit and started breathing again on the way home. We figured he ought to be getting back to his mammy since he was passed out so we carried him back here. Running and everything."

"He's awake. George, you alright?"

George looked up at him and nodded. His head was weak and tired from lack of oxygen but he was still making it.

"But then we was running home on the road and Chito jumped and started screaming and almost dropped George."

"I got bit," Chito said. Koi nodded his head, scratching his hair and looking from his brother and down to the floor and back again. They both waited for either parent to say something.

"You what?" their ma asked.

"I got bit."

"By what?" their pa asked.

"A snake."

Their ma put her hand to her chest and her eyes got big like a bug's.

"What kind of snake?" their pa asked.

Chito looked for Koi to answer. He did.

"A cottonmouth."

"Christ."

"You sure it was a cottonmouth, Koi?"

"Yessir."

"How you know? You see it?"

"Yessir. I killed it."

"Christ," their ma repeated.

"You killed it. You killed it," he said, muttering to himself. "How you feel, Chito boy?"

"My leg hurts."

Their pa walked over to Chito and bent down, gently grabbing the cuff of the boy's pant leg. He nodded to it as if to ask if this was the right leg, the one that was hurting, and Chito nodded back. He pinched the cloth between his fingers and pulled it up. The ankle was there, the bite there too, as bright as day. But the ankle wasn't the same as it had been just a half hour before. It was twice as big, maybe three times. And turning blue.

"Christ."

"Alright. C'mon. Go on out there and get in the truck. We got to get you and your friend there to a doctor this minute."

"Should I go tell George's mama?"

"We'll go to her first. Just come the hell on."

At the doctor, George's ma did the talking. It wasn't much of an office, just a couple of rooms in a storefront. It shared a front door with a tailor.

When he asked about George's history of breathing problems, his ma did the talking.

When he looked at Chito's leg, she still did the talking.

When he handed her a pack of cigarettes and said they were good for asthma, the boy just needed to smoke one or two whenever he started feeling symptoms, she just nodded and took them.

When he said he'd need to amputate Chito's foot at the ankle, his mama turned and looked at the two other parents.

"Christ," Chito and Koi's ma said again. She fell out on the floor. The doctor had to help their pa get her up and laid her on the couch in the other room. She didn't wake up until it was all said and done, and the only way she did was with something the doc called "smelling salts" that he had a jar of. All he had to do was hold it over nose.

"What do you mean by amputate, mister?" their pa asked once he'd put their ma down on the couch.

"Well, sir, I mean I'll have to cut your boy's foot off."

"Why in the hell would you do that?"

"Because it's already dying."

"You ain't got nothing you can stick in it? Or some medicine he can take?"

"Cottonmouth venom is bad stuff, sir. It eats away at your flesh. It's already started on his ankle. Once it gets puffed up like that, there isn't much I can do. I'm going to give him a shot so as to make sure it doesn't spread any further, but I can't make sure of that until the point of infection is gone. I understand this is hard to hear—"

"You better be damn sure you have to cut my boy's foot off before you do it."

"I'm as sure as I can be, mister."

Their pa stared him directly in the eyes. Nobody noticed or had a single thought towards how Chito might feel about this, standing just a few feet away from them and hearing it all. Nobody wondered how he might be feeling about it. Until he spoke up.

"You gonna have to cut my foot off?" He spoke so quiet they barely heard him. The doctor turned and his face softened. Their pa did the same thing.

"Son, I'm sorry to tell you this. But a life without that foot is going to be much better than no life at all. I will give you a numbing shot and some medicine so you'll go to sleep. You won't feel a thing."

The boy was inconsolable after that. They had to pin him to the surgical bed to give him the medicine to make him pass out. And their pa was done talking at this point. He couldn't bear to say anything else. He just stood there and watched the entire operation.

At the end, George's ma still did all the talking. She paid with money that nobody asked where it came from but everyone wondered. And they went home, George feebly smoking a cigarette for asthmatics—a word he'd never heard before that he apparently could be classified by—and his friend Chito walking on a wooden crutch, bandages over the end of his leg, where the foot of a young boy who was just trying to get his friend home used to be. George thought hard about friendship and what it'll make you do. He put out his hand to Chito and the boy reached out and held it.

At Chito and Koi's home, George and his mammy stayed around for a while. Many families from the reservation trickled in late into the evening until the small house was full and they were pushed out into the yard. The boys sat in the grass by the tire swing to get away from the crowd. As it was getting dark, someone walked up to them in the shadow of the tree.

"Who is that?" Koi asked to the darkness.

"It's me." Abi appeared in front of them, stepping close enough that they could finally see him.

"What do you want?" Koi asked.

"To say I'm sorry."

"Okay," Chito said.

"You gonna forgive me?"

"Maybe," George said.

"I feel like it's my fault."

"It is," Koi said.

"No it's not," Chito interrupted, standing up on his crutch and walking over to the boy. "Thank you for saying you're sorry."

The boy started crying and George asked him if he wanted to sit down with them. Koi huffed with an air of drama and got up and walked back inside the house.

6

WHERE DOES TIME GO? As a child, just a young boy, he thought that days seemed impossibly long. He could get so many things done in just the hours of daylight he was given every day. And his ma required that he be outside if he wasn't at school. She said it wasn't no use sitting in the house all day, he should be out doing something. Even if he couldn't work yet. So he had to learn how to fill the days. Most of them were spent with Chito and Koi. And, despite Chito's new disability, the days were no less adventurous. Kids will find a way. And the days of adolescence often seemed never ending as well, like one day might last long enough that each boy could grow a couple inches from morning to night if he concentrated hard enough. And then, eventually, they might not be little boys anymore.

And, at some point, he was no longer a little boy indeed. Those days were as good as gone. He was twelve and he had to spend the days that he wasn't in school working on the only tobacco farm in the state instead of playing.

The owner of the tobacco farm was Benjamin T. Burch. George heard through a co-worker, another young boy who was poor and white and named Timothy, that the T in their boss' name stood for Timothy. He said it with a sense of pride. Some time later, he told George that he felt if he could only just meet Mr. Burch, he could tell him that they shared the same name and maybe the man would take him in as one of his own. Timothy worked harder than any of the other boys on the farm in the meantime, until he could meet the big man. But he would die by the end of the summer when one of the harder-to-handle mules got tired of Timothy's presence behind it and kicked him square in the middle of the head. George would never forget the face that Timothy's ma made when she got there to pick up his body. His daddy didn't come with her, so she had to ask a neighbor man to drive her there in his pickup truck and he'd laid down a tarp in the truck bed as to not get any blood on it. But he didn't even get out to help them carry the young, dead boy and put him in there, he just sat in the cabin with the engine still running, smoking a cigarette and waiting while George and a couple other boys loaded their friend up. George would've gone to the funeral, but he didn't know where Timothy lived, so he figured that was his last moment with his friend.

The days on the tobacco farm were awful, even if you took out the death of the boy. The heat beat down on them and there was only one shade tree, smack dab in the middle of Burch's three-hundred-acre field. The walk to it at lunchtime barely made the few minutes of shade worth it unless a strong wind blew in or they got lucky with a rain shower. In the summer, they'd go down the rows and rows of leaves and pull off the flowers that the boss men called buds and suckers. He didn't much mind picking these flowers because sometimes he'd stuff a few in his pockets to bring home to his mammy. They were pretty and white. They made the boys sick sometimes, causing you to feel lightheaded and like you might want to throw up. Every once in a while, a boy would have to go lay down for the rest of the day and not come back for another day or two. George only had it happen to him a couple of times, but it was awful each instance and he could see in his mammy's face that she wished he didn't have to work a job that would make him sick. But the flowers were beautiful, regardless. When he'd first started, he didn't understand why they'd be pulling them off but one of the older boys who'd been working on the farm for a couple of years by then told him that it's because the flowers *steal the food away from the baccer leaves.* George had asked him *what food?* And the boy said *newtrents, the food is called newtrents.* When George got home that day, one little flower still in his pocket, he pulled it out and asked his ma, *what is a newtrent?* And she looked at him for a couple seconds with a face of pure confusion until her eyes slowly widened and she said, nutrients? George thought about it and nodded and asked what that word meant and she said that *it's the good stuff we get from food.* He asked her if plants got it too and she said yes, taking the little flower from his hand and giving him a kiss on the forehead for being such a smart young fella.

But the flowers weren't the only thing that had to be picked off the tobacco leaves, they were just the easy part. There were also worms. Tobacco hornworms, that's what the boss called them. The first day they had to start searching for them in the leaves, the boss man pulled all the younger boys together and produced one of these caterpillars out of his pocket in the palm of his hand. It was green and smooth and wriggling around in his pale palm. George hated worms with a vengeance and when he realized that he was the closest in the front to the bossman, whose name was Mr. Harold, he started to back up into the crowd of boys.

But Mr. Harold pointed at him and said "Hold on now, George. Come over here and hold this one for me."

George reluctantly stepped forward and held out his hand. The older man placed the worm in his palm.

"Now this is the enemy of your days to come. Don't worry, they won't hurt you unless you let them get that horn out and sting you."

At these words, George almost slung the tiny green creature that he was staring at out of his hand and onto the dirt but Mr. Harold saw him pulling his hand back to throw it and started laughing.

"No, no, George I'm just messing with you. These bugs are harmless to people. They might as well be pets. If you want to take one home and put it in a box to keep and look at, be my guest. But they can't stay here on this farm, no sirree. These suckers like to eat tobacco leaves like George here likes to eat fried chicken, ain't that right, buddy?"

George tried to laugh along with him but he couldn't take his eyes off the worm in his hand. All the other boys laughed with, or at, him.

"Now you just look on the leaves for any places where it might look chewed up and then you look up and around that spot. And you'll find one of these little buggers. Just pluck 'em right off the leaves, alright?"

"What do we do with them once we have 'em?" asked John, the smallest of the bunch of new boys, and a kid who wore glasses even in the field.

"Good question, John. Here's my answer: I do not rightly care as long as you don't put them back on the leaf. Smash 'em in your hand, throw 'em on the ground and stomp on 'em, put 'em all in your pockets and take 'em home to let your mama cook up in a stew. That's what y'all injun boys do anyway, right? Eat bugs?"

None of the boys laughed or twitched at the joke and Mr. Harold's face got a tinge more serious when they didn't react.

"Just kill them things, boys. That's what you're paid to do for the immediate future. Squash them bugs. Alright? Now get out there."

At this, George threw the hornworm on the ground and stomped on it. He started to walk away with the rest of the boys when Mr. Harold grabbed him by the shoulder and turned him around.

"George, you're a smart feller, aren't you?" he said with a tone of inquiry, like he was genuinely curious.

"My mammy says so," George replied.

"That's right, I bet she does. Look, son, I like you. I know you don't like that worm but you still took it from me and I like that. Some of them boys would have refused. Now if you can put that smart brain to hard work out in these fields for a while, I'll tell you what, you might have just enough white blood in you that you can raise your status around here some, alright?"

George stared at him for a moment and asked, "What do you mean, sir?"

"Just that you don't have to be like these other young injun fellas. Or even the poorer white boys. Your papa's genetics must be strong."

He paused and George didn't know what to say to this.

"And don't think some of us don't know who your papa is. It's a secret, well-kept for the most part, but our boss Mr.

Burch knows things that most people don't. Now, get on out there to work, my little friend. Let's get the rest of you strong like your mind is."

THE REST OF THOSE WORM and flower picking months of summer flew by like they knew how bad they were so they wouldn't stick around too long, as a small act of kindness to the boy, and the early fall harvest season was upon them soon enough. It was hard work but George appreciated that there were no more bugs to worry about and hell, it was all hard work. He went home every day bone tired and his mammy complained that he wasn't himself anymore despite the fact that she knew he only worked this job because she practically made him do it. But no money begets working to get more of it. So she'd just complain about how he was a ghost sometimes, almost as a joke to get a little laugh out of him, but she couldn't do anything about it. The form of many, many complaints in their house and in their neighborhood and in their county and in the state of Mississippi and in the country it resided in and the planet altogether.

Near the end of the leaf picking season, after the death of Timothy and the traumatic escapade of loading his body up to go to a hole somewhere, a car pulled up at lunch time one day. It was beautiful, almost exactly like the one he'd seen in his driveway that day years earlier when that strange white man showed up at his house and talked about money and whiteness. George and all the other boys sat there with their sandwiches in hand and watched the car door open and a great big man get out the side of it. He was far off, a couple hundred yards at the least, and just a speck in their vision really, but he was big enough that there was no questioning it. This was a fat man.

"Who the hell is that?" said one of the boys, practically speaking for all of the boys.

"I don't rightly know," another boy replied. And after a pause he kept on, "But he sure is fat ain't he?"

All of them chuckled and snorted and giggled until one of their bosses walked over, constantly looking back behind him at the big man as he came their way, and asked what they were so damn giddy about. Nobody would answer for ten seconds or so, so he asked them again.

"Don't be shy now," he said.

"We were just saying that man over there sure is big," the second oldest boy, Scott, said. He'd worked on the farm for three years by then and had a little more confidence than the rest, whether or not it was earned.

"That man?" Their boss pointed in the direction of the rich man.

"Yessir."

"Let me tell you something, boys. That man is going to come over here in a minute and I expect no, no goddamn laughing, you here?" He was yelling then, but it seemed he was trying to keep it down enough that someone, a certain someone a couple hundred yards away, wouldn't be able to hear it.

"Who is he?" Scott asked.

The bossman walked right over to Scott and knelt down in front of his face, spitting some chew out on the ground at Scott's feet.

"That big man," he said, putting a sarcastic drawl on the words big and man. "Is none other than Mr. Burch himself. Mr. Benjamin T. Burch."

Silence washed over the group of overworked boys and they understood the weight of their laughter. This was after the start of the school year, most of these boys—including George—went to school only two days a week at the beginning so that tobacco season could be ended with all its workers, and they'd all recently been on a school field trip to the cigarette factory just outside of town. It wasn't much of a field trip at all really, several boy's mothers worked in the factory, but it was a day that didn't involve books and learning so they all gladly piled into the raggedy school bus and took the day to see how cigarettes are made. When they got there, one of the boys looked at the side of the building and saw, written in big letters along the white painted brick wall, the name "BURCH TOBACCO," and one of them said, isn't our boss named Burch and another one replied, *no that's our boss's boss* and the first boy said *no shit* and that was the day they found out just how rich the man that owned the field they worked in really was. And as they sat there under that tree on that picking day, now understanding why they shouldn't be laughing, they also realized that the man had been walking their way the whole time they'd been having this conversation and he'd gained considerable ground. He was no more than thirty yards away and he was waving a big white hat in their direction. When he finally got up to them, he was breathing nearly as heavy as he was.

"Now are these," and he paused for a breath, "my tobacco leaf pickers right here?"

"Yessir, Mr. Burch, these are the young fellas we've had working this field all summer through harvest," their boss said, a chippier tone to his voice all the sudden.

"Well would you look at 'em. A bunch of children sweating up a storm and eating cheese sandwiches under this here old tree. Boys, when I was your age, my family didn't hardly own any land. And I had to work from when I was about your age, maybe a little younger. And I remember lunches just like these, praying to Father God that my mama had packed some meat in the sandwich that day and that maybe a little breeze wouldn't come along and give me some reprieve. I remember it well."

He stopped to take another breath and pulled out a metal cigarette pack from his shirt pocket.

"I've heard y'all are all good workers, but admittedly I've come over here from my car to speak to one of you boys in particular. I mean, I come here to check on the field and it looks like y'all are doing good work so I commend y'all for that. But one boy, yes, I've heard he's in this group. Is there a George here? Injun boy, from what I hear."

George's eyes got big and he tried to stay as still as possible for a moment, hoping that if he wouldn't move then no one would report his presence. Maybe they wouldn't be able to see him at all. But he was wrong in his assumption and nearly every person there turned and looked at him until it was painfully obvious he wasn't getting out of it so he raised his hand.

"That's me, sir."

Burch squinted hard at him in the early afternoon sun and said, "Well don't you look just white as can be. Huh. Come with me over here, boy, to my car. Come on."

He waved his hat at George and started back off to the new but dusted vehicle sitting at the farm road. George got up and followed and he could feel the stares of every boy and man on his back wondering what the hell he had done to have his presence requested.

"Now George, your father is a good friend of mine," Mr. Burch said, huffing and wiping his face off as they got to his car. "He's a real powerful man and I respect him a whole lot. And—"

"I'm sorry, mister, I don't mean to cut you off," George interjected.

"Uh huh, what is it?" the big man said.

"Sir, I don't know who my pa is."

The man looked down at him and frowned like he was having a prank pulled on him by this little half-breed twerp, and big, rich men don't have pranks pulled on them by anybody with less money than them. And then his face softened as if he understood and he started chuckling and the chuckling turned into a hearty laugh that turned into a violent coughing fit that George had only seen in fat, rich men like Mr. Burch. Once he'd gotten his breath back and wiped the spittle off his mouth with his pocket hankie, he just smiled at George.

"Well, son, in that case, I won't be the bearer of news that ought to come from somebody else. But I figured you knew him since he said y'all have met before. All that to say, I've got an envelope for you. Cash money, from what I understand. I'd advise putting this in a discreet pocket and not telling a soul out here that you got it. I wouldn't even trust your bosses out here not to take it off you. You understand?"

George said yessir and took the envelope, stuffing it in his waistband and tying his rope belt tight and tucking his shirt back over it.

The man stuck out his meaty hand to George and George took it, or rather his hand was swallowed up, and they shook hands like two business partners in a way that was new to the adolescent. Before the man turned around and got in his car, George had just one question to ask him.

"Sir, what does the T. in your name stand for?"

The big man looked at him and George was suddenly worried he'd asked an offensive question. But he just cracked a little smile.

"Your papa told me you were inquisitive. It's Tyler. Benjamin Tyler, after the inventor of the lever action repeating rifle. My daddy liked his guns. Hell, I do too."

George just nodded and didn't say anything more as the man loaded up in his car and was driven away by what looked to be another native man, but he wondered how his pappy could know he was inquisitive, and could tell somebody else about it so confidently, when he didn't know him at all.

7

"GEORGE, WHY DON'T YOU GO grab some of them tomatoes off that shelf over there," his mammy said to him, in the grocery store. He was fourteen and already taller than her and really didn't like having to go buy groceries with his ma because that was a girl's job but she already told him that she didn't have any other girls to help her out and if he wanted to talk her ear off all the time about the big muscles he'd been growing then he better use them from time to time by carrying some of her groceries around. So, he was there because she was right.

"How many?" he asked. His voice had gotten deeper and he liked talking sometimes just to remind himself of that fact.

"How many?" she repeated, laughing, in a funny, mocking voice that was as deep as she could go. "Get me five, mister big talker."

He grabbed the five tomatoes, slowly checking each one over and placing them in the basket he'd made by pulling the end of his shirt out. It took him far too long, his ma would have just grabbed five that looked decent, but he wanted to make sure they were alright. Better than to get 'em home and have to throw one away after you already bought it. While he was doing this, one of the grocery store employees, a skinny old white lady, walked up to him slowly on his left and watched. After watching him for a bit, and as he was searching for his last tomato, she spoke.

"You gon' pay for those, ain't you?"

"Yes, ma'am, of course," he said, turning to her and making sure he didn't drop any.

"Well no need to get snappy with me."

"I didn't, I'm sorry, ma'am."

"How you intend to pay for them? You got money on you?" she asked. Her eyes pried.

"My ma does."

"And where is she?"

"Just over behind th—" as he went to point, he got a shine of luck and his mammy walked around the closest aisle corner. Seeing the lady talking to him, she walked over.

"Something wrong?" she asked George and the old woman.

"You his mama?"

"Yes."

"I was just making sure he planned on paying for them tomatoes that he was stacking up in his shirt."

"Well why wouldn't he?"

"It must just be bred in you."

"What's that?"

"That smart aleck nature. Can't help yourself. How about y'all just gon' head and pay for your stuff, huh?"

His mammy was not a violent person, let it be known. She hardly ever raised her voice, much less her hand to somebody. If George had to really think about it, she had only gotten physical with him once. When he was just a pup, no more than five, he had taken to curiosity for curiosity's sake. He just wanted to know how everything worked and what it was like to work it. A shovel, a door hinge, the stove. Most importantly, one day his child-brained curiosity had zeroed in on a candle. One of the first memories that he could recall later on in life, him looking up at the white candle with its tiny, beautiful flame on the kitchen table and its little silver base holding it up. He stared at it for a while from the floor and then he got the courage to climb up in a chair to be closer to it. As he moved up into the chair, he noticed that his movements near it coincided with the flame moving. At first he moved his head and the little fire moved a moment later, the same direction. Pretty soon he figured out that waving his hand really did the trick and this held his curiosity pretty much at bay for some time until he heard a clang from his ma doing something outside and he was sucked out of his dream state. When he turned back to the candle, the bright idea hit him. That's what she called it, his bright idea. The idea was pretty simple, how about you pick that sucker up and see what it's like to hold it and move it around? And so, he did. And so, the wax dripped on the table. And so, little George got scarred by the hot wax. And so, he dropped the candle and it hit the table and the flame caught on the thin white sheet his mammy had laying over it and so he was standing there wide-eyed when, thankfully, she walked back in to see her boy setting the house on fire.

After getting the small flame put out all the way with a pot of water she had just filled up outside, she tore his tail up. Spank after spank from her and cry after cry from him. Then, suddenly, she stopped. He turned his head around and looked at her with red eyes as if to ask if she was done and she didn't say anything, just stood up and walked outside.

That was the last time she hit him in anything more than a playful way and he was nearly certain it was the last time she'd hit anybody else either.

So, when this white woman had the gall to talk to her that way, she told George to hand her those tomatoes and go on outside the store to wait for her and she paid for it all without saying another word to that mean white woman. While George waited for her to come out, he noticed a man sitting outside the store, about thirty or forty feet away. He was sitting on the ground and he had a blanket over his shoulders and it sounded like he was singing or humming loudly but he was too far away to make anything distinct out.

"What are you looking at?" his mammy asked, walking up behind him with two big paper bags in her arms. He turned around and took them.

"That man over there."

"Well, we got to walk past him anyway, so you can say hi as we go by." She didn't say anything else about that grocery store clerk.

What happened next is one of the few moments in his life that he would rather forget but he can't, no matter how hard he's tried.

The man stops humming. He looks over at George and his mammy. He is white and he has a beard all the way down past the tattered collar on his dirty shirt. It's so quiet George can hear a bird singing from a tree branch nearby. They try to pass by without harm but George sneaks a look at him and the man shouts at them. *Where the hell are y'all going?* George looks at him and then at his ma, whose face twists with the rage that she held back from the grocery store clerk. She turns and glares at the man. Home. She tries to push George forward and keep walking. But the man stands up. He's only a few feet away. *Why don't you come on over here, pretty thing?* They keep walking away and he starts to follow. *Did you hear me? Turn around. You're mighty pretty for a injun. I bet you full blooded Choctaw ain't you. Own a little land. That boy got a daddy?*

George stared at his mammy the whole time they walked as fast as they could down the dirt path home and the man continued to follow. His voice got angrier as he kept on and George's mammy's eyes strained on the road ahead of them. *I asked you a question, woman. You think you're too high and mighty for a white man or something? Can't be, with the color of that boy's skin. You know what I think? I think you love you a white man.* George's ma stopped in her tracks and he did too. She turned around to the man and he stopped too. He was grinning from ear to ear, an evil grin, a grin that embedded itself into George's brain. A grin like he'd later hear somebody call shit eating. *I'm telling you one last time, we're going home. Please leave us alone.* The man didn't stop grinning. *Say sir and I will.* His ma started to turn away and the man lurched towards her, grabbing her arm. *Say sir.* She tried to wrench her arm back but he held on tight. George found himself stuck in his place, like his feet were cemented. He watched on as his ma took her free hand and slapped the white man flat across the jaw. He let go of her and leaned back and touched his face. His smile only left for a second and then it was back. He pulled out a knife. George only saw the gleam of it in the Mississippi sun for a second before the man lurched forward and shoved the tip of it in his mammy's side. *Red bitch.* He pulled it out and stabbed again. His ma fell. George dropped the groceries and fell on top of her. The man kicked George in the back and ran off laughing. *George.* She tried to talk but she was sucking and gasping for air like a fish out of water. George screamed for help. He ran back to the store and when he walked in the white woman was standing there with her hands on her hips. *Didn't I tell you to leave? I'm gon' have to call the cops on you.* He panicked and had only one idea. He grabbed a tomato and ran. Ran back to his mammy. He heard her picking up the phone and dialing fast. But by the time the policeman arrived, it was too late. She was gone. The bird stopped singing.

8

THE MEMORY FADED AWAY from him and he could hear the sound of the water rushing in the river again. The light of the moon was blocked through the trees and it was so dark he couldn't hardly see a thing then. But in some ethereal trick of the eye, there she was.

"Ma?"

She didn't respond. But she was there and she was walking up to him and he felt like a boy all over again. As she got closer, he saw her more clearly. She was wearing the white dress that she kept around for the Sundays she'd make him go to church and the hat she'd bought just before she died. It was big and white too and it had feathers on it that he never got to ask her what type of bird they were from. In this moment she was just as real as she was back then. But there was something faded about her, something translucent. The edges of her shimmered and, when she walked into a spot lit up by the moon's radiance, her edges shimmered so much they looked to be tiny particles dancing. And, if he wasn't laying there snakebit, he might've gotten up and joined in. Her appearance made him feel like dancing.

Her face wore a smile.

"Mammy?" he said, a little louder.

She stopped walking towards him. She couldn't have been ten feet away.

"Georgie," she said.

Her voice showed no sign of the years that had passed. She was young, like she'd been when she was killed and like she'd always be for the rest of time.

"Ma, why are you here?"

"Does it matter?"

He smiled at the wittiness she always had.

"It's so good to see you, ma. I missed you." He said this through a frog in his throat. Nearby, one sounded off from the riverbank.

"Are you hurting, Georgie?"

He looked down at his leg and was forced back into the realization of his current circumstances. But he didn't feel no pain in this moment. He only felt her light.

"Not right now," he paused. "But I think I'm dying."

"Do you remember what I told you?"

"What's that?"

"What I told you about people dying, Georgie."

"God will take you across the earth to the southwest horizon. Do you remember that? I told you always remember where the southwest horizon is, and you can take heart that God will take you there when you die."

AND HE REMEMBERED THEN. He remembered being just a boy and learning in Christian school about dying. He'd never really thought about it before. Timothy's death hadn't happened yet and he wasn't much exposed to the ending of lives, past his pawpaw when he was just young enough to remember anything and a few elderly Choctaw people who passed recently and who he barely knew from their community.

He'd come home and asked her if she was afraid of dying. And she'd asked him why he wanted to know and he'd told her because he just found out that people died. And she'd smiled.

She told him that *there was no need to worry about death because, when you die, God takes you over the southwest horizon to heaven where you can be happy. Maybe even happier than here on earth.*

He'd asked her how that was possible?

How what? she'd asked back.

Well you'd have to be there for me to be happy, he'd said.

She'd smiled and bent down and hugged him and whispered in his ear that God would make sure they were together one day in heaven so they could both be as happy as they could bear it. And he'd felt better then.

"Are you there?" he asked her.

"I'll be there waiting for you," she said.

"But I don't think I deserve it," he said, voice cracking. "I've been an awful man."

"I know your heart. God knows your heart."

And she reached down, shimmering and shining like one of God's own special children, and she kissed him on the forehead and he felt it. She always knew what to say or how to hug him and make him feel alright. It was her best quality as a mother, one of many. And then she was gone and all was dark around him again and the frog bleated from the riverbank once more and one bird responded with a tune that struck him as familiar and he felt a kind of love in his heart that he'd only felt from his ma and it made him think about other loves, large and minute, and this brought his thoughts back in time and he rested his eyes and let the darkness behind their lids fill with recollection.

9

George had to move in with Chito and Koi from then on, against their pa's will for a few days, but he didn't have anywhere to go and the man eventually relented. Mostly on their ma's account. She had never stopped liking him and the influence she thought he had on her two boys.

On the day of his mammy's funeral, they went with him and sat in the front row of the church pew like they were her family too and Chito and Koi's ma put her arm around him as he softly cried while the minister spoke. He wouldn't remember a word of what that man said. Even though his mammy had been relentless in her first-generation faith, George knew that this man did not know her from Adam and that the words he would have to say were empty and could be reused for any old Sunday. So, he shut off his ears as best he could. He thought about his mammy in the best ways, only pulling memories down from the shelves that he would want to see. He closed his eyes and saw her helping him dig for worms in the back yard so he could go fishing. He opened his eyes for a moment and saw the preacher up there on his pedestal and he closed his eyes again, seeing her smiling at a drawing he'd done at school of their house and the sun and little stick figures with smiles on their faces that stood for him and her inside the house. He opened his eyes once more and saw the preacher waving his hands about and then he felt a squeeze on his own left hand and he looked over and his friends' mammy was the one squeezing it with hers and she looked at him with a face of reassurance that only a mother can do and he looked at her and at her hand again and closed his eyes one last time for the service. He could see her singing him lullabies. He could hear her too. He smiled, sitting in that pew, and her voice carried a tune throughout the church building all around him and the pastor's words didn't matter to him at all anymore.

After the service was through and she was in the ground beside his grandparents, he asked if he might stop by his ma's house one more time to grab a few things. When he walked in—the rest of his new family waiting outside—he saw that dust had already begun to collect on things like it was the new tenant of the home in her absence. He grabbed the rest of his clothes and balled them up as tight as he could to carry them all and walked through the small home looking for anything else he might want, knowing full and well that he could come back at any time since he would be living only a hop, skip, and jump down the road but also knowing that he felt like he might never want to step foot in there again. On the small table that held their radio, beside the two old living room rocking chairs that they used to sit in together after dinner, he spotted her bible. He felt compelled to pick it up, even if he wasn't sure he'd open it for the rest of his life. But in lifting it off the table gently, he pulled the cover back and found an inscription on the front page. It was a short prayer for patience and peace and guidance for her and the son she would soon bear, signed by his pawpaw. He closed it and stuck it in his pocket and looked at the radio for a moment before sticking his head out the door and asking his new surrogates if they would like to have his mammy's radio. They said yes, so he hauled it up in his arms on top of the clothes and walked outside and went on to his new home with his friends.

At their home, just as it was when Chito lost his leg and George learned of his disability the hard way, many people from the reservation were already there. Many of them had not been to the church service, but had food in their arms and waited silently to give George a pat on the back or a loose hug as he walked into the small crowd with his new family. He saw Abi was there again. He hadn't spoken to him since.

"Hi George," the boy said. "I'm sorry."

"You only seem to show up when bad stuff happens, huh?" Koi said, trying to make himself look as menacing as possible.

"Thank you, Abi," George said.

They stood there silently, the four boys all with eyes on the ground from the weight of their world making them too heavy, adults milling about around them. Under his left arm, Abi was holding a basketball. George had played a couple of times at one of the barns down the road where a father had bolted a hoop to the side of it. He wasn't very good but it was something new to do. Seeing that George spotted it, Abi spoke up again.

"Do you boys want to go play basketball? We could play two on two."

"Sure," George said. Abi nodded and his eyes widened with a trace of hope, but then he looked over at Chito as if he remembered he was there.

"Oh, I'm sorry, I didn't even think about your leg," he said.

"It's fine, I learned how to shoot with one hand," Chito said. He grinned. He was proud of it. All three boys looked to Koi, who grunted and nodded in affirmation, and they went to leave without telling anyone. But George wasn't sure they would notice anyway. It wasn't about him. Or his mom, really. It was about everyone there.

A hand stopped him. The boys didn't notice and kept walking. George turned around to see an older lady standing there with her hand tightly around his forearm. He recognized her and the many lines on her face but he couldn't remember her name. He didn't know what to say so he stood there and waited for her to speak, looking back to check on his friends but they were out of sight in the crowd already.

"I see you," she said.

"What's that?" he asked. The voices around them made it hard to hear her.

"It breaks my heart," she said.

"What does?"

"The pain and the suffering."

"Oh, I'm, I'm alright," George said. He wasn't, but he figured he had to be.

"Not now. To come. There is much to come." As she said this, her brow furrowed and she closed her eyes and a single tear fell from one. She still gripped his arm tightly.

"I need to catch my friends."

He tried to pull away from her. She was stronger than he expected. Her eyes shot open again and no more tears followed the first. She let go of his arm.

"Suffering will not leave you," she said. "*Chi iakaya chi.*"

"Okay," he said, not understanding. He turned from her and ran through the crowd, nearly knocking over Chito and Koi's mother, until he caught up with the boys. They were just down the road and had stopped to wait.

"Where'd you go?" they asked.

"I got stopped by an older lady. She said something to me."

"Well, what did she say?" Koi asked.

"She said suffering will follow me."

"Was it Hʋshilusa?" Abi asked.

"Yeah, I couldn't remember her name but I think it was her."

"She's crazy, don't worry about it. You know she got her name because the sun was blacked out when she was born. What did we call it in school? An eclipse, I think. My ippokni told me to not pay her no mind because she was just born to be a little crazy," the boy said, pointing a finger at his head and twirling it around.

"Okay," George said. But her words echoed in his ears and he found it hard to shake them.

Koi and Chito were 19 and 15 by then. Chito, whose growth had stunted—which his ma blamed on the amputation—and whose face remained soft like a child, used a wheelchair most of the time. He wasn't the same after the amputation, no matter how often he tried to pass off like he was the same boy with the same energy and the same love for roughhousing and the same fire for building something with his hands outside with the help of his brother and friend.

After the doctor had removed his foot and ankle, complications had taken over his life for months. First, the venom of the bite left him in a state of disrepair that made him nearly give up on life altogether. It started with stomach issues the likes of which neither he nor his family had ever experienced. He was in the outhouse for the better part of most days for two weeks. He'd come out of the tiny room looking like death had visited him alone and told him of all the bad things that were yet to come, his face covered in sweat that thickened into pools that stuck to the skin instead of droplets that fell off. His skin would be so pale they called him George as a joke to lift his spirits. By the time this passed, he'd lost fifteen pounds and was ravenous. His pa gave up entire meals for a few days to let the boy get back to health. But then, the infections began. The wound was infected two or three times, depending on which family member you asked. It would turn green or yellow, looking more like some alien species' appendage than a nub at the end of a human leg. The skin would crack all over with veins dark black and blue.

After passing out in the doctor's office the first time, their mama slowly recovered and was able to handle the subsequent visits for the infections and reinfections. By the second or third visit, whichever was true for the teller of the story, she'd grown so tired of the doctor's insistence that this was the best he could do that she grabbed a scalpel off his desk and pointed it at him. *Give my boy the best damn medicine you have or I swear to God I will cut your foot off too,* she said to him, her eyes bloodshot and exhausted and choleric. The doctor's eyes had gotten so wide Koi would report later to George that he thought they might pop straight out of his head and land on the tile floor. *G-g-get your wife under control, mister,* the doctor had stammered to their pa, who reached over and gently grabbed the scalpel out of her hand. Once he had it, he didn't set it down though. Koi told George that he just stood there twirling it in his hands and looking at the floor. The doctor tried to talk to him but he had none of it, his eyes stuck on the floor like they were anchored to it. *My point is not over, sir, I expect you to try something that will actually work on my son this time,* their ma said again. The doctor flicked his eyes back and forth between the two adults. His face showed shame and terror and guilt and fear. Then, he looked down at Chito, sitting in his wooden wheelchair and trying to look invisible to them. The man just nodded and turned around, grabbing a bottle off the shelf that none of them recognized from past visits. *Let's get him up on the table* was all the doctor said. In a few days, Chito finally felt better, and the skin where his leg stopped and only the memory of a young boy's strong ankle and foot remained began to turn back to its original light brown.

But even with a clean bill of health and not having to see the doctor anymore—not that he wanted to see their family again either, in fact, he directly said the opposite to their pa as they left that last appointment, giving the name of three other doctors that might be able to put up with the insolence of his bloodthirsty Comanche-acting wife—Chito could not find his spirit anymore. Their ma whispered a word that George caught one time but had never heard. *Akkanlusi.* He asked his ma, before her passing, what this meant and she just shook her head and scrunched her eyebrows together and said *poor boy, just be his friend.*

Koi's fortunes were different. He still lived at home, but this was not uncommon, and he'd finally started making enough money that his parents could afford their own truck. He had grown to be tall and broad, his facial hair growing out thick and black and his voice deep and, sometimes, threatening; and he'd worked his way up in a lumber mill to be a shift manager.

This had only come through the death of a coworker, though. Koi confided in George one evening, the sun setting low over the white oak in their back yard towering at least eighty feet in the air by then, with its tire swing still hanging and swinging in the breeze, that he'd watched an older man die on the job three days prior. The two boys were sitting on the ground, Chito in their pa's shed trying to whittle down a strong walking stick. George looked at Koi and didn't say anything. He had never told them about Timothy and he didn't feel like now was the time to share his story because Koi had almost never opened up about anything to him. So, he just pursed his lips and looked over at the older boy, waiting for him to go on.

Koi told him they'd been hauling logs to the mill. These were especially huge, probably coming from old growth oaks like the very one they sat under. But he wasn't paid to know what type of wood it was, he was just paid to cut it into boards. Because of the size, they normally would add an extra man to carry them, but a stomach illness had been going around and it was just Koi and the other man working that day. *His name was Itilakna.* When Koi said this he looked at George and waited for him to understand the irony there, but he quickly realized that George was still the least educated on the old language out of the bunch. *This means yellow tree,* he said, with a hint of annoyance that mostly came from the emotions that had nothing to do with George at all. George looked from his face down to the ground and nodded in understanding.

"We had carried at least a dozen logs already and we were getting tired. I told him we could take a break. I could see that he was struggling. He was old, in his fifties I think. He was wheezing a little, like you do sometimes."

George nodded in understanding again.

"But he didn't want to stop. I thought if I just sat down, he might join me. H-he might know that he couldn't do it by himself and just sit down beside me to cool off for a minute. So I sat down on the dirt and laid flat on my back. And I waited. But he didn't join me."

"He kept working?" George asked.

Koi was silent. George looked over at him and the older boy was just staring up at the tree, his face turned slightly away from him so that he couldn't see his face.

"I just laid there and waited. I don't know why. I should have gotten up to help but I figured if I stayed there on the ground he might get some sense and come back over to where I was. But then I heard it."

He was silent again and eventually George asked him what he heard.

"I heard a thud. The kind of sound that only a big log makes when it hits dirt. And I heard a scream. I jumped up and ran over and he was under the log. I guess he'd tried to grab it and pull it off the pallet and it slid off faster than he expected. I don't know. I don't see how he could make a mistake so dumb. But I don't see why I was so dumb to lay down and not keep working with him."

He stopped talking and George heard the muffled sounds of a boy who never cries, crying. Like a tiny engine, puttering and expulsing air. He covered his face with his hands. His body convulsed. After a while, George reached out and put a hand on his shoulder. He looked up at George, his face and eyes were red with exertion.

"I don't understand why so many terrible things happen to people like us."

"What do you mean?" George asked him.

"I don't know what I mean," he paused. "Maybe I will one day."

George didn't push him on it. But what he wanted to say was that he was right to not understand. Because everyone was dying around them all the time but it was only the people with their skin and their jobs and their names and then they were gone and no one cared because you had to keep going and live on somewhere else or be promoted in their place, but it didn't change the fact that pretty soon he was sure that someone else that looked like them would die too and it would happen all over again.

One day later on, he came home and their pa asked him over dinner how his job was going now that he was a manager. Koi took a bite of his food and swallowed before answering that being shift manager sounded like he was a boss man but it really just meant he carried the same big ass logs for a little more pay. He said that he had already found out the hard way that being Choctaw meant there was only so high to grow. Or *being of Indian skin of any kind, for that matter,* he said.

His pa hit him, slapped him from clean across the table. He said *don't you talk like that at the dinner table or at work or anywhere at all.* Chito and George ate the rest of the meal in silence while Koi rubbed and nursed his right cheek with the palm of his hand, taking bites off his fork with the other. George snuck glances over secretly and saw a familiar tear well up in the boy's eye before disappearing. The sides of that small wood house grew tighter by the second, until the fireplace was directly under them and one of the two faded white-framed front windows touched George's back and it was cold but only in the spot it touched, for the room was as hot as he figured hell would be and for a brief moment he thought he heard Koi whisper to himself that the walls were closing in.

KOI DATED A GIRL NAMED SUSANNA too, the entirety of the years George lived with them. Her real name, her Choctaw name, was Satina. Koi called her Satty. Her parents were wealthy; her dad built one of the first gasoline stations in Mississippi and now owned a handful of them. She wore pretty dresses. They'd have flowers embroidered—a word she taught all three boys—in them or sometimes more intricate things like animals. Her favorite (George assumed because it was the one she wore most of the time) was yellow and in the middle of her chest was an orange sun cresting over a blue horizon like a lake or the ocean, or what he imagined an ocean might be. She'd ride her bike, always a shiny new one, to their house nearly every other day. Their ma called her daughter, and she helped in the kitchen so much that everyone imagined she practically lived there. And George never asked, but he did notice that she was always coming over to see Koi and never the other way around.

Susanna was the prettiest girl he had ever seen at the time. And if you'd asked him any time later, she might have still remained in that standing. There was no real way to explain it either because everything about her was just lovely. George overheard Koi telling her she was *beautiful inside and out* and he thought that was about right. In fact, he was jealous immediately that he hadn't thought up something nice like that to say to a girl like Susanna, or even Susanna herself.

And she took a quick liking to his two little brothers, Chito and George, one by blood and one by chance, spending hours with them while they all waited for Koi to get home from work. She'd play games outside with them, even roughhousing sometimes. She'd push Chito's wheelchair across the yard, chasing after George, both of them screaming and hollering at him to come back here as he ran and laughed and laughed. For the first time since his mammy's passing, he felt loved by someone in a way that didn't require him to give them anything.

10

One night with Susana in particular stands out and will continue to stand tall in George's memory, until the end of time. It was past dark and past bedtime for the parents and the three boys were sitting in the front yard in the dirt. They'd taken to eating out there. It was Koi's idea and no one pushed him on why he wanted to do this but everyone knew the reason. It was written on his face for two days after the dinner where only George heard his whisper. But even their pa didn't say anything when they took their first meal outside. He just sat down at the dinner table and silently watched the band of brothers march their plates out the door and sit down in the yard.

George was nearly asleep when a bell rang, somewhere out in the darkness of the road in front of them. The moon was bright but had not yet risen past the tree line. No one said anything and they watched and waited for what was coming off the road to them as another bell rung out there.

"Hey fellas," Susanna said, slowly materializing before their eyes like an angel out of shadow as she rode into the yard. She smiled as she whispered this, her voice carrying softly over the short grass and her white teeth almost shimmering in front of them. George, coming out of his drowsy daze, seriously wondered if she might be an angel after all.

"Satty, what are you doing here?" Koi asked, jumping up off the dirt and walking over to meet her where she had stopped her bike in the driveway. The two younger boys got up to follow him over. George could see something in the little basket on the front of her bike.

"I'm here for some fun."

"Fun? It's bedtime," Chito said, leaning on the wooden crutch he'd carved for himself.

"You don't look like you're in bed."

Chito shrugged at her and looked to his older brother as if to ask him what he thought of the situation. Koi looked at the two boys, then his girlfriend who was still smiling at him with a gaze of temptation and then back at the front door of their home. No light escaped the windows. Their parents were asleep, or at least awake and not trying to see anything.

"What did you have in mind?" Koi asked her.

"Let's walk down to the *hatcha*. And drink these," she said, picking up two big glass bottles out of a crate in the bike basket and holding them up in front of her face.

"What's that?" George asked.

"Beer," she said.

George had never seen a bottle of beer before, or a beer at all. It was strictly forbidden in Chito and Koi's household and he never saw his mammy drink a drop of it. She only spoke of it once, lamenting to herself about how so many good men in their community had been ruined by it. He had taken that as enough evidence to stay away from it ever since.

"Satty, what are you doing with that stuff?"

"Trying to have fun, like I said."

"The boys can't have alcohol."

"Why not?"

Koi didn't answer, because he didn't really have one. And by the time he had thought of a few weak reasons why his two brothers couldn't have a drink, he realized that she had laid the bike down and started carrying the bottles back down the driveway.

"Hey, where are you going?" he tried to yell in a whisper.

"To wherever the fun might be."

He shook his head and turned to look at the two younger boys whose eyes were wide as if to say *please can we go* and he shook his head again and shrugged his shoulders and they started down the path after her.

THEY SAT UNDER a small wood bridge at the edge of a creek offshoot of the Pearl, or *hatcha*, River. The water hardly moved here, it was more of a swamp than anything else. The only sounds were of squirrels and raccoons in the trees, frogs and toads in the muddy bank, and a restless fish gator that might come up for air between sleeps in the pitch black.

Susanna screwed the cap off of a beer and handed it to Koi, who took a man's portion swig. Or that's what he said, trying to loosen up or at least give the appearance of loosening up in front of them. Then he handed it to George. The bottle was heavy and still a bit chilled. He leaned down and sniffed the opening. Pungent wheat and yeast slapped back at his nostrils. The boys laughed at him.

"Just take a drink of it, whitey," Koi said. "It ain't a flower."

George took a sip. It was harsh on his tongue but went down okay. It tasted like old bread that had just started to turn. He tried to act like he enjoyed it and took another sip. But his grimace must've been clear as he wiped his lips and handed the bottle off to Chito.

"Don't like it?" Susanna said, sitting cross-legged on a patch of grass.

"You like it?"

"Hm, I don't know. Maybe not."

"Then why drink it?"

"Drink enough of it and you'll get it," Koi said, laughing.

And so, George did. The taste was offensive to him for the better part of the few hours they were out there in the dark, but he did notice that the further along he got onto the beer, the further along it got on his taste buds until he felt like he might like it by the time the bottles were empty. All of them were drunk but comfortable enough with each other that no one became reserved or angry at their sudden inability to function. They were walking on air together.

"I'm feeling lighter than the breeze," Chito said while he tried to stand up and balance on his one foot before nearly falling over and having to be caught by George, who then fell over straight onto his back, the other boy tumbling down on top of them.

"Well you don't feel lighter than the breeze," George coughed out from under him on the mud. They all laughed so hard the frogs started ribbiting back at them like neighbors who were trying to get some shut eye.

Just before they finished up for the night and went on back to the house, they all laid on their backs and stared up at the sky, each one of them amazed at the way the stars moved more when they were drunk. Eventually Susanna turned over on her side towards George and Chito and asked them if they felt like men now.

"Why would I feel like that?" Chito asked.

"Because grownups drink alcohol. You just did something grownups do. Men get drunk."

"Our pa doesn't get drunk," Chito said.

"Well, mine does," she replied.

All of them got quiet again and a meteor flashed over their heads in the moonlit sky and George spoke up after a minute or two.

"I'd never grow up if it meant more of this."

He paused to let out a silent burp.

"Or I'd grow up if that's what it took. Whichever."

Chito nodded his head in agreement and Susanna cocked hers to the side so she could see George and she smiled a knowing smile at him and then Koi pushed himself back up on his feet and stood over them, holding out a hand to Susanna to pull her up too.

"Don't wish to grow up too fast, whitey."

They walked home, all smiling for different reasons. At some point along the way, George overheard Susanna whisper to Koi *why do you call him whitey* and he said *can't you see* and *don't you know* and she told him that it was some way to talk to a friend, a brother and he replied after a breath that there are some things that just matter about a person no matter how much you love them.

In his eavesdropping, George barely noticed that there was another car in the driveway. Neither did Koi and Susanna. It took Chito stopping in his tracks and pointing for them to notice the black police car in the driveway and then hear the voices talking near the front door of the house.

The details here were fuzzy in the moment and the day after and the weeks to come. All George knew and would remember was that Susanna's family woke up to find her and her bike missing so they called the police—the white police, since they lived off reservation land—and told them that they were worried something had happened to her with the boyfriend they knew she had but had never met. They were worried he'd taken her off and done something to her. That was what the cop had said. And George would remember that the police insisted they had to take him in even if Susanna cried over and over again that she had left on her own will to see him, they still had to put those handcuffs on his big wrists and shove him in the back of their tiny automobile and take him to the jail. And George would remember how silent Koi was as they shoved him and then the look on their pa's face as he shook his head and his eyebrows pulled so tightly together that they might become one and his right hand rubbed his face in a way that was so anxious he became unrecognizable.

And George would remember the searing headache at sunrise and Koi returning by foot in the late morning and the look of embarrassment on his face and the words that they never had jurisdiction to arrest him in the first place, no matter where she was from, and that he was too tired to do anything but sleep. And George remembered going back to sleep too since his head throbbed so. And in his dream, as he slept from morning to late in the afternoon, George sat in the middle of that family's house and the walls slowly collapsed on him until he was pinned between all four of them and he could hear Koi and Chito yelling his name and telling him to get out of it but they had already closed shut and then he woke up.

WHAT GEORGE HAD NO PLANS on telling either brother was that on another night not long after that incident had passed and the household had calmed down back into the natural swing of things, whichevery person and family has to do as long as the world keeps turning and the sun rises and sets, when he had just turned 16, he went outside to relieve his bladder and, having finished, turned around to find Susanna stepping out of the door and sneaking up behind him.

"You know you are my *nafki* right?" she asked, getting close to him.

"Yes, of course," he replied. His childlike innocence was unsuspecting.

"Do you know what *nafki* is?" she asked, standing so close to him that he could smell her breath, sweet like she'd had a piece of sugar candy.

"Brother. You say it all the time." He tried to lower his voice when he talked to her since she was so close, the moment calling for it.

She smiled at him. Their eyes were locked, and he started to back up. But he couldn't get over her eyes. And her lips and her cheeks and her jaw and her hair, for that matter.

He leaned out and kissed her, once, softly, his first. She returned it, if only for a brief moment before she pulled her head back. When he opened his eyes, he expected a look of shock or a palm across his face. Instead, she only gently smiled.

"I'll give you that one, just once," she said.

"Okay," was all he could muster.

She winked at him and put her finger up to the lips for a silent *shh* and then turned and went back inside immediately. No other mention of it. He knew then that, if he couldn't have Susanna, he would want a Susanna in his life. He knew that there was some part of his innocence gone, all because of this girl with her kindness and her beauty. Innocence wasn't even a word in his vocabulary yet but he wondered about it then. He wondered if he'd ever had any innocence. Or if he'd lost some of it, if not all, on the day his mammy died. If he had any left. Because that's what this felt like to him. Some other form of another event in the history of his life.

As he stood there in the front yard, his pants not even buttoned all the way up, he began to struggle to breathe. Under the pressure of the moment, his lungs began to feel as if they were collapsing in on themselves. He dug that pack of cigarettes out of his pocket and he lit a match and he took a drag of it. He sat down and smoked the asthma cigarette until it was a nub and he rubbed it on the ground and laid on his side and fell asleep there in the yard.

And George would have to start searching for another Susanna. He couldn't have her. Because she and Koi were married by the end of the year, and moved away to a house down the road where they could start an adult life together. The house was beautiful and white all the way around with new brick foundation underneath the boards and there were talks all around town about how this poor boy who worked so hard every day had gone and married into a family that had enough money that he would never have to work again and the house was on white folk land bought especially for them and no one spoke about the arrest anymore because it no longer held any weight over him.

11

He could hear a voice, whispering to him. A familiar voice, like a dream. It whispered to him to wake up but he wondered why a dream speaker would want you to wake up and end your conversation with them for good. It whispered to him in a familiar tone and cadence. It sounded like that of a teenage girl.

"*Nafki, nafki,*" the voice whispered in dulcet tones. The voice warmed him from the inside out when it, she, said this and he was grateful in that moment for any warmth that could be afforded to him on this riverbank. He wished for a blanket, he wished this voice would bring him a blanket and cover him up and tell him to close his eyes for sleep. But it whispered on with nothing of the sort.

He opened his eyes and scanned around him in the darkness but couldn't seem to find the source of the voice.

"*Nafki,*" she called out to him again. "Brother."

It sounded as if it spoke from the river and he rolled his body so that he could view in that direction. It was then that George saw a faint light near the water, barely visible behind a tree. He felt the voice and the river pulling him over. But he was so tired and his body ached.

"Who are you?" he called out, coughing from the pain he still bore from the rope.

"*Nafki,* come here," it said.

"I can't," he cried.

"You were strong as a boy, you are still strong now as a man."

George rolled himself from his side to his stomach and pushed his hands into the soft dirt, giving what felt like all the strength he possessed to push himself up and onto his knees. His leg felt like it was on fire from the snake bite up to the thigh. He grunted and moaned at the pain, but pushed once more and rose onto his feet, wobbling like a child. The walk towards the river and the mystery woman took ages in his mind. He kept having to latch ahold to a small tree or stop to catch his breath.

He remembered his inhaler then. Oh, how life had moved on and advanced since he was a pup. But when he reached into his pocket, he remembered that those boys had taken the inhaler from him. They'd patted him down when they took him, looking for anything dangerous. When one of the boys found the inhaler, he turned and asked the others if it was worth taking. They'd just nodded and shrugged. *Do you know what it is?* one asked. *I think it's one of them 'halers.* Then the others had shrugged again and said *just throw it out* so he did. But now George figured it didn't matter anyway. He was going to die here, he knew. It didn't matter by what.

So, he pressed on. When he finally turned the bend around that tree obstructing his view of the voice, there she was in front of him. Susanna, as she was the last time he saw her. Young and married and lovely.

"Susanna," he whispered.

"George. Come sit with me." She turned, her body but a glimmer, and sat down on the bank of the river with her feet and legs in the water.

He sat down beside her and stared over at her. Even with the appearance of his mammy before, he was struggling to understand.

"Why are you here?"

"I don't know if I can be the one to answer that question," she said. "Why are you here?"

"I don't know either."

"Are you sure?" As she asked this, her eyes implored him in the way they always had, looking for him to think inwardly more and look for more in himself than the outside world might expect of him.

"I don't know, Susanna," he said. Tears began to roll from his eyes, growing in size and number, and he began to violently shake like a child. His breathing turned to wheezing and the wisp of a woman he once knew leaned into him. Her warmth clouded over his body like a shroud and his weeping ceased.

"Do you see these?" Her transparent hand pointed towards the ground beside her and the round wood stump that stuck out of dirt.

"The cypress knee?"

"Do you know what they do? Why the cypress tree has them?"

"My mammy used to say that it was the only tree that had roots that needed to breathe. Or maybe it was Chito and Koi's ma who said that. Someone said it to me, when I was a boy."

"But were they correct?"

"I don't think so."

"You don't think so?"

"Well, do you know?"

"You are the one with the memory," she said.

"No, I remember watching a PBS show and they said we still weren't really sure what they are for."

"But there has to be a reason."

"Yes. That would make sense."

"Then why are you here?" As she said this, her legs shifted and her knee touched his above the water and one of her feet grazed his under the water and he felt just like a boy again. A boy who was in love with a girl. A girl he could never possess. His heart fluttered and for a moment he forgot the snake bite and the failed hanging and he only remembered that kiss she'd graciously given to his virginal lips in the softest of ways.

Before he could answer her question and after he snapped out of his remembrance, he realized that she was fading away. Whatever made up her ghostly particles slowly drifted and dissipated until they and she were no more. He laid down on his back, his feet still in the lightly moving water. He pushed them in a little further, until the bite was submerged and the chill of the water rushed over it.

12

There were few things as promising to a seventeen-year-old boy of the time, who felt himself to be a man or at least be damn close to it, than the prospect of the state fair.

For nearly a month, Chito had been telling George in hushed tones about the possibility of them getting tickets to it. George had asked him the requisite question, thinking his friend was just daydreaming in the way the crippled boy could do and forgetting the fact that the Mississippi State Fair had long been a segregated affair only for the whitest folk. And neither of them had even been to Jackson in the first place, or even close, so they'd have to get past going to the city they'd been told was made for white men, for the first time, to immediately enter a large event made for, catered to, and completely populated by white folks.

"Chito," he said. "We're not white, how are we supposed to get in?"

Chito stared at him, and his forehead furrowed just a bit.

"One of us isn't white."

"I am not white enough for these white men. Is that better?"

"It doesn't matter no way," Chito said, before explaining his plan.

Chito had recently become employed, his first job, at a shop in town that specialized in creating furniture and knick-knacks out of fine wood. It had been a great deal to get him this job, or any job at all, on account of his disability. But his brother's successes at work and newfound family that had tasted more success than any of their family had ever dreamed, had created more opportunity than they knew of. The white man who owned the woodworking shop sourced everything from the mill that Koi managed and had cut a deal years back with Koi's father-in-law for cheaper gas since he had to haul so many pieces of furniture to homes all around the state. So, the white man put Chito to work, whittling knick-knacks like little wooden birds and other animals and large tree limbs that could be turned into coat and hat racks or lamps and picture frames and figurines with movable arm and leg joints that would be painted by the owner's daughter to be sold as baby dolls. And Chito was good at it. It took only a week or two for the white man to warm up to his new hire and accept that he was the best at carving wood of any employee he had had or would ever have.

And, at this newfound employment, Chito met the owner's son. His name was Nehemiah. He was a blond-headed boy who said he was nineteen. From the day Chito met him, the boy was attached to his side at work. Despite the fact that Nehemiah wasn't very good at carving or whittling or anything that required much patience and hand aptitude, he was his father's son and that allowed for a position with no prerequisites. But it didn't matter much to Chito, because the boy's taking to him and desire to be Chito's friend came with perks. Chito eventually was picked up for work every morning, and dropped off after too, by the boy in his shiny vehicle. He also enjoyed lunches on the boy's dime, getting to forgo the peanut butter sandwich that his ma would make him early in the morning. And, on rare occasions, he was invited over for dinner at the owner's house too, even though the boy had never taken Chito up on an offer to have dinner at his place some time and meet George and Koi.

After months, this friendship culminated in a conversation that had taken place three days earlier. Nehemiah had walked over at lunch time and taken a near-finished canary out of his hands, replacing it with a cold ham sandwich.

"Buddy, I have an idea," he'd said.

"What kind of idea is it, Miah?" Chito asked, taking a bite of the sandwich and discovering a thin layer of mayonnaise. He loved mayonnaise on sandwiches and his friend had remembered and he grinned slightly as he chewed it.

"A good one."

"Well, what is it?"

"You ever heard of the state fair, my injun friend?"

"Course."

"Would you like to go to it?"

Chito stopped his chewing and cocked his head to the side but he didn't see a hint of joking or any manner of messing around on the boy's face. Yet, he still had to ask. The one major flaw about Nehemiah, along with his shortcomings with his hands, was that despite his general good nature and kindness he was dumber than a bag of rocks most days.

"Are you messin' with me?"

The boy's face lost a hint of its brightness.

"Why do you ask that?"

"Miah, you just said it yourself. I'm not white. Can't go unless you're white."

"Oh. Hell, you think I haven't thought that part though?"

And, he went on with his plan. Chito would come with Nehemiah to the state fair, which he'd gone to by himself for the first time the prior year, and he could bring his brother or the friend George that he talked about all the time. As for the matter at hand regarding their skin color, Nehemiah had asked his mama if she would be willing to color their faces a shade whiter with some makeup. After that, they were to wear long sleeve shirts and pants, which Nehemiah could lend them.

"What about our hands?" Chito asked.

"You sure do think about everything, don't you, buddy?"

"You have to."

"Stick 'em in your pockets for all I care. I'll pay for everything so you don't have to take them out no time. Folks won't be none the wiser."

Chito thought about this for a moment and figured it to be as foolproof of a plan to get him and George, as he already knew what answer he would get from Koi if he were to ask, to the place they'd only had false dreams about.

As George listened to all of this, he just nodded along and stayed quiet. At what appeared to be the end, he thought for a moment and said, "Okay."

"So, you're in?"

"I can't turn down the fair. But I might hate all that powder on my face, and—what are we supposed to do if the powder starts to come off?"

"I'm sure she can loan us some too just in case."

"These people sure do like you, Chito."

"You trying to say something?" Chito asked. Insecurity crept over his face like a long shadow, despite the moon's shining above them in the front yard. They could hear their ma out back filling up a bucket to wash dishes with. The wind blew over the flat ground all around them and the leaves in the oak tree shifted and the tire hanging from it lightly swung. George thought carefully about what to say and decided to soften up on his friend, who as a result of staying home more than George or Koi all these years, had grown more naïve than a white person's domesticated dog.

"I'm just tired, don't worry about me. I'm in for the plan. Let's go to the fair."

Chito's face lit back up and his hair blew a bit with a gust of wind.

"Oh, and I forgot the best part."

"There's a better part?"

"Nehemiah said he read the Jackson paper and they wrote that the circus is coming to the fair for the first time ever."

"The circus?"

"The circus. Lions and bears and women with beards and flame jugglers."

"I'll be damned. The circus."

"You remember that book Koi stole from school for us to look at? With them black and white pictures of that circus. Barnum or something. They had that big old tiger. Had stripes on its back and big teeth and they had it jumping through hoops."

"I remember," George said, leaning back and laying down in the grass.

"Won't that be grand."

Above George's head, he saw a cloud in the light of the moon and as it moved and reshaped slowly he saw the head of a lion, or at least a head as he'd seen in drawings in the books of his youth. He couldn't help but feel a bit of excitement despite all the worries in the world.

Nehemiah's mother was a short lady, wearing the fat of the rich along with all the jewelry too. She had long, blond hair though and in her face was the remnant of a woman who George guessed must have been quite nice to look at when she was he and Chito's age. She met them at the door on the day they were to board the train to Jackson wearing a white house dress. When she opened the door, she just stood there in the frame for a moment taking George in. She even put her right hand on her hip and her left on her chin, pondering openly about them as the door swung in and hit the wall beside her. After a beat, she spoke directly to Chito.

"Now Nehemiah told me you were bringing your brother," she said.

"Yes, yes, ma'am," Chito stuttered, giving a quick nervous glance over to George. "Well, he is basically my brother."

"But he looks about white, Chito," she said with a long drawl on the first syllable of his name and a sharp upwards movement of the final vowel. George figured she was from somewhere else with the accent she had, but he had no clue where it might be. George looked at his friend who seemed to be lost for words.

"Miss, um," George said.

"Joy. Miss Joy."

"Miss Joy, my mammy was Choctaw just like Chito here. But I didn't know my pa, and still don't think I know him. But by the color of my skin and a few things people have said to me, I can only guess he was or is white."

"Mm," she grunted, before smiling lightly at him. "And what would your name be?"

"George, ma'am. My name is George."

She nodded and, apparently considering this all satisfactory, turned and walked back into her home, raising her right hand and moving it just enough to indicate the boys were to follow her in. They followed her down a long hallway that was dark from lack of windowlight until they came to a parlor in the back of the house on their left that was nearly all windows on two of its walls and which looked to lead off to another room.

"George, please have a seat here in the parlor. Chito, you come on in here with me first."

And so George did what she asked. He watched his friend enter the open doorway off from the parlor and saw the mirror on the wall then and the bench of makeup and then she went in behind him and closed the door and George was left to his thoughts.

He took to looking around the room from his seat, afraid to get up and touch anything in case it might go missing and he get blamed, or even getting caught looking around and being accused of the desire to make something go missing. The room was full of knick-knacks, just like the kind that he knew his friend made. There were at least seven different types of birds that he could count of varying size. Some looked so small that he'd be worried about breaking them if he was offered to hold one. Beside him was an identical chair to the one he was placed in. He hadn't noticed as he was sitting down, but it was a beautiful thing. Its seat and back cushions were green with beautiful red embroidery that looked like trees and bushes against a lush forest.

All was quiet for some time. He guessed at least a half hour. And then, the door opened again. His friend emerged from the room and stepped into the light of the parlor and George had to stop himself from sneering at the boy. He was white, that was for sure.

"Don't laugh at me," Chito said, seeing his mostly failed attempt at keeping it together. "You have to do it too."

George heard Miss Joy calling his name from the room but he couldn't see her. Chito said it was his turn so he got up and made his way past his friend, still smiling at his transformation.

"Who's whitey now?" he whispered in Chito's ear as he passed him.

When he entered the powder room, he was met with a myriad of smells, most of them floral in some way. He turned and closed the door behind him, seeing a quick view of his friend trying to look at himself in the reflection in the window glass, before turning around and surveying the place. George saw chairs to his right with pink upholstery and a row of mirrors that went the entire length of the room, much longer than he could see from his angle outside, with a bench in front of them the whole way down. The room was long and narrow and at the very back was a baby blue curtain that seemed to section off another part of the room that he assumed couldn't be very large unless the house really did go on forever. He felt that he might get a headache if he was in this house, or at least this part of it, for too much longer, from the sensory overload of smells and colors around him. But, with all of that going on, there was no sign of the matron of the house anywhere in the room.

"Miss Joy?" he called out as he started to look around for any other doors he might have missed. Just then, he heard a rustle from the back of the room behind that curtain.

"George, just one moment," she responded from back there. "Please, make yourself comfortable."

He sat down then in one of those chairs with the pink cloth. They seemed to be extra cushioned, and he couldn't help but feel comfortable. He sat there and waited for a couple of minutes and she didn't come out, despite a random rustling sound every once in a while. Eventually, he got so comfortable sitting there that he leaned his head back and closed his eyes. Within just a moment, he was asleep.

George woke to a touch on his thigh, a gentle caress. He opened his eyes, with his head still back, and didn't see anything but ceiling at first. But when he lifted his head off the top of the chair and lowered his gaze, he couldn't believe what he was looking at. Miss Joy was there, on her knees in front of him, one hand on his thigh slowly moving a finger up and down on it, and she was as naked as the day she was born. She had put extra makeup on her face to make her cheeks pink and rosy and her breasts hung there in front of him plump and soft like something he'd never seen before. And he hadn't. Not really. His view of her stopped just above her naval, but behind her he could see in the mirror her back and buttocks and legs and feet down there on the ground.

He started to say something, but she reached up and placed the hand that had been on his thigh to his lips and whispered a shush. When she moved her arm, he couldn't help but to see her corresponding breast jiggle and he couldn't hardly believe what he was looking at. He wondered if he was dreaming still.

"Am I dreaming?" he asked aloud, on accident.

She looked like she might laugh, but the face she was making that he'd later recognize to be an attempt at sultry did not break.

"Don't sound an alarm," she said, still whispering. "If you do, I'll say you forced yourself on me. Do you hear me?"

George thought for a moment. Her southern drawl was so awful and drawn out that his first thought was that he could stand to never hear her speak again. But here was a woman, a full grown woman, naked in front of him. Alas.

"Yes ma'am," he said, his own voice coming out of him like there was a ghost inside that had been waiting to take control of him at some point, and the point had been reached. When he said this, she smiled and winked at him and proceeded to yank at his pants legs to get them off. He felt compelled to help her with this, to make things easier for her so that the woman could maintain some amount of decency and keep up that shroud of whatever it is you'd call that she was putting up. With his trousers off, she leaned back for a moment.

"That'll do," she said. Then she leaned forward again, taking his privates in her hands and putting her mouth to them. He felt like squirming all the way out of the chair and into the dirt and just dying and staying there but there was nowhere to go and it wasn't all that bad after all and eventually he felt like putting his head back again and closing his eyes.

After some time, he felt her stop and he looked back down and she got up from her knees. Her stomach appeared above his legs and she would have been less appealing to him, had she not immediately climbed on top of him and made his view nothing but breasts. For the next few minutes, she rode him on that chair with the pink upholstery that surely her husband had made, or at least had ordered someone else to make, like her very own son or Chito. And she told him to let her know when he was close and at first he had not the slightest idea what she meant by that but when the time came he understood and told her and she stood up off of him and he excreted onto his leg for the first time in his life.

"Can't have no mixed babies, no I cannot," she said, standing over him watching it happen. Then she turned around and grabbed a rag and handed it to him and told him to clean up. Once he'd wiped his leg off and pulled his pants back on, tucking his shirt back into them, he looked up to see the woman standing there with powder and a brush in her hands. She must've noticed the look on his face because she stopped and smiled and spoke with an air of detachment he'd rightly never seen.

"Did you forget the reason you came over here, honey?"

It only took a few minutes to make him a shade whiter and for her to feel satisfied with her work. She leaned back and looked at him real hard. She turned around and placed her tools back on the counter and he tried to stand up but she turned back to him and placed a hand on his chest to stop him. Then she leaned in and kissed him one time. He realized then that this was the first time she'd kissed him throughout the whole thing.

"That was fun. Don't get hurt down there in Jackson and we ought to do it again," she said with her nose nearly pressed to his. Then she backed up and went back to her business, seeming to forget about him completely.

So, George stood up and checked himself over one more time, shaking his head at his own reflection. There was no time to consider the damage. He headed out to the parlor where Chito sat there. Chito looked him over and George thought he saw a trace of a laugh on his face but nothing else and his friend asked him what took him so darn long. He just shrugged instead of trying to think up a lie and they headed out to catch the train to Jackson.

THE TRAIN WAS LOUD sitting there at the station and the platform around it was bustling with white men and women of all varieties. They met Nehemiah there at the ticketing office. He was in a tailored suit and wore a shiny new top hat. His luggage was on the ground beside him and there were two more hats in his hands. When they approached and he saw them, he reached out and handed the hats over.

"For you gents," he said. He was smiling ear to ear and George felt an affinity for the boy immediately, even if the circumstances of their meeting had changed so drastically within the past hour and he was finding it difficult to look him in the eye. But before he could think about it too hard, George was wearing a new hat—the first nice hat he'd ever put atop his head—and the boy was shaking his hand vigorously.

"Got the tickets?" Chito asked him.

"Slow your horses, buddy. We don't depart for another half hour. You boys must have run here with all that dust on you. Go on over there and get you a rag from the shoeshine boy to dust yourselves off. I'll get them tickets for us, don't you worry."

And so, they did as he said, and the shoeshine boy, who looked familiar to George as they approached, obliged them immediately. When the boy lifted his head to George, he recognized why. It was the younger brother of one of his old farm coworkers. Suddenly, George became aware of how he must have looked to anyone that might know who he was. He searched for any hint of realization in the young boy's dark face but the kid only waited patiently for his rag back. The makeup was better than George had assumed, he guessed then. But he couldn't help feeling that he had to get out of this town and away from anyone that he knew not named Chito or Nehemiah while he wore this god-awful makeup to make him look whiter than he already was. As he handed the towel back to the boy, covered in their dust, Nehemiah appeared beside them and flipped a coin to him.

"All aboard," they heard the conductor yell out behind them.

"You boys ready?" Nehemiah asked.

"Let's go see a fair," George said. He tried to hide the concerns on his face.

"And a circus," Chito said.

As they boarded the train, the conductor took the three tickets from Nehemiah's hand and gave a quick glance over the three of them. His brow furrowed and then returned back to its natural curve.

"Enjoy the ride, fellas," he said. And they were off to Jackson by rail.

13

It was lunchtime when they arrived and their first stop in the big city was a place to eat. The streets were bustling with people and horses and cars like George and Chito had never seen and they were surprised to find that the overwhelming smells of the city were shit and gasoline. They kept pointing out little roadster cars that were veering in and out of the foot traffic in the road at speeds they didn't know automobiles were capable of and storefronts where beautiful dresses were on women's bodies, except for the bodies weren't real but instead wire shaped into the sculpture of a woman. Nehemiah saw them pointing and asked if they had never seen a mannequin before—saying it like man-ee-kin. And he laughed a big hearty laugh when they told him no, the kind of laugh either of them had only heard from the boy's father. George figured that the boy was doing an imitation as a way of trying on being a grownup while away from the old man.

The trio passed three sandwich shops before Nehemiah came upon a French restaurant with a name the two others couldn't pronounce and wouldn't try to. He turned to them and asked if this spot looked good enough for them to grub before they went on to the fair. George looked inside and saw a horde of white folks sitting down eating.

"Says white folk only right there in the window," Chito said.

"You forget yourself, buddy," Nehemiah said.

It took a moment for the recognition to hit Chito's face, but George saw the lightbulb go on behind his eyes and then he nodded back.

"Alright. This is gonna take some getting used to, I think. But the place looks expensive."

"You're on my dime the next day or two, fellas. Don't worry about it."

The two boys turned to go in and George had a thought pop in his head.

"Hold on. If we don't apply some of that powder to our hands, it will be pretty noticeable to the waiter while we're eating."

So they went into an alley beside the storefront and applied the white stuff to their hands while their friend stood out in the street taking it in. George had a wave of embarrassment wash over him like he'd never felt before and suddenly he didn't want any part of this situation. He was not who he was supposed to be. He could imagine the horror on his mammy's face, or his pawpaw's face—that glimmer of memory he had of the old man's cracked face in one of the first visions he had that his brain let him keep—if they had seen him doing such a thing.

"You ready, George?" Chito said, catching him thinking about this and staring off into nothing.

Their lunch was the most expensive food George had ever eaten or been close to eating. Despite how ridiculous he felt in the new clothes and hat, they seemed to do some good in costuming him with all the rich folks. No one batted an eye at them. But he wondered to himself if this wasn't simply because they were so focused on themselves that they didn't notice anyone else. He thought this was pretty certain when he heard the way they spoke to the wait staff, especially the one black waiter. They spoke in such hurtful ways he couldn't think of speaking to somebody else, or someone that he didn't know from Adam. With every passing minute he felt himself growing more and more distant from the place that he was in and more so desiring to be back in the safety of his second family's home.

"Maybe I ought to just—"

He started to speak his mind and ask for a return train ticket from this boy he barely knew when the waiter appeared carrying their food. So he quieted himself and thanked the man for the food and decided that he had to at least eat what had been set out in front of him. It was a plate of grilled fish on top of some kind of cream with half a lemon there beside it to squeeze on. All three boys had gotten the same thing.

"You know what they say?" Nehemiah asked them. George and Chito looked at the other for help answering his question.

"No, what do they say?" Chito replied.

"Bon Appetit," Nehemiah said with a laugh as he picked up his fork and knife and dug into it.

George had to admit that it was delicious and richer than anything he'd ever had. He let himself get comfortable and ate the whole thing as slowly as he could, despite his stomach's grumbling. After they'd finished, Nehemiah ordered them little coffees to "warsh their palates" as he said it. George had never had a sip of coffee so strong and bitter and in such small quantity. The waiter called it espresso and he called it nasty. But he drank it nonetheless because things like this felt like once in a lifetime opportunities to him at the time. Nehemiah laid a twenty dollar bill on the table and they got up and left, George noticing that Chito's eyes darted back and forth across the restaurant around them for anyone who might have caught on.

"You boys ready for some fun?" Nehemiah asked them as they walked on in a direction that he seemed to know pretty well.

"You sure we're headed the right way, Miah?" Chito eventually asked after they walked for no less than ten minutes, taking multiple turns that didn't make any sense to them.

"Just hold on," he replied.

And they did. They came to the end of a row of houses and saw a herd of people walking by in front of them and Nehemiah smiled and murmured *last* turn and then they came out into the view they'd been waiting for. As they merged into the busy highway of white folks, the vision of a mighty Ferris wheel came before them in the distance, just behind and sticking out above a wooden fence. It was yellow with little lightly swinging cars attached that amounted to twp-seater metal benches with rain covers and bars to keep you from falling off and a red base. All along its bars and poles, green lights shimmered and danced as it spun slowly. It was as if the sun had come down off its pedestal in the sky to Jackson, Mississippi.

"Thar' she blows," Nehemiah shouted out to them, punching Chito playfully. They started laughing and George let out a yelp that made a few of the other people around them laugh too and Chito gave one back.

THE GATE WAS NO PROBLEM and they entered as men free to do as they please in what could only be described at first glance as a magical kingdom.

"Where to first?" Nehemiah asked them.

Both boys replied "I dunno" in unison.

"How about the Ferris wheel?"

They nodded in response. Their eyes were as big as muscadine grapes fresh off the vine. As they shuffled through the crowd, Nehemiah made sure to point at nearly every single vendor and game along the way so that the boys didn't miss a single thing to get excited about. George had the feeling that if he was overwhelmed by the sights and smells in the powder room of the mother of the boy currently leading him through this crowd, he ought to pass out in the excess of smells, sights, and sounds around them.

He smelled dough frying and clouds of powdered sugar.

He smelled cotton candy and located it in view quickly as a small child was handed some blue and red on a paper stick.

He saw bright and flashing lights on signs that said things like "World's Smallest Pony" and "Mississippi's Best Frog Legs" and "Best Photographer in Town" that were clearly meant to draw people in, and looked to be working by the lines in front of them.

He saw young fathers with little children on their shoulders. He heard the children shout things like "Pa, look, you can ride a horsey over there!" As they shouted, he saw the trail of sugar around their little mouths. He saw the sweat on the fathers' foreheads.

He saw women with all kinds of colorful dresses on and big hats with veils on them and big fans to blow air on their faces and their hair out of the way of their eyes.

He saw men that Nehemiah referred to as "carnies" standing around with big mallets in front of little structures with bells on the bottom and signs on the top that said "How Strong Are You?" and the largest weight scales he'd ever seen with signs that said "I'll Guess Your Weight" and these carnies yelled out obscene things in the name of making money like "I bet you can't even lift this hammer, scrawny farmer boy" and "Lady, I'll guess your weight and don't worry, the scale stops at 250." But as folks passed them by, they just laughed at these men and George began to understand that there was a newfangled social code in this place that involved the allotment of a certain level of crass because you were there to have some fun.

He saw a lemonade stand made to look like a big lemon, the size of a small shed. It looked to be cast of papier-mâché around a wood frame. He smelled the tangy scent of the hundreds of lemons the boy working the stand was squeezing and the big pour of sugar that he was putting into every cup. George stopped to take it in. He loved lemonade. His mammy used to make him lemonade every Sunday afternoon.

"Daydreaming?" Chito asked him after he and Nehemiah realized they'd lost him and turned back around.

"Want one?" Nehemiah added.

"No, I don't need one," he said.

"Well, whoever needed a lemonade anyways?" Nehemiah asked with a long drawling emphasis on *needed*.

"Nobody I guess."

"Exactly my point," the boy said as he approached the big lemon and that scrawny white boy sweating away inside of it, building muscle on his arms every time he had to squeeze more of the fruit. He threw up his hand with three fingers flashing at the boy, who he nodded and got to working on making their drinks.

"Is this what life is like for them?" George asked Chito as they stood behind and waited.

"What you mean?"

"White people. Just going and buying things. You want a lemonade, you get a lemonade. You want food from a restaurant served by a black fella, you go get food from a restaurant. You want to go to the fair, you go to the fair."

"Seems like it."

"I'm damn fed up with this makeup, Chito."

"Would you look at that Ferris wheel though."

"I don't like pretending to be somebody I'm not. My ma would have my tail for this. And so would yours. Your dad might have a heart attack."

"It's beautiful. Big and spinning."

"Chito, what did you even tell them we were doing for the next day or two?"

"Who cares?"

"Me."

Nehemiah was getting the three drinks from the stand and Chito turned to George and looked him sternly in the eye, standing on his crutch. George felt a coldness come over him from the glare he received from his friend.

"They think we're getting some extra schooling on leadership from Mister Joy. George, you think I enjoy this whole thing? I've got to walk around on a damn crutch around this big city. My arms and my leg are exhausted."

George nodded back. Nehemiah approached.

"But I see that Ferris wheel and I see all these people having so much fun and I think, why can't I have some fun for once? My whole damn life is wrapped up in getting bit by that snake and my best friend's ma dying and my pa being so afraid of something else happening to us. I'll do what I have to do to have this fun."

"Here you fellers go," Nehemiah said. He scanned their faces as they took the drinks. "Everything alright?"

"Yessir, just my body getting a little tired is all. Let's get on that big ol' wheel over there and see what it's all about and I'll get some rest while I'm up there."

"Now, ain't that the spirit?" Nehemiah asked, beaming.

The lemonades were gone by the time they got to the ride. George couldn't believe how sweet it was and yet, how tart, and he let it fill him like a brightness and he tried to understand what his friend had told him and, for the most part, he did. And then they were at the base of the behemoth and Chito was smiling looking up at it. The three boys standing there were statues then, for only a moment, of awe and anguish. The carnie there, an ugly woman with long, long hair down to the backs of her knees and wearing a tattered dress that was muddy from the field they were in but so high up that you had to wonder if she had been rolling around in it like a pig just before they got there, told them that the two-person-to-a-bucket rule was strict and they'd have to break their little posse up. George relented immediately. He figured Nehemiah deserved to not be on it alone, given that he bankrolled the whole thing, and by God he wasn't going to be alone with the boy for the duration of a Ferris wheel ride with the smell of his mother still on George's body. They boarded first and then lifted up and Chito let out a yelp and Nehemiah laughed and George smiled up at them and the lady looked at them with complete and utter indifference, even scowling a bit, but George had to wonder if that was just the way her face rested when she wasn't putting on a better one. The next bucket came around and she told him to hop in, dropping the bar in front of him.

"Hold on to that hat of yours. Long drop," she said. Her voice was like sandpaper, but he tried to be polite, so he took the hat off and held it in his lap.

The big wheel began to lift again and there was no one else getting on after him. He watched as she flipped a big switch and it started to move a bit faster. He rose and the next buggy didn't stop when it came around for pickup, they only kept rising as the other side came back around. He realized then that he had never tested a fear of heights out and he might have a problem with how high he was about to be up in the thing. But there was nowhere to go, he could only assume that the wheel had no reverse. So, a bright idea popped into his head and George closed his eyes. With the wind rushing around him faster as he lifted and lifted, he waited until he guessed that he was nearing the peak of the ride. Above him, he could hear the two other boys talking but couldn't hear what they were saying. He could only make out Chito's excitement in his yelling over the sounds around them. Nearby he heard the whoosh of a bird past his head. After what felt like long enough, and a little help from Chito yelling out *would you look at that view* loud enough that he could hear, George opened his eyes.

"Wow," he whispered to himself.

He nearly dropped the top hat from his lap, where it might've landed directly on that homely woman's head and made her a touch more handsome. He couldn't believe his own eyes. The green and blue and yellow and red and brown and gray and white earth displayed before him.

He could see the entirety of the fair.

He saw people walking in giant tents where cattle were being led in and out on the back side.

He could see a horde of folks standing around a little racetrack where tiny pink blobs ran around in circles. He assumed they were pigs and he had to laugh at the idea of watching a pig run.

He watched as long lines of little people walked together towards food stands. They looked like ants.

He smelled nothing but cool air.

He saw a stage. It must have been the largest he'd ever seen, much bigger than the one at church. He saw large speakers being set up in front of it and workers, carpenter ants he thought with a giggle, hauling boxes around.

He saw, in the distance, past the stage, the biggest tent of all. It was round and had stripes of red and a dirty white. In the center it was open to the elements and a tall pole stuck out of it. Behind the tent, he could barely make out what looked to be cages, big containers made of metal bars. But he couldn't see what, if anything, was in them. He wasn't sure on distance anymore, being up so high, but he figured it must be a mile away.

He saw the horizon and trees in all directions.

He turned his head and saw back to the entrance of the fair and the city behind that, jostling and bustling. He saw the smoke from engines rising above the buildings there.

He wondered if this is what God feels like.

The ride descended and he placed the hat back on his head before coming around at the bottom to the loading platform.

His friends were waiting there for him as he hopped off the bench seat.

"Worth it?" Chito asked him.

"I was gonna ask you the same question."

"I wish everybody could see that."

"Fellers, all that lookin' around has made me hungry for a little snack. Maybe some corn on the cob. What do you think?"

"Can we ride it again later?" Chito asked.

Nehemiah grinned at him and they started off in the direction that George knew the circus was in but was mighty far off and he felt like an explorer going on a journey in an unknown land with unknown creatures as they reentered the area where people did their best to get somewhere. He thought of the stories he'd been taught in school. Greek men who were half God who went on long journeys or were punished eternally for taking things that weren't theirs. Or Jesus himself, journeying all around the desert and being kind to people and throwing tables when he had to. He hoped he was the hero of this tale.

14

THEY STOPPED at a corn on the cob stand for Nehemiah, who bought two and ate them before they could find a trash can to throw them in, so the boy just chucked them on the ground off the path a bit. They saw an ice cream stand and George couldn't hardly contain himself. He'd only had the treat once, when he was a pup and he'd followed his mammy into town and a man that had been coming over to the house for a couple of weeks met them there and went into a diner and came out with a cup of vanilla ice cream for him. By God, it might not have been a tall tale to say that he'd thought about it every week since, even if that man did not last much longer than the ice cream itself, melting in the light of George's mother's gaze. He ordered vanilla ice cream here again, even as Nehemiah urged him to try chocolate or even strawberry for the chunks of frozen fruit in it. George ignored him and, once he had the small cup cold heaven in his hand, he simply told Nehemiah that he could keep the other flavors for himself, he only needed one. This one is to her memory, he thought, as he scooped a bit onto a tiny wooden spoon and into his mouth. Cold rushed in like a wave and he smiled and he ate it too fast and by the time it was gone the roof of his mouth felt like it might fall off.

After walking for no more than a minute or so past the ice cream stand, they ran into a crowd. George couldn't remember seeing them before and he reckoned, by the sun and a general awareness he thought he had, that it couldn't have been more than a half hour since he'd been up on that giant spinning wheel looking out over the whole of it. But here was this mass, this glob of people. On first glance, from what he could tell, they were all white. A mix of men and women, many blond women holding their babies up on their chests or some of those same fathers before holding them on their shoulders. Nehemiah tried to lead the charge through them so they could keep on sightseeing, but the crowd was impenetrable. They stopped there and he turned back to George and Chito and looked at them as if they'd know what was going on. The two boys just shrugged back at him. It was his thing after all. So Nehemiah tapped the closest man on the shoulder.

"Hey mister, what's all this for?" He asked.

"It's a rally," he replied.

"For what?"

"You come all the way to the fair today and don't know what for?" The man chuckled and turned to another man beside him as if someone else had to be in on the joke. Nehemiah's face turned a little redder than it was before.

"No, sir. I just came to the fair."

"That's it, huh. Well, it's for the man running for governor. Randall Knight."

"Alright. Thank ye, mister."

Nehemiah turned back to them and asked the boys if they wanted to stay and hear what this politician would have to say. He said he'd heard his father mention the man and that he was thinking about voting for him so it couldn't hurt for him to hear what this man was all about in case he'd want to do the same. George had figured enough of the boy to know that he would vote for whoever his father voted for but there was no need in calling his bluff. Chito turned around and they followed his gaze to find that the crowd had swallowed them whole. There was a mass behind them by then.

"Well, I reckon we got nowhere to go anyway," Chito said, with a shrug. Nehemiah grinned a little and craned his neck to see around them.

"That does seem to be the truth."

Just then, as if the decision would be made for them in every which way, the shriek of a microphone blasted through the big speakers surrounding the stage and the crowd winced, turning towards where it came from. George could see just enough over the heads in front of him to watch as a white man in a pale, khaki suit stepped out onto the platform. He squinted at him, recognizing something familiar in his gait and the hat he wore, but he couldn't place it. It felt like something far away. Like a bird had picked the memory up as if it were a seed and transported it somewhere secret, where he'd never find it. At least not looking at him from this far away. The man stepped up to the microphone center stage and looked out over the crowd. George imagined what it'd be like to look out over a horde of people that look just like you. The idea was short-lived.

"Well, I'll be," the man started. The microphone was so loud that his voice became a boom, not like that of any human George had ever heard.

"I don't think I've ever seen a crowd of people quite like this one in my entire life. Thank y'all for coming on this beautiful day and taking time out of your recreation at our glorious state's fair to listen to this old feller speak."

The volume had been turned down and, like a revelation from God, George was transported back to when he was just a pup and he went home looking for that knife and there was that man, there was this man, standing in front of him just as he stood today but only closer, towering over him and speaking to him as if he were his own while his mammy looked on with horror in her eyes and then he saw the man leaving and still watching him more intently than any of his mammy's visitors had and then he was driving off in that car of his. And then George was sucked back into the present. The man was still speaking and he'd missed some of it but none of that mattered because he felt like vomiting up that ice cream right then and there. His whole body grew cold like he was feverish.

"Hey, you alright?" Chito whispered in his ear.

He turned and nodded and looked around and remembered that there was nowhere to go. He sucked some air in and felt for his pack of asthma cigarettes in his pocket and it was still there. He took deep breaths until his hearing returned and he could hear this man again. He was speaking of the terror that politicians in Washington had laid upon Mississippi and the south as a whole and how someone had to do something about it before the country sucked them dry of every bit of culture and history and export that this great state had. Nehemiah watched intently.

George felt himself turn back to Chito and whisper to him something that did not come from his brain in the sense that he thought it and decided to speak it. It just came out of him and he couldn't do anything about it.

"I think that's my pa," he said to his friend.

"You what?" Chito asked, turning to him with a look of disbelief.

"I think that's my pa."

"That man up there?" He pointed towards the stage and his voice grew a little louder and a man beside him gave him a look of *shut the hell up, kid*. George's eyes seconded the message.

"Yes."

"How do you figure?" Chito asked, back to a whisper.

"I met him. When I was little. He was at my house talking to my mammy."

"Well son of a bitch. You sure you're alright?"

"Yeah. Can't go nowhere anyway."

They both turned back to the man and he spoke of getting money for the poor farmers of Mississippi. He spoke of politicians who'd rather send our nation off to war again in Europe and spend all of the hard working Americans' dollars on bullets that would kill people that we have no sense in killing.

"What sense does it make for one of your husbands or brothers or sons to go over there and fight Hitler and Germany because he's waging a war with the Jews? I don't see a single Jew in this crowd. And even if there were one, Hitler can't touch you from all the way over there."

The crowd laughed.

Then, he grew silent for a moment and George imagined that the man's face grew weary as his tone changed.

"But I'll tell you what I'm most of all worried about. The main point I want to go Washington and set straight. That's the race problem. And I've got some ideas I believe can fix every problem we have."

He began to speak of miscegenation, a word George had never heard before but learned soon that he knew well—better than anyone else in the crowd he figured.

"If we continue to allow interbreeding of white folk with Negroes and Injuns then, my God—" He stopped to wipe his brow in a manner of utmost drama. "My God, we will be allowing the end of our great nation much too soon. In less time than we have had since Washington's great revolution and creation of this wonderful country that I do love so dearly, we will have no more whites. We will have no more Negroes. We will have no more redskin people of old. We will only have mongrels. Yellow-skinned. To be turned into nothing more than some poor imitation, some shoddy reproduction of a Mexican or a Chinaman. No, my God, no. The record shows that the average rate of marriage between Whites and Blacks in the 18 states where this unholiness is deemed legal is now over 600 a year. Ten years, it's 6,000. In less than 300 years, there'll be no White people in this county. There'll be no Negroes in this country. We'll all be brown. Facial features that don't look anything like the people to your right and left. You know what, do that right now. Turn to those around you. Turn to your brother. Turn to your wife. Look at them faces. Do you want that face to be lost to history? Do you want that face to be gone from this nation?"

Everyone around them shook their heads and looked at each other and then George noticed a boy in the crowd, no more than twenty feet away, staring at him. He was tall and white and young-looking and his mouth was open and his head was cocked to the side and he looked to be no longer listening to the speech at all.

"I'll leave you with this, great people of Jackson and all around our state. A vote for me is a vote for Mississippi's history."

Randall Knight paused for extra dramaticism. The boy was maybe five feet closer to George. People were packed in so tightly that he was having a hard time getting to them. But he wouldn't take his eyes off of them. He just kept shoving through.

"And, and a vote for me is a vote for Mississippi's future."

People cheered. The boy gained ten feet faster than George expected.

"A vote for me is a vote for Mississippi's farmer."

His voice grew louder. The people cheered again. The boy was in George's face. Nehemiah and Chito turned as he approached.

"You ain't white boys," he said to George and Chito. His accent was slower than molasses. He chewed on tobacco and spit after he said this.

"What?" Chito asked, earnestly.

"A vote for me is a vote for Mississippi's race lines," Knight said.

His voice and the crowd were deafening around them.

"You ain't white boys."

"Why do you say that?" George asked. He tried to keep his voice steady and his eyes calm. His hands shook in his pockets.

"A vote for me is a vote for a nation that respects this land of ours and the people on it."

The crowd exploded in yelps and hollers.

The white boy took his thumb up to his mouth and swished his mouth around and licked his thumb and placed the thumb, wet with slobber, on Chito's face and pulled it down so hard that every bit of white powder disappeared into the spit on the boy's finger and the brown of Chito's face was on display once more. The boy's eyes got big and George would swear later that he could see a fire burning in them, a fire straight from hell.

"Hey, what the hell are you doing," Nehemiah yelled, stepping in between them.

"These two boys are injun," the boy shouted. "These two fellers right here ain't white. They ain't supposed to be here."

His voice was loud but not loud enough. In the moment he began to yell out, a marching band appeared on the stage and fired up their instruments to play the national anthem. The microphone picked it up and suddenly everything around them was drums and horns and pure noise. George could only see the boy's mouth now. He was still yelling the same thing and trying to get anyone to take notice.

Nehemiah turned and looked at them with panic in his eyes like he'd just then realized what he'd done and George saw his mouth tell them to go and run and get out of there and so George grabbed his friend by the arm and pulled him and Chito bounced on his one leg and crutch and they forced their way through that jubilant crowd and George looked back to see Nehemiah trailing them and hand fighting that boy and then Nehemiah shoved a man in front of the boy and the man turned to the boy, thinking it was him who did it, and Nehemiah's eyes said turn the hell around and get going and so George did. He ran, practically holding his friend up in the air, all the way until there was no longer any crowd and he realized they were standing in front of that giant tent from earlier and George pulled out an asthma cigarette and lit it and sucked in as many puffs as he could.

15

"THAT WAS UNBELIEVABLE," Nehemiah said as he ran up behind them and stopped, bending over with his hands on his knees and huffing air. He looked up after a moment and his eyes spelled confusion. "You're smoking a cigarette after that? Just standing here smoking a cigarette?"

"It's—"

"I would've gotten thrown in jail with you two and you're just standing out in the open smoking a cigarette."

"Hey," Chito said, making his voice stern. "It's for his amsa."

"What?"

"Asthma. He meant to say asthma," George replied. Smoke rolled out of his mouth.

"Oh, you're one of them boys who can't breathe?"

George nodded.

"Well good to know for next time we have to run away, I guess. One can't breathe and one is crippled. What the hell was I thinking?"

"What's the matter with you?" Chito asked.

"I can't get caught."

"I mean, neither can we. What's the big deal? We're already here. In the damn thick of it."

"If I go to jail again, Pa will kick me out and fire me and I'll have nowhere to go."

"Again?" George asked. He picked up his foot and stubbed the cigarette out on his shoe and took a deep breath in and for the most part he was alright again, if not just a little horse.

"I got in trouble last year. I was s'posed to go to college and I got real drunk one night with some other fellers and I woke up in jail with a bloody nose. Simple as that. Pa said he'd keep a roof over my head and food in my belly and some money in my pockets if I'd stay clean and then maybe he'd pull some strings to get me back into college after a year or two."

"And you're just now considering how this adventure of ours might be dangerous?" George asked.

"I guess so."

"Well, I'll be."

"Hey," Nehemiah's face got red and his eyes got squinty. "You don't get to talk to me like that, boy."

"Boy?" George asked.

"What?" For a brief moment, Nehemiah's face dropped to innocence and he scanned George and Chito's faces for a context he was missing.

"Who you calling boy?"

"Oh," the white boy replied, looking like he realized. "I'll call you whatever the hell I want to call you. I took you on this trip. You could at least show me some damn respect. I've paid for every damn thing."

"I didn't ask for none of this."

"You took it though."

George reached both of his arms out and pushed the boy. Chito got in between them as Nehemiah reared up to respond with his own shove. His face was as red as a tomato.

"Guys, let's relax," Chito said.

"To hell with you," Nehemiah yelled. He looked around as he did this but there was no one there to look at him with embarrassment so he kept going. "Just like one of you to get all high and mighty after you ate that ice cream like a child. Want to act like you ain't a dirt poor redskin. Like you're better than me."

"You sound like that man we just listened to," George said. He felt like he'd reached a point of anger at this boy that bottomed out into something completely different. A calmness washed over him. Like his mammy was right there beside him. Like she'd appeared through that ice cream and would again be there to protect him in the way she always did. He wasn't worried about anything. Not anything at all.

"Nehemiah, just calm down. We'll go check out this circus and cool off a little. Just been a long day. That crowd and all that noise has got us running thin. We just need some time," Chito said, still standing between his two friends.

"Aw, shut up, Chito. You ain't no better than him. I can't believe I thought this was a good idea. Risk my livelihood on two injuns. Here I was thinking you was a friend of mine but all you care about is seeing some damn circus. You just used me to get here, same as he did."

"Miah, you wanted me to come. And I appreciated it."

"Shut the hell up. I done said my piece." The more the boy screamed, the worse his English got, George noticed.

"Come on, Miah."

As Chito said this, the white boy took a step back and it looked as if steam poured out of his ears and he balled his fist up and swung, swung real hard at Chito. His fist hit him square in the temple and the crippled boy fell down immediately, like a hammer hitting a piece of wood standing up on its end. Before George knew what he was doing, he did the same to Nehemiah. He punched him across the jaw and punched him one more time for good measure and the boy stumbled back, putting his hands to his face. Then they both stopped, George with his fists still up like a boxer. He'd seen other boys get in this stance so he fell into it, expecting to have a fight on his hands against an older, bigger boy that he figured he wouldn't be able to win. But Nehemiah lowered his hands and his face was real pale and he stepped back one more time. He shook his head and grinned a little. Blood trickled out of the left side of his lip and there was already a bruise by the eye on the same side.

"Go to hell," he yelled out. "Why don't you boys figure out how to get on home on your lonesome."

George considered shouting back at the boy as he turned and walked away but he figured it best to check on his friend there on the ground. He knelt down and touched Chito's face and he opened his eyes and looked up at George.

"You alright?" George asked.

"Yeah."

"You hear any of that? Or did he knock you out?"

"I guess so."

"He's gone."

Chito's eyes got wide like he'd seen a ghost and he pushed himself up and grabbed his crutch. He turned his head back and forth as if to check and see if what George had said was true. A cut above his eye bled slowly.

"Where is he?" he asked frantically.

"He left. Said he was going home."

"Well, we gotta catch him."

"Why?"

"Are you serious?" He was yelling now, and George found it curious how much he sounded like Nehemiah. "He's our ride home. We're in Jackson, George. Jackson."

"He left us. He just coldcocked you and left you on the ground. Didn't even check if you were alright. He don't give a shit about you, Chito. He talked to me like I was shit on the bottom of his boot. You, too. He's just another white boy."

His friend stopped looking around and stared him directly in his eyes. There was a coldness there that he had never seen, or at least hadn't noticed before. Chito took a step back from him and a tear welled up in his eye but his expression didn't waver.

"We're dead if we stay here."

"We'll figure it out. I'm not gonna go find him and suck up to him."

Chito nodded and looked like he was thinking.

"He go that way?" he asked, pointing in the direction Nehemiah had run off.

"Yeah."

"I think I gotta find him, George. I can't not get back to my family."

"I won't apologize to that son of a bitch."

"I already got this makeup on anyway. What is it to suck up to one more white man?"

And with that, Chito started off walking in the direction of the gates. George watched as his friend pulled the white powder from his pocket and started reapplying where he felt like he'd been hit. George knew then that if he didn't follow him he'd probably be stuck there in that god-awful city with all of those god-awful people. And if Chito was gone, he had no one. The only other person in Jackson that he knew or who knew him in the slightest was the man who'd called him a mongrel from atop that stage. But he couldn't move his legs towards Chito and towards Nehemiah and towards the gate. He just stood there and watched as his life went on past him. And he recognized that he was never going back home again then. But he didn't move his legs. He thought that maybe home wasn't there anymore and hadn't been for a while. He thought that he'd figure it out. He thought that if he'd been able to figure it out when his mammy died and he was just an adolescent, he could figure it out in this moment too. And he heard a sound behind him. Like a man shouting. He turned and there was a carnie, dressed up in a bright red outfit and standing in front of the entrance to the big circus tent. He was yelling that the show would start soon and people were beginning to file past him inside where it was dark and George couldn't see in. He considered his options. He looked back once more and Chito's outline was barely visible, moving away as quick as he could on his crutch. And George's head turned back and his legs began to move towards that tent.

HIS EYES HAD TO ADJUST to the dim, dirt-floor, candle-lit tunnel that was the entrance of the circus. He blinked furiously to get his vision on track. Beside him and in front of him and behind him were all white people doing the same and making small comments and jokes to their wives and husbands and children and other family members, *the candles aren't hardly doing anything and where the heck are you taking me, Bill?* As they continued into the darkness, sounds began to break through the symphony of voices around George. He heard what sounded like a trumpet but unlike any trumpet he'd ever heard, one that didn't care about the quality of its notes. He heard people cheering and hands clapping. And through cracks in between the heads and shoulders of the folks in front of him, he saw light at the end of the tunnel. As they got closer to it, the tunnel opened up into a giant room where rows and rows of people were standing in a circle and he turned to the right, following the crowd of people, and saw then that there were rows of seats going up high like in an auditorium. He followed the herd until an open chair caught his eye, way up near the top, and he ran up to get it before anyone else could. He sat down and looked out and saw an elephant standing there. Right before his eyes, in the center of the room. It was standing in a big circular space that had thick netting all around it. People stood on the edges on George's side of the netting and they were hollering and laughing at the big animal. The standing room and the auditorium seating went up on three sides of the ring and there was a back wall where there seemed to be nothing there but the tent. The elephant was trouncing around and a small man stood beside him carrying what looked to be a sack of apples in one hand and a lasso in the other. George figured it had to be the biggest living creature he'd ever seen. On the ground was a giant ball, red and blue with a star on it, and the elephant would slowly pick it up with its giant trunk and throw the ball around before chasing after it and starting again. But before chasing after it, every time it threw the ball the little man in there with it would hand the great elephant an apple. People threw peanuts at it through the netting, most just falling on the ground by its feet. Every once in a while the elephant would pick a group of peanuts up and chuck them into its mouth and more people would throw handfuls in at the sight of this. After some time watching this elephant go around and round, the man pulled out one final trick. It was a big wooden ring. He picked it up and held it out in front of the animal and the elephant let his trunkdown and curved it up and into the ring and lifted it out of the man's hands. Then it began to move its trunk around in a circle, slowly, and the ring bounced and jumped around on that big gray nose and everyone there shouted and cheered for the thing. A little boy's voice appeared from somewhere near George and it said "Do it again! Do it again!" as the elephant lowered its trunk and gave the ring back to the man. At the back of the ring, the tent opened up then and the man and the elephant left, disappearing into whatever was back there. As the act ended, men appeared all around wearing the same outfit of brown pants and a white shirt and a red vest and they all had little curious red hats on atop their heads and they were holding out many bags of peanuts each and yelling out into the crowd for people to buy them. And then into George's ear, another voice appeared, that of an old woman's. He ignored the voice, scanning his eyes around the tent and watching the hundreds of white folk enjoying themselves as they waited for the next act. He'd almost forgotten about his troubles and Chito and Nehemiah and his father and that white boy. He was enjoying himself. But then he realized that that voice in his ear was speaking to him.

"Honey, you hear me?" it asked.

George turned and found a lady beside him, staring into his eyes. She was old, older than any person he figured he'd ever seen or at least that he could remember. His first instinct was to wonder how she was in the circus tent in the first place, how she walked all the way to it.

"No, no, ma'am. Sorry, I didn't hear you."

"That's alright, it's hard to hear in a place like this. I know best." As she said this, she smiled without showing her teeth. Her lips were cracked with the years, like the rest of her, but George had a notion in that moment that she must've been beautiful a long, long time ago. "Is this your first time at a circus?"

"Yes, ma'am."

"Would you believe that I once was in a circus?"

She smiled at him again and he made a face of exaggerated shock to humor her. She laughed and continued.

"I used to ride horses around. Well, one horse. His name was Lightning. You can figure out why." She shot her eyes over at him and grinned. "They'd put up these big rings we'd jump through and these big blocks we'd jump over and we'd run around the circle of the ring over and over again. He had so much energy that it was hard to get him stopped once you started him up. So the grand finale was always a ring of fire that we'd jump through. He'd run up a ramp and leap through it and I'd lay down on his back and spread my arms out like they were wings and I was flying. And we'd set it up so that as soon as we went through it, Lightning would just run straight through the back exit of the tent and we'd keep on going into an open field because I mean it when I say that boy couldn't stop running once you started him. I'd have to talk to him in whispers while we raced around outside and the show kept going."

"That sounds beautiful. I've never ridden a horse."

"Horses are like people. If they look at you as a friend, they're good to you. Better than people can be."

George looked over at her and nodded and watched as it seemed that her eyes were glazing over in memory and for a moment he imagined a tear, a single droplet, leaving her right eye. He felt bad for staring then so he looked back out to where the center ring was and saw that they were setting up some kind of small platform out there.

"Do you miss it?"

"What's that?" she said, her eyes returning to his face and back to the space they were in.

"Do you miss the circus?"

"Oh. I don't know. Maybe. I miss Lightning."

"What happened to him?"

"The same way all the show horses go. He broke his leg and they put him down. I couldn't bear to watch it, so I went somewhere else. They came and told me he was gone." George caught a glimpse of that glaze over her eyes again. "I regretted that for a long time. Not being there with him. I thought about how he must have been afraid. And especially after all he'd done for me. Even when he broke his leg, he didn't let me get hurt. It was our last show. Of course, I didn't know that at the time and I'd assume Lightning didn't either but it was our last show together. He jumped through that ring of fire at the end and buckled a little but caught himself and kept going. I remember wondering what it was and looking back at the ramp to see if he'd busted a hole in it as he raced on but it looked to be in working shape. We got out of the tent and he made it maybe thirty feet before he just stopped and leaned down real slowly, to let me off. He'd never done that before. I got off and saw right then and there that his front right leg was broken. Just snapped, the bone was sticking out. I guess he'd landed wrong. But he hadn't fallen into that ring or nothing. He made sure I didn't get hurt with him."

"He was a good friend."

"Better than most people."

"I always wanted to go to the circus and so did my friend, but he left me here," George said. "So, it's just me here."

She didn't say anything for a while, just looking out over the crowd and the empty ring in front of them, and he didn't wait for her to say anything. He figured she might have been tired. And then, the room began to dim. George realized then that there was one big light, hanging from the roof in the center of the room. It slowly got darker and darker until it was completely off. The only light in the room were candles on the walls and he could barely see past his nose. He heard a whooshing sound, and, at the opposite wall, he watched the tent open just large enough for one person to walk through and he saw the light of the early moon shine through the opening, but he couldn't see the person who had entered the room. He became aware of the heat in the room then, with all those people packed in so tightly surrounded by candles and thick canvas walls.

A person somewhere far off to his right yelled something unintelligible with a sense of urgency.

"Why did they leave you?" the old woman asked him. He didn't answer immediately, because he wasn't sure how to answer the question honestly with her being white, and she reached her hand over and touched his knee. When he turned his head to her in the darkness, she spoke again. "What's your name?"

"George, ma'am."

"Mm. And why did your friend leave you, George?"

"He had to go back home."

"Where is home for you?"

He started to answer her and then he wasn't so sure, again, that he had an answer for her. His mind returned to how he felt outside and he thought about Chito and Koi and their ma and pa and Susanna. But he thought about the police officer. He thought about Miss Joy. He thought about how things can change so suddenly. One person dies. One person is arrested. One person leaves. And then a tie is gone. And when a person only has one or two ties, or anchors, to a place that they called their home and those ties that bind vanish suddenly like a leaf taken downstream by a fast-moving river, that sense of home is gone. There was a hole inside his brain now and inside his heart and he couldn't think of an answer to her question. And then there was a whispering in his ear.

"I grew up on a reservation. I'll bet just like your grandparents did. And that home was taken from me. Was it taken from you?"

He swung his face towards her and she was close to him and he could smell her breath, like cherries, and her eyes there in the glimmer of candlelight told of so many thousands of memories that you could not fool her with some poorly applied white woman's powder. He started to ask her something like *what* or *what are you talking about* but he couldn't bear to be defensive in the light of this face, this face that bore the weight of everything lost that he never had the chance of knowing. He thought then about how many ties she must have had to her home and how they were broken and whether it was slow or sudden. He started to ask her something like *how did you know.* He started to burst into tears because he hadn't done so in so long.

But before he could, light, hot red light, appeared at the corner of his vision and they both turned to see.

Fire. There was fire there, in the center of the room. First, one flame sitting atop a large stick that was in the hand of a person that he could not yet see. Then, the flame met another piece of wood to its right and lit the other ablaze and there were two fires standing there in the air in the hot, dark room. The light from the second fire showed a face. A girl. Her hair was amber brown in the light and her face was beautiful in its mystery. George could make out a nose, a button nose, and two big eyes that might have been blue or green or hazel but he was too far away to tell for sure and lips that were pursed together in effort and concentration and he couldn't help but wish that they'd loosen their grip on each other because he knew that they must be beautiful lips, and he would have wondered to himself why he was thinking so suddenly like this about someone that he was just seeing for the first time and could barely see at all but then that girl, standing there so still with the flames jumping at the slightest bit of draft, began to move about.

She twirled the two flaming pieces of wood in her hands faster and faster until they were spinning like automobile wheels going down a road, if only the wheels were red and orange and dangerous. George was mesmerized immediately. And then she threw them, yes, threw them up into the air as they still spun upon some hidden axis, rising and rising in the air and rotating like two new suns. They barely missed the top of the tent and sure disaster and plummeted to the dirt. The crowd gasped. She caught them, just as she'd been holding them by their cool handles before letting them go.

George heard a woman scream and a man yell.

"Well, I'll be," the man yelped.

Then they all watched as this girl with her fire, like Prometheus, from the Greek story that he'd been taught by the white teacher in his last year of school before he stopped going because he had to work, the one who stole the fire from them Greek gods and gave it to people, yes, she was a female Prometheus, however that would sound in Greek, maybe her name was Prim, this girl with her fire. She turned her back to the front of the crowd, where George sat, and she walked to the back of the room where her entrance and exit was and she turned to the right and she knelt down and tipped one of her flame batons to the dirt and suddenly the fire exploded onto the ground and followed a trail around the ring, making a semicircle of fire there on the ground around her, only leaving enough space for her to exit out of the back.

"My God," George heard a woman cry out.

Some people began to clear out of the room at this, terrified of being in the room that was so hot and felt as if the canvas walls may go up at any moment. They rushed out in the aisle in front of George to the exit. And he heard that old lady beside him again, she was chuckling. The laugh of someone so old that the air has a hard time getting out, as if it might be worried that there isn't enough left in her to leave behind. In front of them, the girl with flame in her hands had returned to the middle of the room. George thought that, yes, some kind of small god might be the only way to describe what he was looking at. She was no ordinary woman.

The girl began to twirl her fire batons around and she threw them in the air once more and caught them just as she had before. Then she bounced on the balls of her feet and danced, continuing the work she was doing with her hands, as she traipsed around the room. He'd never seen anything like this before. Her movements looked as if they had no goal, nowhere they had to get to or would end up even by accident. She hopped and skipped and gyrated and the flames kept working round and round in her hands. She juggled the batons with flames on their tips and spun around at the same time. She next threw them up across to each other and caught them behind her back.

"How is she doing that, mommy?" a little white boy shouted somewhere in the not-too-far distance in the crowd.

She danced some more, turning the batons over and sideways and spinning them and holding them both in one hand as she did a cartwheel, throwing them in the air just as they would have hit the ground and catching them as she stood back up. The room was so hot George felt his skin might melt clean off. But he couldn't leave. He couldn't even stand up. His legs felt like they weren't there, his body too. His eyes were separate from his body and his head and they were only for the use of watching this divine creature and her fire. She stopped in the middle of the room again and George could see her chest protruding and caving in and repeating as she caught her breath.

She knelt down once more there and picked up what looked to be a third stick from the ground. And this it was, because she tipped it into one of the two already lit in her hands and lit it all the same and then she had three. Before her was the platform that had been set up before her act and she had all but ignored it throughout the act so far, so much so that George had forgotten about it, like it disappeared from view until she made note of it and he now had to notice it. She walked up it. It was black and made of metal and had stairs that led up to a platform just wide enough for one person and a beam protruding from the front of it that held up a small platform. The size of a foot, maybe. She got to the platform at the top of the stairs and began to juggle as she had been. She did this for not long, a minute or two maybe. George noticed then that there hadn't been a boring moment throughout and how impressive that was but there wasn't enough time to think, again, because the crowd was gasping and when his eyes readjusted he saw that she had all three sticks aflame in her left hand and she was hoisting herself up on that tiny platform on the beam.

"How is she doing that, mommy?" that little white boy repeated in the dark.

"I have not the slightest idea, honey, but you are never trying it."

"Aw, but it looks fun," the boy cried.

The girl got herself up on the small platform and she put one foot down on it because that truly was all the space allowed and she lifted her other leg up and pointed her foot in the air and her legs made a right angle and then she passed one of the flaming batons to her empty hand and she stood there like a statue for a moment before throwing them all in the air at once. She juggled them. Like it was easy. Like the air was only there to lift and carry each of these sticks on fire to the hand waiting to catch it. Like she had a pact with God that he would make sure her balance was perfect and her hands were perfect and her vision was perfect and these batons were perfect and the platform was perfect all so that she could appear perfect before a crowd.

The back of the tent opened once more and two men came in carrying what looked to be a mattress and they slid it under where she stood in front of the platform's steps and then she jumped.

A chorus of onlookers cried out.

She jumped in the air and turned so that her back was to the ground and her face to the sky and she flung the three flaming batons in a flick towards where those men still stood off behind the platform and they let them hit the dirt instead of trying to catch them and then, like a dove or an eagle or some other beautiful bird, she landed on that mattress with as graceful of a thud as a thud could be.

The crowd was quiet and the mother of that little boy gasped.

The girl stood up and looked out onto the crowd from atop the mattress and took three bows in every direction where folks sat. And as she walked back to the exit of the tent, the crowd stood up in response and cheered for her in a roar like the sound of a train approaching. George felt his legs work again and he was standing with the rest of them, lifting his fingers to his mouth and whistling loudly. And then she was gone, just like that.

George felt a tug on his shirt sleeve and he turned to see that old woman again. The big light in the center of the room came on and he could see her more clearly and her face showed something that was familiar to him. Her smile was wide and she tugged his sleeve again to get him to lean in. The crowd was still cheering and a man came into the center of the ring and yelled out thank yous to the crowd for coming to see the first circus in the history of Mississippi and the crowd continued to cheer and holler and whistle and clap their hands together and make a ruckus. George leaned down and in so that he was close to the old woman.

"Isn't she lovely?" she asked him.

"Yes, yes, ma'am, she sure is," he replied. All around them, folks began to file out.

"Where are you going now, boy?"

"I don't know rightly yet, miss."

"You will figure it out," she said, and he had to lean in even closer to hear her as she continued. "It may not be a better place, but there is always another place. They can drive you out but there is always somewhere else until you find the place where you know that you must make a stand because it's the place where you should be. But if the ties are cut on the place you're in, do not try to put them back together. Go find the next."

He nodded and she smiled once more at him and squeezed his arm and looked at his face hard.

"And before you leave, put some more of that powder on your face, dear."

He laughed and she smiled again. He looked away for a moment.

"Could you tell me about your reservation?" he asked her. But when he turned around, the crowd had moved towards the exit and she was gone inside of it. He searched for her but saw no trace of the lady. He wished he could learn more from her. He wished he could know her better. He wished he could know more about heritage and the old ways. He pulled the powder out as discreetly as he could and popped some on his face before he followed everyone out.

IT WAS DARK when he walked out of the circus tent. The air was cool and the moon was barely visible above the trees in a crescent. Its light was cool like the air and you could hardly see more than twenty feet ahead of you. But George could still see the random signs dispersed all around him for different snacks and goods and wares at the shops. And carnies were still yelling things out in the distance. The fair was not done just because it was night and, for some reason, that comforted George. He thought about it for a moment, still standing in front of the tent entrance, and figured that the longer the fair was open, the better it was for him. He thought too about what that woman had said to him. He thought about Chito and Nehemiah and he wondered if he should be wishing that they were still around somewhere on the fairgrounds and that they had reconciled and they were just walking around trying to find him so they could all go home together. But that woman's words rang in his ears and he felt confused, but not so confused, like he was forcing himself to think it over too much.

So, he stood there for a few minutes. He'd liked to have told someone, if they'd asked what he was doing, that he was thinking his options over. But that wasn't the truth. He was just standing there breathing in the air and smelling the fragrances of popped corn and fried chicken and, behind him, the smells of animal shit from the circus. Devoid of options, he didn't have any to consider. He started to walk away from the circus for good and back into the thick of the fairgrounds when he heard a voice.

"There he is," the voice said, it was male and seemed like one he'd heard before.

George turned around and scanned the area but he couldn't find where the voice was coming from. For a second he wondered if the fair was haunted. A silly thought. That girl with her fire had made him think silly thoughts.

"You sure that's him?" Another voice, less familiar to George, asked. It came from somewhere to his right. As George looked over there, trying to make his movements as inconspicuous as possible, he realized that, who it was, was likely in the small thicket of trees by the circus tent that he'd figured marked the boundary of where folks could go. He tried to slowly start walking in the other direction, towards the stage and the ice cream stand and everything else.

"Hey, redskin," the first voice called out.

George kept walking and tried to ignore it, his steps gaining speed away from the voice.

"Hey, Geronimo," it called out, louder this time. "I know you heard me, boy. I get the name wrong? Is it Tecumseh?"

George turned. He didn't want to be angry anymore. In some odd and potentially naïve way, he didn't feel like he could be angry anymore. He just wanted to keep on going. But he calculated in his mind then, just like he'd done in school with little numbers when their classroom ran out of pencils and paper and the white teacher told them they had to just figure it out in their heads unless they had a stone tablet to pull out and the teacher had laughed and none of the boys had understood the laughter, he calculated in his mind then whether running would even work. He was in a place full of white people. There was nowhere for him to go where he would find a friendly face. He turned around and his eyes took a moment to adjust to the lack of light at the edge of the thicket where the trees covered up the moon from view and them from the view of the moon and then he saw the two boys standing there.

"What?" George said. His voice was quieter than he expected it to be and he wondered if he was scared. He wasn't sure.

"You think you can just run off like that?"

"What are you talking about?"

The boys got closer, and George saw the face from his father's political rally. The boy who had wiped the white off his face.

"You break the law and come here with white powder on your face and you get caught and you try to run off. You go to our circus like you own the damn place."

"I think you've got the wrong idea."

"I don't get wrong ideas, buddy," the boy said. They were now face to face, a few feet apart. George could see in the boy's eyes now and there was a hunger there that he did not know. He didn't pay any attention to the other boy, who wasn't saying anything but just walking a step behind. The first boy licked one of his big thumbs and reached out, just as he'd done before, and wiped the powder off George's face. He stood stock-still and could smell the tobacco in the boy's spittle.

"Well, would you look at that," the second boy said.

"I told you. You think I was lying?"

"I just never thought I'd see something like this."

"You think you can come in here and dress up like a white man? You think that?" the first boy asked, now pointing his glares back to George.

George didn't know what to say. He was scared. He wished Koi was around. He realized that having an older brother might have been a luxury he didn't appreciate enough.

"Now he's mute," the boy said, laughing. The other boy laughed with him. George snuck a glance at this other boy and he was skinny and wore glasses and his teeth, lit up by the signs behind George now, were crooked and half missing. He had a fleeting thought that, if it broke down, this boy was not something to worry about. But the thought left and was replaced by another that told him that everything had already broken down.

"I'm not trying to cause no trouble, fellers," George said.

"I hope not. You've already caused enough just by being here," the bigger boy said with a false comforting tone. "So, are you actually an injun? Or are you mulatto? What the hell are you?"

George didn't answer again.

"Huh? I asked you a question."

"I'm Choctaw and white," George said. He didn't know why he said it this way. He'd never done it before. Possibly because of the confirmation he'd received earlier by way of seeing his father again and looking him in the eyes from afar, or maybe out of fear.

"And white?" the boy asked, his smile big and sardonic.

"Yeah."

"That boy look white to you?" the first boy asked the second boy.

"Well, with all that lady's makeup on he sure does," the second boy answered. They both laughed like wolves howling.

"How bout you just go ahead and wipe the rest of it off?" the first boy asked the second boy. The boy hesitated for a moment but then he walked straight up to George and wiped it off his entire face as best he could. Their eyes locked for a moment as he did this, inches from each other, and George remained stock-still and quiet and hoped the boy would find some humanity in himself but once he was done wiping off George's face he walked away.

"What you think now?" the first boy asked the second boy again. The second boy stood back and took in his handy work.

"That looks like a pale injun," he said.

"What do you two want with me?" George finally worked up the courage to ask.

"How about you do some Choctaw shit for us? Some real Indian shit."

"I don't know no real Indian shit."

"Ain't that a shame. Parker, ain't that a shame?" he asked directly to the second boy.

"Aw, now he knows my name," the second boy replied with real aggravation in his voice.

"It don't matter if he knows your name, dipshit. What's he gonna do, go tell the cops?" The first boy said this and then looked back over to George. "His name's Parker and my name's Colt. You got an injun name or do you really not know any of that shit?"

"My name is George."

"George, ha, George. He said his name is George."

Both boys laughed. A carnie yelled into a microphone somewhere behind him that the next Ferris wheel ride was free if you could beat him in arm wrestling. Somewhere else nearby, it sounded as if a band had come on the big stage and had started playing. A tune of fiddles and guitars filled up the air and the wind carried it in gusts over to where the three boys stood. George's leg was twitching and his hands were still in his coat pockets where he was fiddling with the cloth on the inside.

"George, I don't take kindly to you people thinking you have the right to break the law—hell, break God's law—and waltz on up in here like you're white. Like you can go ride on that Ferris wheel and go see that circus. Or you can go listen to a great politician talk. Do they even let y'all vote? Don't answer me. When I saw you from across that crowd at the rally I knew I had to come have a word with you and you had the audacity to run away. And with two other boys, and for God's sake, one of them white. I bet that son of a bitch was the one helped you get in here. A race traitor. Now, I got one more question for you before we get on to business. Where are those two friends of yours?"

"I don't know," George replied, trying to keep his voice calm and deep and unshaking.

"You don't know? What, they up and left you?"

"I said I don't know."

The boy's eyes got big like they'd done earlier that day in the middle of the crowd. He stepped up into George's face. There was no smile on his lips. He was inches from George and he looked him in the eyes and his eyes were black in the night with the moon behind him.

"You get a tone with me, boy?" His breath smelled like fried food and beer and tobacco.

"I don't like people calling me boy."

"I don't give a shit what you like. You can't figure that out yet?"

George didn't answer and Colt's feet stayed put but he turned his shoulders enough that he could see his friend, Parker. George couldn't see his face anymore and he wondered if he should just punch this boy right then or push him down or grab him or run away. Anything to get an upper hand. But he was afraid to do anything first.

"Parker, he thinks I give a shit. You think I should show him how much I don't give a shit?"

"Colt, well, maybe we should just call it off."

"You scared now, buddy?"

"Maybe it's a bad idea," Parker said. He was standing there awkwardly and George felt for the boy in an odd, disassociated way.

"I don't think you're right," Colt replied. Then the boy turned around for a moment and everything was a blur.

He reached out and shoved him, his hands moving with a purpose beyond his own volition. Colt turned around and shoved George in response. He nearly fell back on his butt but his feet stumbled until he caught himself and the boy was charging him now. George ducked out of the way to the right and the boy reached out and grabbed him by the coat collar. He pulled George in and punched him with his off hand in the gut. George buckled over. Colt laughed. Parker said something about quitting that was mostly unintelligible to George and unimportant to Colt.

As Colt laughed, George hauled himself back up straight and pushed him back. Colt stopped laughing and his face got red the way Nehemiah's had. He charged George again but this time George didn't try to get out of the way. He lowered himself and tackled the boy head on and, to his own surprise, drove Colt to the ground. On top of the boy, George punched him square in the jaw. The boy was stunned for a moment and George paused. He didn't know why.

"Colt, just let him go," Parker yelled. Neither of them noticed.

When George paused, Colt reached up and grabbed him by the shoulders and slung him over and jumped on top of him and George felt an instant regret for pausing his blows to the boy's face. With the boy now straddling him, George fell victim to three or four punches, the count didn't matter at some point, to the face and then the arms and then the forehead. Colt was just looking for anywhere to get his knuckles to hit his head. George closed his eyes and felt his bones bruise as each hit landed. They stopped and he opened his eyes. He watched the boy reach in his mouth with his right hand and yank the wad of tobacco out of his lip and his left hand grabbed George by the side of the head and pinned him down. He took the wad of sludge and yanked George's mouth open and shoved it inside.

"Swallow, you fucking animal," he whispered, smiling.

George reached up and, with a grunt and all the strength he had left, grabbed the boy and threw him over. On their sides now, he spit the tobacco out and pushed himself up off the ground and onto his feet. Colt got up too.

"Colt," Parker started to speak again.

"Shut the hell up, Park. I'm gonna kill this redskin."

"Colt, come on."

"I said shut the hell up," he screamed.

And then, the boy pulled something out of his pocket. It was as if time slowed down and George finally got to really take stock of things. His hand came out of his pants with a small straight-blade knife. It looked to have a bone handle, possibly deer antler, and its blade glistened in the cool moon's lumen. He turned it over in his hand and held it like a brute or a child might hold a fork at dinner, his thumb tucked in and his fingers wrapped around it. As he did this, Colt stood there swaying in the night air on the balls of his feet like a dancer.

"I'm gonna cut him up," he said, then repeating it like a singsong. "I'm gonna cut him up. I'm gonna cut him up. I'm gonna cut him up."

He kept saying this as he charged George, his left arm out looking to grab and his right arm with the knife tucked in to his side. George ignored the left and reached down and hit the boy's right arm with his palm to stop any forward movement. Then he headbutted the boy. He'd never done such a thing before. He shot his forehead down and through the boy's nose. Colt fell backward and stumbled some and then ungracefully met the ground with his back. The knife fell on the dirt. His nose began to bleed and bleed. He garbled something that didn't make any sense to anyone. George looked at the knife and looked at the boy with blood pouring down his face and then back to the knife. In the top corner of his vision, he then saw that Parker was eyeing the knife and him as well.

"Don't do anything stupid," Parker shouted. He started to move towards the blade on the ground and George jumped forward.

George punched the boy square in the jaw. He felt like a lion or a wolf. He felt like he could go on like this forever. Like he could never die. Like his blood was pumping so hard. Like he was a warrior of old. Like he could never die. Parker stumbled back and George reached down and snapped the knife up. When Parker realized this, he backed up a few steps and put his hands in the air.

"I don't want no trouble," he said. "I never wanted no trouble to begin with. Please."

The boy started to cry like a baby and George had the urge to tell him to shut up just like Colt did. This would have bothered him at any other time. He was normally so calm. That's what everybody told him. That's what his mammy told him. His calm disposition preceded him. That's what a schoolteacher told him. And here he was, so fucking angry that he couldn't hardly see or breathe or hear. He could only feel that knife in his hands. With Parker standing there bawling, Colt had come to again. He lifted his head up and wiped his face with a shirtsleeve, the blood staining his clothes immediately. The boy stood up because George let him. Standing then, he started to laugh.

"I've been bested by a mongrel, huh," he said. The blood kept coming out of his nose and he didn't bother wiping it again. His face was pale and already showing dark bruises. "You gonna give me that knife back? Or at least let us go?"

"Why would I do either of them things?" George asked.

"I wasn't gonna kill you. I was just talking big."

"You wasn't?"

"Naw, I wasn't. Tell you what, keep the knife. Just keep it. To hell with the knife. Park and I will leave you alone. Enjoy the fair some more."

"I don't think so."

"Alright."

The boy took one last charge at George. Like he wouldn't see it coming. Like he knew it was his last option. When he got close, George shoved that knife in his hand forward in one clean, swift motion like you would pop your fist under a table as a boy to make a fork jump off of it. The knife fit into the boy's abdomen like it was made to go there. Colt jumped back and let out a grunt. The handle stuck out of him. No blade was left in the air. It was all inside of him. He looked down at it.

"You fucking stabbed me," he said. His voice was hoarse and weak. He put his hand on the bone of the knife but didn't pull at it. "You stabbed me. Son of a bitch. You stabbed me."

George stepped forward and swung his fist as hard as he could into that boy's nose. He felt cracks and pops and breaks and the boy hit the ground like a sack of potatoes. On the ground, his eyes were closed and his nose plum sideways and that knife still stuck out of his shirt but blood began to pool around it. His nose was beginning to dry as if the blood had to divert to the new wound.

"You killed him," Parker screamed. "You killed him. You killed him."

The boy ran over to his friend and fell on his knees and began to pat at his face but Colt no longer moved. George wasn't sure if the boy was dead but he knew then that he didn't care either way. Parker kept screaming and crying and he looked up at George and said it one more time.

"You killed him."

Then, the boy got up and took off running towards where the rest of the people were, still enjoying the fair without the slightest idea of what was going on. George watched him go. He was pretty fast. George thought his life might be over.

When the boy was gone and out of view, George stood there over the possibly dead body. He reached down and tore the knife out of the boy's stomach. He wiped the blood off of the blade and then reached back down and took the sheath for it out of the boy's pocket too. He stuck them in his coat. In reaching in the boy's pocket, he'd felt something else in there so he reached back down and dug around. The boy still didn't stir. George pulled out a small wallet. Inside were dollar bills that he quickly shoved in his own pockets. There was also a small card that George had never seen before. It said Driver's License on it and had the boy's name—Colt Norris. He put it back in the wallet and took it too. He felt like he was watching himself do things from up above himself. Like life was moving on without him but he was still right there. He wondered if he should run. The cops would probably beat him to death in Mississippi for killing a white boy. If they didn't kill him right there, they might hang him without a trial. He wondered if he could kill another person. If it was just one police officer. Then he heard a voice whisper from behind him. The voice of a woman.

16

GEORGE'S FEET DANGLED in the river still, water rushing around the toes that he could hardly feel. When he heard footsteps crunch beside him, he didn't move or open his eyes. Whoever it was sat down beside him and George waited for them to speak.

"You ain't even gonna look at me?" they asked. He opened his eyes. It was that angry boy, that godawful racist boy. He closed his eyes again.

"I don't think I need to."

"Mm, alright," the boy mumbled.

"What do you want with me? Closure or something?"

"Naw."

"Then what is it?"

"Why do you think I had something to do with this?"

"You're the one who showed up."

"I'd rather be on a beach," he paused. "I only got to see a beach once. On the Alabama shore."

"Why? Just tell me why you're here."

"You don't get it, do you?"

"I guess not."

"Mm."

They sat in silence for what could've been a minute or an hour. Time was gone for George.

"Aren't you going to leave?" George asked, slicing the silence.

"Why would I?"

"Why would you stick around here?"

"Not my call. Never has been."

17

"Who's there?" George asked.

"Is he dead?" the voice of the girl asked back. He figured she was standing inside the tent entrance by where it came from. But he didn't step towards her as to not scare her anymore than she might have already been.

"I don't rightly know," he replied.

"It looked like you killed him."

"It did look that way." He paused for a moment, looking down at the dead boy with blood smeared down from his nose across his lips and cheeks and chin. Black and blue bruising up and down from his forehead to his neck. "You gonna call the police on me for it?"

"I don't think so. I saw the whole thing. But are you gonna kill me?"

"I don't think so. Don't have a reason to."

"I hope not. But okay then. Come over here. In the tent."

George looked around once more. He didn't know why, he just did it. There was no one coming yet.

"Wait," he said. "You think I should move the body?"

After he said this, there was a moment of silence and no response from the disembodied voice coming from the circus tent. But then, without saying anything, she appeared out of the darkness of the entrance. It was her. The girl with the fire. She was now dressed in blue jean overalls and a white shirt and a chore coat. She had no shoes on. The closer she got, the more George could see her face. And he knew it was her from her gait and from her beauty. Her face was wonderful now that she was right there in front of him. She studied the body on the ground as she approached, not even noticing George standing there staring at her. Her hands were in her overall pockets.

"Grab his legs," she said, still looking down.

"You sure?"

"Just grab 'em." She had a hint of irritation in her voice. As if he was being ridiculous for asking a question. It only made him more mesmerized by the girl.

So, he did what she asked and grabbed the boy's feet and she grabbed him by the armpits and they carried him into the woods there by the tent. Every time he figured they'd walked far enough and started to slow down, she just kept plowing through. Even when the bramble in the thicket got so rough that he felt a tear in his coat, she wouldn't stop. After they'd walked for what felt like forever, she stopped suddenly and dropped the boy's head and the legs practically fell out of George's hands. She began to kick dirt and leaves on top of the body and he followed suit, letting her decide when enough had been done. Eventually she stopped kicking and wiped her hands off on her overalls and looked up at George, which he realized she still hadn't done yet. He stood stock still while she looked at him. Her gaze was curious and her eyes searched him over. He hadn't the slightest clue what she was thinking about. She did this for long enough that he felt awkward and looked around instead of at her. Something about her stare was powerful. Like she had that fire of hers stored behind her eyes for safekeeping when she wasn't performing. He felt as if he could melt in it, despite the chill in the air.

"What you got them fancy clothes on for?" she asked, her head cocked to the side.

"Oh, these?" He looked down at his garments and suddenly felt self-conscious of them and ashamed that he was dressed like a rich boy. She would think he was something that he wasn't. But then again, the powder was still mostly there on his face too. "A buddy gave them to me, so I put them on."

She grinned a little.

"Give me that knife," she said.

"What?"

"Give me that knife."

"Why?"

"You just killed a boy, did you not? Jeez. I'm not gonna let you get all angry and kill nobody else. Just hand it over. Simple precautionary measure."

Just as he'd been doing since he'd gotten in step with this mysterious girl, who apparently had more to her than just the ability to juggle flaming pieces of wood and balance at the same time, George did what she asked and handed the knife over along with the sheath it came in. She grabbed it and shoved it into a pocket and started off to her right. It wasn't the way they'd come in the woods.

"Are we not going back?" George asked.

She stopped and turned back and stared at him with her mouth wide open in disbelief.

"You aren't a dummy, are you?"

"What? No," he replied.

"Why would we go back the way we came?" she asked, exasperated. "Do you want to get caught or something?"

"No, I don't."

"Mmhmm," she paused. "You alright?"

"I don't know. Hey, wait, what's your name?"

"Charlotte."

"That's a, a pretty name," George said. He didn't know why she made him stutter. Or maybe he did know.

"And your name is George."

"How do you know that?"

"Maybe you are a dummy," she said, before smiling and returning to the direction she had been going. He shrugged and followed behind and they walked in silence. Eventually she began to make an arc in what felt to George like the direction of the circus tent and the fair, but he knew he was only believing this because she seemed reliable and resourceful. There was no reason to think differently yet. They marched on, the leaves on the ground crunching under them. It was still early fall and many of them were colorful in the daylight and kind to the eyes but George hated them then. He cringed at every footfall and every loud crackle that followed it. He began to worry that the police would be there, waiting for them when they got back. But the truth was, when they walked out of the woods, they were then behind the tent and all he saw were those big metal cages and tents behind them where folks stood around drinking from flasks and eating out of tin plates and standing by fires and talking to each other. There wasn't an officer in sight. As they approached the crowd of people, a huge man wearing no shirt and leather pants saw them and stepped out to greet them. As he approached, the man got taller and taller until he was up close and George figured he must have been seven feet tall. He had a thick mustache and thicker eyebrows and his chest was covered with dark hair too.

"Charlotte, where have you been? We've been looking all over for you," he said. George recognized his accent as one from up north, even through how deep the gigantic man's voice was. He'd only ever heard a few accents like it. They rarely made their way into Choctaw lands.

Before she could answer, the man looked over at George and his big eyes on his big head squinted and his forehead tightened.

"And who are you?"

ALL THINGS CONSIDERED, George found the man fairly peaceable. He was worried that he might come over and grab him by the head for the trouble he was causing and just rip it clean off and then squeeze it until it exploded like he'd seen real burly boys do with old watermelons. The man surely had the muscles to accomplish it. He might've weighed 400 pounds. But despite the appearance, the man showed an attentiveness to Charlotte's telling of George's story that was to be admired. He didn't speak over her or ever look like he wasn't listening. When she finished up telling everything that she knew, which started not too long after those boys had come out of the woods and started the whole mess, the man nodded for a while like he was thinking and it was the only way he could get his brain to work. Eventually he turned to George and stopped nodding.

"You have anything to add, boy?" he asked.

He thought for a moment. He considered how much he should share and how much this man or Charlotte or, hell, anyone could be trusted anymore. But he'd gotten into feeling like he had nothing to lose and he wasn't shed of that feeling yet.

"How much do you want to know, sir?"

The man said all of it. George wondered if he was Charlotte's father. Then, he explained his troubles. He started at the woman putting the powder on his face, before retracing his steps and explaining his heritage, and then moved on, skipping the rest of the parts about that woman and what she'd done to him, to the train and the restaurant and the city and the Ferris wheel and the rally and then to the circus, where he'd seen Charlotte. The man listened with a similar but detached attentiveness that he'd shown the girl.

"And that's where it ends, and her story begins. Honest truth." He stopped and remembered himself. "Sir."

"Alright. Charlotte brings a murderer here. A coldblooded murderer." He said this and squatted there in front of them, shaking his head and grinning a little. "You think you've seen it all. But then, you run a circus, you can't ever expect things to be normal. No such thing as normal in a circus, no, no, no."

He paused and rubbed his chin, before slapping his knee and standing up straight.

"We haven't seen any police over here. But the first place they look is the circus. Every time. We never have nothing to do with anything but the first place is always the circus. So, we have to do something about you. You say that boy will recognize you? The dead boy's friend?"

"I'd imagine so."

"Yes, I bet he would. Let me think."

As the big man said this, he turned and motioned for someone else to come over, a young man with long hair. When the man came over, he told him to bring Charlotte and this boy some food. He was back with two bowls of some kind of stew quickly and they ate in silence. George didn't realize how hungry he was. He was on the comedown from whatever kind of high the rage of killing had given him and he felt like dropping onto the ground and staying there forever. But the stew was good and hot and he ate it.

"Boy, how are you in tight spaces?" the man eventually asked. George's mouth was full and he swallowed as quickly as he could.

"I don't know."

"I guess we'll find out."

"I'm sorry, sir, I don't mean to question you or anything," George said. "But you're being mighty helpful to me. Why?"

"I'm helpful to Charlotte. Big difference," the man said. "You understand?"

"Yessir."

"Good. Charlotte, take him back to the trunks. Find one that he fits in and come back when you're done."

She didn't say anything in response and got up from her seat, leaving her bowl of food half-eaten, grabbing George's arm and pulling him up too. He nodded to the big man and followed her. Seemed to him that had become his life then, just following this pretty girl around wherever she pulled him. He would've laughed if not for the murder he'd committed and the reason she was helping him at all. They walked through the little circus compound and he saw all sorts of people in a blur as they sped through towards the back. He passed men with handlebar mustaches, children with monkeys on their shoulders—real monkeys, like out of story books that he'd read as a boy, like little men covered in fur—men feeding horses that were white with black stripes like he'd never seen before, women with pencil mustaches and big muscles lifting barbells and grunting, and a band of musicians sitting around a bonfire in a trashcan playing a mix of instruments so eclectic—horns and guitars and banjos and violins and drums and harmonicas and some he didn't recognize as anything from this country—that the music they created wasn't hardly music at all. Then, they passed where all the people were and they were surrounded by those big cages. Inside of them was every animal George could imagine. Horses and pigs and the elephant from the act that night and a large tiger that George had to stop and stare at because he could not believe his own two eyes. It sat in its cage licking its paws and hardly noticed him or ignored him if it did. Beside it was what looked to be the ribcage of a cow, nearly licked clean.

"Come on," Charlotte said, pulling him on past. He obliged, but kept his eyes on that big cat for as long as he could. She stopped in front of a big trunk finally. They were out of the light from the fires behind them but George could see well enough that it was a wood box painted green with brass hinges and locks. She opened it up before him and told him to climb in.

"What's the tiger's name?" he asked.

"What?"

"The tiger. Does it have a name?"

"Benjy," she said, letting a deep sigh out. "You're an odd boy."

"It's a lot to take in," he said.

"I'm sure it is," she said with a slight grin. "Now hop in."

He put his feet in the trunk and saw that it was empty and then she motioned for him to sit down in it, so he did. She handed him the knife back and told him to poke two or three little holes in the back for air, so he did. And she told him to keep the knife, for evidence's sake. Then she stepped away for a moment and the air was cool and quiet then and George stared up at the stars. She came back with a large blanket and started to drape it over him.

"I'm sorry about the smell. It's usually for the monkeys so they don't get cold."

And it did smell but he let her lay the blanket over him completely and then it was dark and so he closed his eyes since they had no use.

"You sure you're alright?" she asked.

"I guess so," he said.

"Okay. Danny will have a plan. If you hear people walking around here that don't sound like me or him, don't make a sound. Just sit there still. We'll come back for you eventually."

He didn't say anything and then she closed the trunk down over his head and he heard her lock the clasps down and walk away. Her footsteps gradually grew quieter until there was no sound left in his ears but his own breathing. George wished then that he had a light and a book. But he couldn't read quick enough to make it matter anyhow. He positioned the blankets where they'd be under his head a little and still on top of him and he laid down on his back. He thought about that Ferris wheel ride and Chito yelling out *would you look at that view* and how, at the time, George could see the very place he was laying but it all looked so miniscule and far away that it hadn't seemed like a real place he would ever have ended up. Yet here he was. Placed inside a trunk, awaiting sentencing by God for what he'd done. And then the blanket atop him began to feel heavier and heavier and the weight was on his shoulders and stomach and even his back although it was on the ground. *I killed a man*, he thought. *A boy, someone no further along than me. What would mammy have thought of me.* He remembered that white man who'd jumped them and who'd never been caught even though the police said they would do their best. He knew they didn't mean a part of it because she was Choctaw and it happened on white people land, and by the hand of a white man for God's sake. They weren't going to do anything about it and they didn't and that man might have still been out there on the same Mississippi soil as George then. And George thought, *now we are both killers, ain't it all the same?* And the walls of that trunk grew tighter and tighter and closed in on him and he sobbed so loud that he had to shove the blanket into his mouth so he wouldn't make any noise and it tasted so godawful that he had to stop crying. His eyes were tired, even behind shut eyelids, and he let himself be calm for sleep in the hopes that dreams would be better.

In his slumber, George dreamed of home. His ma was there and they were outside. She had a baseball in her hand, and she threw it to him and he caught it. They did this, lobbing it back and forth for some unknown minutes. Neither of them made a sound, they just smiled at each other. The sun was high in the sky and there was not one single cloud and he could tell that it should be hot, but his skin felt fine. Then, all of a sudden, there was a great big boom in the sky like thunder but as if it were right behind George's ear and he stumbled back and looked up towards the sun and there were still no clouds up there. He shrugged it off as if nothing happened. When he looked back to where his mammy stood and started to throw the ball to her again, he found that she was not there. And then the house behind where she had been slowly faded. The grass turned from green to brown and then to dirt and even the dirt faded to gray. The wind picked up around him and he looked around for any sign of life but there were no trees, not even past the fields that surrounded the house where there had always been acres of woods. And he heard a voice and he couldn't tell what it was saying but he knew he should be afraid of it and he wondered if it was God speaking to him but he thought that he was told God did not speak in ways that Christian folk could not understand. He listened as hard as he could and the voice became clearer.

"Mister, Danny was it? Danny, we saw the blood out front of the tent and yet there was no body there. Now, if no one else was around, how could it have gone off somewhere on its own?" the voice asked. It was a man but George was certain it could not be God, yet he knew of what the voice spoke. It was somewhere else in his mind and not in this dream. Another voice spoke.

"I do not know anything about no body or no killing. We finished our show and we come out back for the rest of the night. Simple as that, no other funny business." This voice was familiar to George but he knew it was no God either but a man who was lying and George knew that God told no lies and he didn't know how he knew this man was lying but he was so certain of it. The wind had died down around George in this open field but there was still nothing around him. He only held the ball there and then he realized that he didn't want it either, this little thing that was the last of whatever world he was in, so he chucked it as far as he could and it hit the ground some twenty yards away from him and disappeared from view.

"Are you able to attest for where every member of your crew was tonight?" the first voice asked. His questions were pointed and seemed to come from a place of frustration.

"I am able to attest that we have no killers in our crew."

"A circus has no people of questionable behavior? Isn't that the point? How do you get all these people then?"

"Sir, our circus has people who want to perform for crowds and eat a hot meal and go to bed and be safe. Nothing more."

The voices were so close to George that he could hear their footsteps too and every movement they made.

"So if I check any of these trunks, I won't find anything?"

George suddenly shot awake, and his eyes opened to the darkness of the blanket on top of his face. He realized what was going on and he began to shake even though he didn't want to and knew he wasn't supposed to be moving at all. He tried to hold his breath for as long as possible.

"You'll find supplies and other things that are always in our trunks."

George then heard what he guessed to be the officer opening the latch on a trunk nearby and rustling around in it. Danny mumbled something incoherent behind the man. A minute passed as the man kept opening boxes and trunks and George was starting to sweat through his shirt even in the cold of the box. He heard the cop open the trunk to his left. And then he heard new sets of footsteps approaching, with new voices attached to them.

"You aren't supposed to be back here," a new voice shouted, and George recognized it as Charlotte. Even her voice was on fire.

"I'll go wherever I have to go to find Colt," another voice responded. It was Parker. His voice shook. "Mister officer, you found anything?"

He heard the cop, still standing there by the trunk beside George's, turn around.

"No. Son, you aren't leading me on a wild goose hunt, are ya?"

"No, sir. You, you, you saw the blood with your own two eyes."

"Mhm. And how do I know you didn't do it?"

"Because he was my friend," the boy cried out. "That damn injun boy did it. I saw it with my own two eyes."

"Then how about you stop bothering me and blubbering about? Damn Indian did it. Like he was a cowboy out in the wild west and got scalped or something."

The officer chuckled and moved to George's trunk. He slipped the clasp off the front and opened it. George could hear the wind over the open box. He took one last small breath and laid still. Nothing happened for a moment.

"I'm not gonna waste my time no more with blankets and boxes," the officer said. His feet sounded as if they turned around again. George continued to hold his breath. "Maybe your friend got up and walked off. Hell, maybe he's out there on the grounds looking for you and you ran off."

"But he was dead. I saw it," Parker said.

"I'm beginning to question what you saw. Come on. Look, I'm sorry for bothering you, Danny. Let me know if you hear anything or if you see anything out of the ordinary with one of your, well, your unordinary folks you got around here."

Danny grunted in reply and George heard the officer and Parker walk away. He waited until he could no longer hear any footsteps and took in a deep, wheezing breath. That doctor, long ago, had told him that moments of neurosis, he had called it, could possibly bring about his asthmatic attacks, so he tried to calm himself. But before he could focus on it too hard, the blanket on top of him was snatched up and the burly man Danny was peering at him from up above.

"You alright in there?" he whispered down to George.

George nodded and the man grabbed him by the hand and lifted him out. Charlotte stood behind him and offered a nervous smile.

"Quite the close one. I got worried there for a second. Could see it all happening. Could see him catching you and blaming me and then our whole operation going down in flames," Danny said. "But, lucky you are. Lucky we are."

George still didn't say anything. He didn't have anything that felt appropriate for the moment.

"Well, George. We're supposed to pack up and leave tomorrow. I figure you aren't sticking around here, are you?"

"No sir, I guess not."

"Mm," Danny grunted, his hands on his hips.

"Do you, do you think I can join y'all?"

"Join us? Join the circus you mean?"

"It seems like my best option."

"I'd like to say I expect a better attitude but hardly anybody joins the circus because it's their dream. Alright then, welcome to the circus," Danny said. His big eyes had a kindness to them.

George thought about what that old woman had said to him and he looked over at Charlotte who twiddled her thumbs and he saw burn marks on them for the first time and he saw how pretty she really was.

"Always a new place," he mumbled.

"What was that?"

"Nothing, nothing. Thank you, sir."

"Alright, I guess that settles it. A murderer, huh."

"He's not a murderer," Charlotte said.

"I'm just messing. And, George, as your new employer, what's your full name?"

George thought about it for a second. He remembered that driver's license in the wallet in his pocket. That boy out there in the woods, as dead as a door nail. Deader'n hell. He considered that maybe no one would ever find him. He considered that the person he was before that night might as well be dead too. He spoke, without thinking.

"Norris," he said. "It's, it's George Norris."

"Mhm. That sure ain't any Indian name I've ever heard. But who am I to judge?" the big man said. He started walking back to where everyone else was in the camp and George and Charlotte followed. When they passed by that tiger, it had its head laid on its paws and its eyes were closed, but it opened one of those big eyes with green pupils as they walked by and George could feel its hot stare.

PART TWO

18

GEORGE STOOD in the center of the circus ring, scooping elephant shit off the dirt floor. It was mid-afternoon and he was alone, which was not very common in his newfound home and profession. He whistled to himself a song he'd only learned recently from one of the traveling musicians. He'd called it "A Tisket, A Tasket." He scooped the dung into a small wheelbarrow and took it out to the trees behind the tent and dumped it. It stank, as shit does, but he'd gotten used to it over the few months he'd been a part of the circus and appreciated that it was one of his few chores that involved some peace and quiet. The circus had proven to be many things, but not peaceful, not quiet.

As he pushed the wheelbarrow over to the woods, Charlotte ran up on him from behind and kissed him on the cheek. He stopped walking and leaned into her. She smelled like smoke because she always did. The girl did nothing but practice and eat and sleep.

"You stink," she said.

"You too."

They smiled at each other, and she followed him over to the woods and stood back while he did his job. They were in Georgia. They'd been there for a few days and the first show was that night. He'd seen people driving by slowly all week, gawking at the big tent and the peculiar people that walked in and out of it all day. He'd seen the newspaper advertisement for it and the opinion article that accompanied it from a local minister who called the circus a "sinful affair." Apparently the man didn't appreciate entertainment, and especially not entertainment that involved a black tiger trainer or a girl who wore a leotard and danced with fire. Charlotte had giggled and blushed when she'd seen her own very act be mentioned as one of the man's main issues with the show. He even added a note that he'd heard from a minister in Alabama, where they'd just been for over a month doing show after show, that Charlotte could only be described as "promiscuous" and a "harlot." George had never heard either of those words before and he had to ask what they meant. He was offended when Danny told him but Charlotte told him not to worry about it too much.

The couple walked back to the tent together now and he left the wheelbarrow off a bit away from everyone outside where it could air out and not bother anybody. They entered the tent ring and stood there together. She liked to go in on the days of performances and visualize her act from start to finish and he liked to go in and watch her do this. She went through each motion as if she were doing it for real. George liked to watch her feet as they bounced effortlessly and her legs as her muscles tightened and released. She was wearing shorts and he could hardly contain himself. When she finished, he clapped and whistled with his fingers in front of his teeth, just like he'd done the first time he'd seen her.

Their courtship hadn't taken long. Most of the holdup was George and his emotions. He'd been catatonic for some time, watching the fight in his head over and over again. When he lay down to sleep, when he woke up, as he worked during the day. He was hardly a person for a while, more so a walking ball of shame and muscle. Charlotte had broken him out of it, without even trying, it seemed to him. And there wasn't much to their courting once she'd untied the bandages around his soul and knocked him down a couple of times with her sense of humor. In fact, he felt as if he hardly had anything to do with making it happen. Danny had given him the job title of "help where you're needed" and had offered him a bed in the tent with him and George had become one of the crew. They were an inviting crowd. So, with him being around all the time, he just stayed close to her whenever he could. She didn't tell him to bug off most times unless she made a mistake in her practicing and then she'd need time to herself. After a few weeks of his just being around and their friendship growing, one morning she walked right up to him and asked if he wanted to be her boyfriend. He'd stammered on for a moment, barely producing a yes, because it was true, he wanted nothing more than this, he felt so bonded to her after what he'd done and what she'd seen him do and what they'd done together, and she smiled at this almost-answer.

"Alright," she'd said. By the time he'd figured out his tongue again, she'd already walked off and that was that. Their first kiss had been just a week prior to this day. They'd just finished up with the last show and a lot of the crew were drinking and some of them were going out drinking but most were just staying at camp, so as to not cause any trouble. Danny once told George that the life of a circus performer is to be cheered on and loved dearly inside the confines of that tent and to be wished to simply disappear when outside of it and George said that sounded familiar but he didn't explain any further because he wasn't sure that he could. So most of them stayed around the camp that night and got good and drunk off cheap liquor. But George had heard from one of the other "help where you're needed" boys, a tall and skinny kid named Jack who had freckles and said he was sixteen but everyone knew he was only fourteen, that there was a river just a short walk down the road that had a small lake off of it where you could go fishing or whatever else you want to do. Jack had never been with a girl and it was obvious that he admired Charlotte—it was obvious that many boys and men around admired Charlotte—and George knew what he was implying with that last part, so he only responded to the fishing comment, telling the boy that he hadn't gone fishing in years.

Instead of drinking that night, which George wasn't sure that he wanted to do ever again after the night Koi was arrested, although he also wasn't sure that he could withstand the peer pressure, he asked Charlotte if she wanted to borrow some of the fishing poles that Danny had in his tent and go check out this lake. She'd thought about it, giving the expression that she had to contemplate it real hard before answering, and then said yes, of course, with a smile.

"Have you ever been fishing?" he'd asked her.

"No. Can't be too hard though, can it?"

THE WALK TO THE RIVER and the lake took longer than Jack had made it seem. George had to go ask the boy for directions, who grinned from ear to ear with imagination as he told them where to go. The boy had said it was a straight walk down the dirt road that ran in front of the tent and then one left turn onto a cut-through in the woods that he said would be obvious for the wood sign painted red that said Private Lake—No Trespassing. When he'd heard this, George started to say "are you kidding me?" but Charlotte beat him to the punch and simply said "okay" and that was it and they were off. It took no less than half an hour to get there though, and by the time they were in the woods and they could hear the sounds of lapping water on dirt banks and frogs ribbeting, it was so dark they could hardly see except for slivers of moonlight that came down between pine trees. George set the poles down on the path right before the lake opened up as it was too dark to get any real fishing done anyway.

But what he soon realized was that Charlotte had hid something from him. Despite her fearlessness, she was afraid of the dark.

"This is so dumb, George. This is so, so, so stupid. I can't believe you convinced me to do this," Charlotte said, creeping around the bank of the dark pond, shoeless. With every step, George watched her in the shimmers of light as she felt for anything that wasn't grass or dirt or rock. She screamed once and George reached down and picked a caterpillar off her foot, flicking it into the foliage nearby.

"Shh," George whispered. "Do you hear that?"

She stopped beside him.

"No, I don't think so," she said, her voice irritated.

"Yes, you do. Give it another try. You just gotta focus. There's so much sound right now if you focus."

She sighed and got quiet again, but George imagined that her thoughts were probably cluttered with the fact that she couldn't see a thing. He found himself amused by this contradictory girl.

Then, a *plop* in the water, from a fish presenting its side belly to the air and diving back down. Then, a movement in the trees above. After a couple seconds, the sound was accompanied by the rustling of the wings of a small bird.

"How was that?" he asked, coming closer to her so that she could see him smiling in the light of the moon breaking through the shadow. She didn't answer.

"C'mon," he said. "The water's right here, let's test it out."

She followed and watched as George took his shirt off and rolled his pants legs up and dipped his pale toes in.

"It's pretty warm," he shouted, in as low a voice as he could, slowly crouching until his knees were submerged up to his rolled-up pants.

"You go ahead," she said, arms crossed, staring at him and the black water. To his right, a flurry of bubbles appeared, and the skinny bodies of several fish urgently exited the bed they'd been holed up in. George laughed and even tried to grab one.

She sat down on the pond bank in front of him with her knees up into her chest. She was completely silent, her toes hedged up as far from the water's edge as possible. The moon was almost directly above them then. Small waves bounced against the dirt in front of her from every movement George made and she watched them come and subside, come and subside, in front of her feet, like it was an invisible barrier that separated them.

"I don't think I'm going to get in," she said.

George nodded and neither said anything for a while. The little fish swam around George's legs. He saw a turtle pop its head up a few feet away from him and then go back down and he went over to grab it but it had already swam off. When he turned around, she was standing up and walking further down the bank.

"Hey, where you going?" he shouted, jumping onto the bank and grabbing his shirt.

Charlotte kept walking as he tried to catch up with her. A big toad hopped near her foot and into the water and she jumped away from it. Then he watched as she approached the water's edge and reached her hand down to the black abyss, shaking slightly, but she couldn't quite reach. She took a step closer, looking as if she was mustering up as much courage as she could.

"Wait, Charlotte," he said from behind her.

"Shit!" she screamed as her ankle hit something hard and she toppled over sideways, falling face-first into the shallow water. He jumped over and reached out quickly to catch her, but it was too late and her upper body was covered in mud. She pushed herself out of the water and back onto the bank, her hair soaked and her face splattered with brown sludge. She spit some dirt out of her mouth and George wiped her face off with his shirt.

"What were you doing?" he asked and she began to cry, still sitting there on the bank.

George sat down beside her and waited as tears softly fell on her pretty cheeks and she sniffled, air pushing in and out of her lips. After a while, she told him that her father had died in a river when she was a child. He wanted to ask then if Danny was not her dad but he didn't want to interrupt her so he kept his mouth shut. She said that he had been a fisherman in Louisiana and they even owned their own boat with a small crew and everything. He was a successful man for their little village. And he was a good dad and she loved him and he taught her to juggle. But one day he went out to work on a morning that didn't seem like anything out of the ordinary, there wasn't even a cloud in the sky, but a bad storm popped up out of nowhere and then he never came home. They didn't find his boat for a year and, when they did, it was up in a creek and cracked and charred in ways that looked like lightning had struck it. Her ma had tried to make the best out of it with just them, but he was the one with the job and the one who put food on the table and she had only been a mother since they'd gotten married. One morning, Charlotte woke up and her mother was not there in the bedroom that they shared and she wasn't in the kitchen or the sitting room either. She went outside and found her hanging there from a tree. Little Charlotte ran away from home that instant and just kept running and running until she was so tired that she collapsed.

As she told him this story, her eyes closed and she reached over and gripped his hand tightly and he closed his eyes too.

"I woke up in the middle of the night, still there on the side of the road I had been running on. In the distance I saw lights from fires and heard music and people talking so I got up and walked to it. I remember I was so hungry. I was nine years old, I think. It all runs together eventually. When I got to it, it was the circus camp, if you'll believe it. I just walked right in like I knew somebody or like I was going to at least find somebody I knew and I remember that Danny saw me from across the camp and walked right over and leaned down and asked me who I was. I told him what happened to me just like I'm telling you now and I swear he had tears in his eyes. He was bigger then than he is now. And he had tears in his eyes and I recognized that he was a big softy then. And he took me over to where people were eating and sat me with one of them women of the crew and they fed me and gave me a change of clothes and I've been with them ever since."

She stopped talking and took in a deep breath.

"So you're afraid of the water?"

"Terribly so."

"I'm sorry for bringing you here then. I wouldn't have if I—"

"You didn't know," she said, cutting him off with her words and then cutting him off further by leaning in and kissing him on the lips. Her mouth tasted of the pond water but her lips were so soft and he immediately felt so warm that he didn't notice. He kissed her back and started smiling with his lips still connected to hers and she realized and smiled back. They separated and he looked down at the water because he didn't know where else to look. He watched as her feet moved over and touched his in the mud and they sat there for hours, kissing on and off and not saying another word until it was time to go on back to the camp.

On the way back, she spoke once, breaking the silence that had gone so long it startled George. They were still holding hands as they walked down the path.

"You know what's funny, too?" she asked him.

"What's that?"

"My grandmother was in the circus. Sure was."

"Oh, really? What did she do?"

"Rode horses, I think. But she quit way before I was born."

George looked over at her and she was looking up at the stars and he tried to hide the realization on his own face but then he thought *there's no way* and he shook his head and kept looking down the path and every once in a while, Charlotte would squeeze his hand and smile at him and he would return it and he didn't hardly feel any cold despite how wet he still was.

"Wanna learn how to juggle?" she asked after she finished practicing her act that day.

"Oh, I don't know," he stammered.

"It's not so hard, come on." She motioned him over and handed him one of the batons. "Throw it up in the air from one hand to the other."

So, he did. It was heavier than he expected and cold and he wondered how she could ever throw more than one of these up in the air and catch them, or how she could catch just one of them when it was lit on fire. But he did what she asked a few times until she reached over and grabbed the baton as it came down to his left hand and then handed it back to him with a second one. She nodded at him to go on with it but he had no idea where to start and he just stood there looking at them and thinking about the best way to go about it.

"You sit there and watch me all the time and you can't figure it out?" she asked.

"Well, I, I don't—"

"You don't what?" Her hands were on her hips and she feigned anger.

"I don't know that I watch your hands every time."

"Mm, right. I won't ask what you're watching then. Alright, so hold them both in your right hand and have one between these two fingers and one between these two and then chuck the first one up to your left hand. We'll do the easy way to juggle first to get you used to the rhythm. Once you've got that one halfway through its arc to the other hand, throw the other one up in the air in the same motion. And then when the first one hits your left hand, just toss it under back to the right hand, just a little swift motion. A straight pass from one to the other, don't throw it back up in an arc or anything."

He listened as best as he could, trying to imagine what she was saying but he wasn't so good at the visualization stuff she practiced so often. He nodded and gave it a shot, but he took his eyes off the first one as he threw the second and dropped it. Once he dropped that one, he forgot about the second too and was whacked on the top of the head by it as he reached down to pick up the first. Charlotte laughed a little and told him to try again. Keep his eye on the first one. He gave it a second shot and caught both of them, but he forgot the little toss back to his right hand. On the third try, he did it alright, if not for a bit of fumbling.

"Now, once you have done all of that, just repeat the cycle. High toss, low toss, high toss, low toss. Just keep your eye on the high one at all times and remember to keep your right hand open for the bottom one."

He went at it for God knows he long and he might've strung together a rally of four cycles at his best. But he thought it was a fun game to play and he liked being in the light of her gaze. After a while she told him he'd done alright and he stopped and she came over and planted a sweet kiss on his lips and he dropped the batons as soon as her face touched his.

"Wooo, look at you two," Danny's voice rang out from behind them. They stopped and turned around at him and George could only imagine the blush on his face. "Young love, young love."

"What's up, Danny?" Charlotte said. She sounded half annoyed.

"You have that boy learning how to juggle?"

"He's doing a fine job at it too." George thought he'd stopped blushing but his face got hot again and he figured he just couldn't stop.

"And here I was, coming to see if he wanted to take a break from shoveling shit or cleaning cages to see how strong he was. Eventually we'll need a new strongman since I'm retired."

"And you were thinking of me?" George asked with a finger pointed to his own chest. Danny laughed a big hearty laugh at this.

"You've killed a man, you must be pretty strong, right? Charlotte said you fought well."

"Would you keep it down about that?" Charlotte said.

"We are surrounded by a circus with no audience, Char. The police want nothing to do with these misfits unless we're in the middle of putting on a show. Stop worrying about it. I've been doing this longer than you've been alive. Anyway, no, I'm just joking. Hey, let me see those batons."

"You want to give it a try?" George asked, picking them up and throwing them over to the big man.

"Who do you think helped this girl get better at her act? God or something?"

He threw them up in the air in the fluid motion that Charlotte had been trying to get George to learn and juggled them for a minute or so, eventually stepping around like a boxer, rigid motions that he'd say later were for lack of practice. He finished and took a bow that made George and Charlotte laugh and then he threw the batons back to George and made him show him what he'd been learning. They went on like this for a while and laughed so hard they cried as George fumbled the low toss once and dropped it on his toe, making him lean over and whack his head with the other again. George watched as Danny picked Charlotte up and held her over his head while she juggled and he couldn't stop hollering and clapping at the odd father-daughter couple and how they kept looking to him for affirmation. In the midst of their fun, he figured that he'd not been happy like this in a long time. In a long, long time.

THAT NIGHT, they had their first show in Georgia. One thing he had learned since joining on as a crewmember was that he had only seen a tiny snippet of the wide variety of acts that made up the circus. In total, there were more than twenty acts that took place each week. That's why it stayed in town for so long, so folks from every nearby town could have a chance to see the act they were most interested in. Danny said it was a business model he'd invented himself. Not even PT Barnum had thought this one up, he'd say, and George would nod along, having no idea who that was but thinking it was a pretty interesting name.

Their first night always had to start with a bang, Danny would also say every time. It involved trapeze artists, something George learned was when a woman or a man, three women and one man in this crew's case, would climb high in the air on thin ropes tied around their ankles or wrists with big hoops in their hands and they would twirl way up high in the air and dance around like great falcons who controlled the wind and they would sometimes meet up there near the ceiling and two of them would join hands and they would curl and spin around each other. The band played classical music by people from long ago that had hard-to-pronounce names and the band members said they were from places like Germany and France. And that they were written on piano but hauling one around would be too hard so they had to rewrite it for whatever instruments they had. George thought it still sounded lovely and the audience seemed to enjoy it as those people floated up there.

The night's act also included Benjy. George had gotten to spend a considerable amount of time with the tiger by then, mostly because his cage often required cleaning and nobody else wanted to do it. What he'd learned was that tigers only get bigger the closer you get and that they're pretty nice as long as you don't look them in the eye and you're keeping them well fed. Or at least that's how Benjy was. George had gotten so used to being around the big cat, who still had to be chained to one side of the cage while it was being cleaned, that he usually offered to do the chore even if Danny told him that Jack could do it some days. He'd also learned that tigers moo like cows and he thought it was funny, so he took every opportunity to hear it happen again.

Benjy's act was fairly simple but it was always a crowd favorite. His keeper, a man named Nathaniel who was kind to no one but Benjy, would walk around the cage and throw balls and pieces of meat up in the air and the great tiger would run around, catching them and sometimes even bringing them back to his keeper. Danny had once told George that Nathaniel was a son of a bitch in every capacity and he drank too much and stole from others often and had even been caught sleeping with the wives of other crew members, but he knew that tiger like a boy knew his brother, so they had to keep him around. Folks would stand up in the aisles and rows the entire time the performance went on and they would be completely silent except for oohs and aahs as Benjy did amazing things. The final part of the tiger's act was to stand on its hind legs like a human and, miraculously, catch a small rubber ball in its paw. This would really work the crowd and George was just like the rest the first time he saw it. But he learned later that the trick was it was a sticky ball and the tiger just had to slap at it, which cats love doing. Not that it mattered to the crowd.

The final act of the night was Charlotte. Since George had seen her the first night, he had suggested to the band that they ought to play music behind her like they did the trapeze artists. Everyone thought it was a pretty good idea and so they played shrill music meant to induce anxiety upon the crowd, until the last bit of her act where they'd play softly and slowly get louder in what they called a crescendo, playing folk music from the mountains because Charlotte had requested it. She'd given him a kiss on the cheek when she found out about his music suggestion and he'd just shrugged it off.

"How good you are to me," she'd said.

"You're the one who's done the real stuff," he'd replied. "I'm just helping a little."

Her act went off that night like it always did, beautifully. Men yelled louder than the women, even ones with wives. Some of them yelled out that they wanted to marry her and, very often, she would return to the camp that night to find all assortments of flowers and chocolates left for her with little notes that she never read. George didn't find himself getting jealous anymore after just a week or two because he loved eating chocolate so much. That night, she'd even been gifted a full chocolate Santa Claus, as it was closing in on Christmas time. She shared it with him and they laughed while they ate the jolly man from head to toe and made themselves sick off the sugar.

But when she went to clear out the rest of the gifts she'd gotten that night, she noticed that Danny had pulled one from the mix and put it in his pocket.

"What was that?" she asked.

"Nothing, nothing. Junk," Danny replied.

"No, I want to see it. It's mine, isn't it?"

The big man nodded in a solemn way that made George question if she should see whatever it was either. He pulled out a little book from his back pocket and handed it to her. It was a small, leather-bound bible.

"What's so bad about this?" she asked, turning it over in her hands.

"The inscription. On the inside," Danny said, his eyes to the ground.

But Charlotte couldn't read very well, having never gone back to school after leaving home. She opened it and urged George to read it aloud to her with a quick shrug of her shoulders. He squinted and read slowly, as that was all he could do. It took him a minute and when he realized what it said, he asked her if she was sure she wanted to hear it.

"Do I look like a damsel in distress to either of you? Read the damn thing," she shouted.

"Okay," George said. "It says 'All sinners will be punished unless they get right with God and, and change their ways.'"

"Oh," Charlotte said. Danny nodded in agreement with her sentiment and reached over and pulled the book from her hands.

"Let's just get shed of it," he said, walking to one of the bonfires they had going and chucking it in.

19

THE SHOWS WENT OFF as they always go off for two weeks after that and, if you took Charlotte's nights out of the equation, you would have thought that Georgia had been dying for a circus to visit their state. They sold more tickets than Danny said they ever had. The money flowed in so well that the crew started having "fancy dinner nights" as one of the band members, the fiddle player, called it, where they had a local restaurant bring whole roast chickens and potato dishes and they all got to sit at a real table and eat like civilized people. Danny said it didn't make sense to save all the money for a rainy day when you could make one day a week a little sunnier. And George agreed, but he found it odd when Danny would ask Charlotte over and over again if she liked whatever food was brought in and when he started having the catering nights scheduled for only the evenings that she would perform.

But it only helped so much with her moods. George found that the words in that bible had taken a bite out of her energy and especially on the days that she was supposed to perform. She was still mostly the same for the first week. But then her second show happened.

Everything seemed normal when she came out and lit her first baton on fire. The crowd was hushed as they always were at the beginning and the band had just started to play quietly, when a shout rang out in the crowd.

"Heathen," a man yelled and then repeated three times. "Heathen, heathen."

The band played louder to cover him up and Charlotte kept going and you couldn't see her face yet in the darkness to tell her reaction. George was sitting nearby this man and found him quickly as he was the only person standing up. He ran over and stood in front of him and the man sat down quickly.

George bowed out his chest and tried to make himself look bigger. The man, wearing a long beard and a small hat and a black suit, cowered a bit.

"What are you doing?" he asked the man.

"I am doing God's work," the man responded.

"You can do God's work somewhere else then," George said, grabbing him by the arm and yanking him out of the building. The man protested outside that he could not be treated this way and George reminded him that it was private property and he would call the police if he didn't get going so the man did.

After dinner that night, as George sat with Charlotte in her tent before bed, she didn't speak for a while and he couldn't see her face as she sat in her bed, turned on her side, and he wondered if she was sleeping. But she spoke as he started to get up and leave.

"Did you hear that man tonight?" she asked.

"The one in the crowd?"

"Yes."

"I took care of him. You don't have to worry about it."

She said okay and he kissed her on the cheek and bid her goodnight. When he went to the tent he shared with Danny, the big man was still up, reading by candlelight. He stopped when George walked in.

"Thank you for taking care of that nuisance earlier," he said.

"No problem," George replied, climbing into his cot.

"Is Charlotte okay?" Danny asked. George thought about the answer for a moment because he wasn't sure.

"For now, at least."

To take her mind off it, George proposed they have a date. Danny provided him with a suit. George tried to ask him where he got it and Danny shook his head before he could get all the words out of his mouth. It was blue—indigo was what one of the trapeze artists said when he walked by wearing it. On the shirt, there were frills like George had never seen. The jacket and pants were a cool blue and the collar was a little darker. He was proud of himself when he put it on, but as he turned around to the mirror he remembered the last time he wore a suit and a shudder flew down his spine and he didn't want to look at himself anymore.

The date wasn't much. That was what he told her once he'd walked over to her tent and "picked her up" for it. She wore a yellow dress with tiny flowers sewn into it. When George complimented it and how pretty she was in it, she told him that it had been a gift from a fan. One of the few that she'd really appreciated and kept. It fell just to her knees and he had to keep himself from staring at her legs in the waning daylight. They sauntered together to the edge of the campsite, where a small table sat. A chair on either side, the finest China that anyone in the cohort owned sitting atop the table. He pulled her chair out for her and sat down and Jack appeared, seemingly out of nowhere, with a bottle of wine and two glasses. They were then served the best gumbo George had ever eaten.

He watched her while she ate, the way her mouth moved with each chew. The tightening of her jaw accentuated her cheeks and, in turn, her eyes.

"What are you staring at?" she asked between bites.

"Oh, nothing."

"You know what I was thinking?"

"No, what?"

"You're so good at asking about me, I hardly ever get anything about you."

"Well, maybe that's alright," he said, trying his best to not come off as defensive, even if he was.

"No, I want to know more about you."

"Why?" Before she could say anything, he read the signals that her eyes were beaming across the table. They had a way of squinting with anger without ever really squinting at all. "Oh, alright, okay."

"What was your mama like?"

"She was, she was really nice," the words had to be yanked out of him but he knew he wasn't getting out of it so he kept on as well as he could. "She was beautiful. And she was good to me."

"Tell me a memory of her."

"Oh, okay, well. She liked going over what I was learning in school, English mostly, and teaching me some of my people's language too. She said it was important. But that was how everybody was there. All of the older people thought it was important."

"Do you not think it is?"

"I guess I do."

"Do you miss it?"

"My mammy?"

"Well, yes. But your home in general."

"Not at the moment. I think this is fine. Going pretty well," he tried to grin at her and turn the conversation, but she didn't notice or did and chose to ignore.

"Teach me some of it."

"The language?"

"Yeah. Teach me a word."

"Like what?"

"I still wonder the same things about you that I wondered from the first time we talked. Anything. First thing that comes to mind when you think of me. Whatever."

"Mm, chi i hullo li," he said before taking up another spoonful of gumbo. After he'd swallowed, he saw that she still waited to hear what he meant when he said that combination of sounds. "I love you."

She blushed. He loved when she blushed too.

"Thank you," she said. "How do you say thank you?"

"Yakoke."

She said it back to him.

"Do you know a lot?"

"Only a little. What I was able to learn before I left."

"Do you wish you could've said goodbye?"

"I don't know how much good it would've done," he said.

They finished their meals and poured the last of the wine. He cleared his throat.

"How are you doing?" he asked.

"I'm great, of course."

"No, I mean, with everything going on."

"Let's not talk about all that, George."

"Are you sure? I don't think it's right to not talk about it. You are not alone. It's okay to share it with me."

"It hurts," she said.

"Yeah?"

"Maybe I've been doing my act this whole time just to be seen by someone. But I didn't know what that could mean. To be seen by the wrong people. They think of me as sin in the flesh, don't they?"

"I don't know what they think, Charlotte."

"Yes, you do. Don't play coy with me," she snapped.

"Okay," he said.

"I'm sorry, I'm sorry. You don't deserve it."

"Maybe I do."

"No, you don't. You're such a good boy. And you saw me, first. Maybe I should focus on that," she said.

"I do see you."

"Can we talk about something else?"

She grabbed his hand. She did not speak. Her eyes did for her, speaking a new language. She leaned over the table and kissed him. They forwent their chairs for seats on the grass and once it had gone quiet in the camp, they made love right there in the weeds and the dirt.

"Yakoke," she told him as he dropped her back off at her tent at the end of their night together.

"For what?" he asked. He blushed to hear the word spoken by someone else, even if it was spoken in a foreign accent.

"Everything."

The man returned to the next show with two companions.

"Heathen, heathen, heathen," he screamed as Charlotte's act began.

"Sinner, sinner, sinner," his friends screamed in unison.

George hadn't considered that he'd come back, or at least not with extra help, so he had to run outside and grab Danny and Nathaniel to help him throw them out. They shouted the whole time they were being pulled out that God wouldn't put up with this.

"This tent will be struck down in a mighty fire," the first man yelled as George pulled him by the arm. When he did this, it startled Charlotte and she looked out into the crowd where they were for a moment and dropped one of her batons. But she remembered herself and picked it up quickly, getting back to the show. George whacked the man in the head with an elbow and the man fell down in protest. He pulled him out by both arms, the man's legs dragging on the dirt. Outside, they threw the men on the ground and Danny stood over them.

"Fellas, there has to be a better way to handle this. I'm a businessman. I don't like you hurting my business," he told the three men, lying there under his shadow. One of the men spit out of the side of his mouth before speaking.

"Money has no place in the kingdom of God and neither does that harlot you put out there with her devilish fire," he said.

George watched as Danny's face turned red. He thought he might stomp on the man's head then and there and get it all over with. But George knew the consequences of this all too well and he tried to imagine stuffing the big man in a trunk to hide him but the thought was almost funny and he knew it to be impossible. As soon as his face had turned red, it calmed back down to the pale white it was behind his thick beard and eyebrows and his face loosened up.

"You fellas want a refund?" he asked them.

Their faces were so stunned and bug-eyed that George nearly laughed. One of the men started stammering.

"No, no, keep your money," he said, pushing himself off the ground in a motion that created a few extra feet of space between the two groups. The two other men did the same. They all stood up and brushed themselves off.

"Alright," Danny said, putting on a fake southern drawl and a smile. "Well, we thank you for your donation then. Hope y'all get on home safe."

"May God str—" the first man started to say. Danny threw his right hand up in the air.

"Amen, amen, thank y'all for coming."

The men walked off with scowls on their faces. George and Nathaniel stood there staring at their backs and eventually Danny turned back to them and his face showed a sudden aging of a decade. The wrinkles on his forehead were doubled and he looked tired.

"Why don't y'all get in there and catch the end of Charlotte's show?" he said.

"Do you think they're done?" George asked.

Danny shook his head a little, as if his neck was tired too. "No, I wouldn't put money on it. Go on, go on," he said. George and Nathaniel nodded and walked back into the tent.

His bet was a good one. The men kept coming back for weeks. Charlotte performed once a week and they were always there, that man and his growing posse of interrupters.

George noticed that she had taken to sleeping less. Some nights she wouldn't go to bed until long after midnight had passed, just sitting outside by a fire and staring up at the moon, and he would give up on staying awake with her. She'd hardly talk throughout the day and when she did it was about nothing at all or the men. George would ask her if she wanted to go for a walk or go into town and do some shopping with the bit of money she'd gotten in gifts—she was still getting the gifts as usual. She'd just shake her head, her gaze off in the distance and her mind somewhere else.

"George," she'd said one night just as he decided that he'd get up and head to bed.

"Yes, Charlotte," he said, sitting back down beside her.

"What have I done?" she asked.

"What do you mean?"

"What have I done to deserve it?"

"Oh, nothing. You haven't done anything at all. These aren't good people."

"But what if they're right?"

"What do they have to be right about?"

"What if I am of the devil? Maybe I'm cursed. That would explain it all, wouldn't it?"

George didn't know what to answer to that so he just shook his head violently. He was angry at her for believing any of it but he knew he couldn't express it. She was too fragile then. It made him wonder how someone could go from so strong-willed to this so quickly.

"You can shake your head all you want," she said then. "Oh, I don't know. Maybe I'm being crazy too. But I hear them while I perform and it's getting harder to go on performing when they scream these things. At night, I dream of my mama hanging there in the yard or I dream of the lake that my pa would fish in. He's not there. I'm alone and I'm standing above the water like I heard Jesus did one time. The water is still and then I start moving over it with the wind. The wind carries me around a bend and I see his boat washed up on the shore and then the wind stops and leaves me far enough away that I can't get to it but I still can see it and I can't go anywhere to get away from it. I have to look at it, like somebody has brought me there to see it and punish me for it."

He put his arms around her and she didn't cry, she only breathed hard. He got one of his asthma cigarettes out and handed it to her. It was the last one in the pack but he figured he'd just get Danny to add some to the next goods order.

"Don't worry about me," she said after a while.

"I have to, Charlotte," he said.

"No, you don't."

She didn't say anything else and got up and walked to her tent. He didn't follow her. He sat in the chair by the fire and nodded off and woke up later to the cold of the night and walked to his tent in the dark. Danny rustled when he stepped inside it but didn't wake, so George never said anything about the conversation to him.

By the fifth week, there were more than twenty of them. Danny had taken to stationing George, Jack, and some of the other men at the entrance before the shows as folks filed in. He told them to say they were ushers if they were asked. It had been fine for a couple of weeks and they were able to identify the men as they walked up and tell them politely to leave, stopping the ruckus at the gate. But this time, they were overwhelmed by the clergy men. They approached in a horde, all wearing outfits of black. Danny was standing there with the boys and he whispered under his breath something about them growing exponentially and George didn't put too much thought into whatever that must have meant but he could use context clues well enough. When they got closer, Danny stepped out in front of them with his arms out wide.

"Fellas, thank you all for coming," he said, his deep voice booming. Some of the other folks unrelated to the mess that walked by turned to see what was going on. Leigh, who was running the ticketing that night, tried to keep everyone focused on getting inside the tent for the show. The group of men tried to walk by him and Danny stood there like a log and blocked the front few with his arms. "I'm the proprietor here and I'd love to have a chat with you."

"We're here for the show," one of them said from the middle of the crowd.

"Well ain't that great," Danny said.

"Yeah, so why don't you just let us on by?"

"What act are you here for? What are you looking forward to most?" Danny asked, backing up as the men pushed into him. But the men didn't answer and they walked on by. George and the others tried to get in the way but there were too many of them. They walked in the entrance without paying for a ticket or anything. Nathaniel was performing when they all stepped inside the big room, George and the rest following behind trying to do anything to help it.

Nathaniel and Benjy had just started their act, Benjy running around the room in all of his powerful beauty, when the men breached the room and began to chant. At first what they were shouting in unison was unintelligible to George but as he ran closer to them he could slowly make out what they were saying.

In a call and response, the man who they'd long identified as the leader of this group shouted, "And Judas said: Bring her out, and let her be burned."

And the men responded in tune, "Bring her out, and let her be burned."

And they did this on and on, raising their volume until they were screaming and you could no longer hear the band.

The crowd was watching them instead of the act. George stood in front of them beside Jack and they both had their hands on their hips because they didn't know what to do. George felt fear for the first time in a long time.

"I've never dealt with anything so ridiculous in my life," Danny yelled.

Some of the crowd around them started to boo the protestors and the main man began doing something that George heard someone call "speaking in tongues." He threw his head back and was shouting in a language George had never heard. It sounded like gibberish. George had heard English and Choctaw and some Spanish and this was nothing like any of them and, while the man did this, the rest of these religious zealots kept shouting their line. No one was watching the center of the ring any longer and then George heard a growl coming from there and he wondered if he was hallucinating and if none of this was real at all but then the growl happened again and he recognized it as the voice of Benjy.

"Whoa there, whoa there," screamed Nathaniel. The men kept chanting and yelling but everyone replaced their gaze back on the act. Benjy was growling and whipping his head back and forth at the noise. "Benjy, calm down, buddy."

And then time slowed down, like it always seemed to do when an awful thing happened, like God wanted to make sure that you understood what was going on in front of your eyes, like life wasn't hard enough in regular speed. The great tiger leapt forward. It was angry and Nathaniel was prey. It was only doing what it was made to do. The crowd gasped. Those men kept chanting. Nathaniel fell down. The tiger jumped on top of him. Nathaniel screamed something and his voice was hoarse and high-pitched and George would think later that he wished he had another memory to remember the man, but this is what he and everyone else there got. The scream halted the Christians' chanting and they all turned and followed everyone else's gaze down to the man and the beast. Benjy didn't do anything for a moment as he stood atop Nathaniel. He only lifted his head and looked out at the crowd with his paws on the man's shoulders holding him down, his nose wiggling as he sniffed around the room. And the room held its breath. But nothing good ever lasts.

Benjy started at his right arm, sinking his teeth in and wagging his head until it pulled clean off. Nathaniel yelped. Blood gushed out of his shoulder. Then the tiger slapped him across the face with its claws out and George could've sworn later on that he saw the animal's trainer's eye fly out of his head and into the netting. Nathaniel yelped one last time and went silent. A woman in the crowd screamed and the crowd gasped and a child yelled out something and pandemonium ensued all around. People jumped up out of their seats *en masse* and stampeded down into the path towards the exit. Danny sprinted past George, his big body moving faster than you would believe possible, to beat the crowd out of the room. The religious men stood completely still and silent, watching what unfolded about them.

As the room was emptying out, the tiger had taken to eating the body of the man there on the ground and George could no longer watch. Danny ran back in past him and down to the center of the room and George saw then that he had a rifle under his right arm and he pulled the thing up to his shoulder and took aim at the tiger and fired. The tiger jolted as the bullet hit it in the shoulder and it slowly turned towards Danny. He bolted the rifle again and fired. The tiger bounced back like it had been punched in the nose and the beast collapsed. He bolted the rifle one more time and fired it into the animal's head again. The room went silent and the big man turned around with the gun still in his hand and he looked at that group of men still standing there. No other patrons were around.

"Get out of my tent," he said, low and full of rage.

"Are you threatening us?" the lead man asked.

Danny lifted the gun up to his shoulder once more. All their eyes grew three sizes and they turned and filed out of the room around George, some of them bumping his shoulders as they passed.

"May this place burn to the ground," he heard one of them whisper as they passed. After they were gone and the sound of their shuffling out had ceased and the room had gone silent again, George saw a movement behind Danny, who was still standing there staring at the exit with nothing behind his eyes and seemingly no breathing. He stepped up past the big man and looked at the center of the ring and there was Charlotte, standing over the tiger, and she was crying there. She reached down and caressed its face and got on her knees and the tears fell from her face onto the man and the beast and the ground like the heaviest of rain and George did not step any closer to her as he felt wholly insufficient for whatever great pain she was feeling. She looked up at him and her eyes were red and her face was nearly blue in her suffering.

"Did I do this?" she asked.

Danny walked out of the tent exit with the rifle slung over his shoulder and George wanted to tell Charlotte no, that they did this, but the words would not come out of him, they could not leave his lips, and she bent back down over that tiger and cried.

20

"Folks," Danny said before pausing at the early morning meeting he'd called the day after the incident. It was Sunday. There were beads in his eyes. "Folks, there are no words for what happened last night. I don't have them. This was no accident that comes along with the trade, nor was it the fault of Nathaniel's or any of us. I've never felt so helpless. I've never felt so helpless. But we have a show to do tonight. If we give up now, I fear that we'll have to give it up forever. We can figure it out. If you don't want to perform tonight, someone else can step in for you. But we can't give up as a whole. There are some forces beyond our control at play here but there are things we can control and performing the acts we came here to perform is at the top of that list, I believe. Does anyone have any objections?"

No one spoke.

"Okay, then we have to get to work." And he ended it with the same big clap of his hands that he always did but there was no smile on his large face to go along with it.

George looked around for Charlotte but she was nowhere to be found. He walked over to her tent as everyone dispersed and got back to the tasks at hand. There was no one inside when he peered in but the candle by her bedside was still burning, nearly down to the end of the wick. He went back out and found Danny standing in front of the empty tiger cage.

"Have you seen Charlotte?" he asked.

"No, why?" the big man said. When he turned around to face George, there were the remnants of tears just below his eyes. He wiped them off with his shirtsleeves. "She not just sleeping in or something?"

"She wasn't in her tent and the candle was still burning by her bed."

"Mm. She might've not gone to bed last night. That would have been a reasonable thing to do."

"She's been hardly sleeping at all."

"Mm," Danny grunted.

George asked every crew member that he passed as he walked around camp but none had seen her. He checked inside the big tent but no one was in there except for Jack, who was pouring buckets of water on the dirt where the tragedy had happened. The boy stopped working for a second and waved at George as he stepped in.

"Nasty work," he said.

"I'm sorry you've got to handle that."

"Could be worse, I guess. You needing something?"

"Have you seen Charlotte?"

"Oh, I saw her early this morning. I woke up real, real early, couldn't keep myself asleep for no more than a couple of hours after seeing all that last night, and I saw her leaving camp and walking on down the road that way." He pointed and George's first thought was it was the way those men had come from and gone to, but he figured there was a whole world in that direction and he shouldn't jump to conclusions so quickly.

"You ask her where she was going?"

"Naw. I'm afraid of that girl."

George smiled a little and said that was a fair thing to be, she was a little scary at times, and he thanked the boy before leaving the tent, hearing the slosh of water on the dirt behind him and shivering a little at the memory. He went and found Danny again, lifting weights with his shirt off, his wide, hairy chest open to the cool wind, and relayed to him the information from Jack. He said he was going to go see if he could find her, leaving out his concern about where she might have gone to. He said this and then immediately turned around to leave. He didn't want the man to stop him from going out so he wasn't going to give him the opportunity. But Danny blurted out to give him a second, he was coming too, and George turned around to ask why. The man was putting his shirt on and apparently could sense what George's question would be.

"I have no show, hell, I got no life without that girl. You're not going by yourself."

"Somebody has to be here to run this thing, Danny."

"They haven't needed me for any of that for a long time, buddy. I'm going with you. Let's go."

THEY WALKED FOR A MILE down the road and a few cars passed by them, mostly beaten down things that sounded as if they were on their last legs, along with a couple horse-drawn carts. Old women sat in them, staring out the back and not turning their heads to get a glance at them walking there on the side of the path. George wondered where they were heading and why they looked so solemn about it.

"I remember the first time I rode in a car," Danny said. "I thought the world had changed right before my eyes. We couldn't have been going very fast. Them things just couldn't go fast. Good horse would outrun 'em easily. But it felt like a new age had come. Maybe it had, I guess."

"We never owned a car. But my pa did. I saw him ride away in it once. It was nice. Sleek and black. Fast, at least looked fast going down the road."

"You didn't know him or something?"

"Or something, yeah. Turns out a lot more people knew him better than I did. A whole state's worth of people. And I'm better off for it, I think."

Danny looked over at him with a curious gaze and nodded and let the conversation fall. Up ahead of them then, George saw the white outline of a little church. He started to say something but he saw that Danny was already squinting at it in the distance, maybe half a mile away. Neither said anything about it and they walked in silence for a few minutes until the full church, a small building with faded white paint over weatherworn boards, was in view and that same group of men were standing in front of it. At the driveway they passed a sign that said Dry Branch Pentecostal Church in black lettering. George had never heard of this type of Christian church. They could hear singing and piano music inside as they approached the front door. It was slightly ajar and Danny entered first.

Inside, they saw rows of pews filled to the brim with men and women and children. They were all standing and it was so loud in there that hardly anyone noticed Danny and George had entered the room. Danny found an empty space to their right, in the very back pew, where a family of three was worshipping. The little boy there, holding his mother's hand, turned and stared at them both, wide-eyed and possibly afraid. The congregation kept on singing.

And though this world, with devils filled,should threaten to undo us,we will not fear, for God has willedhis truth to triumph through us.The prince of darkness grim,we tremble not for him;his rage we can endure,for lo! his doom is sure;one little word shall fell him.

George did not sing along but he listened intently to the words of the song. He found them to be the words of a people that must have been constantly afraid, at battle with something bigger than themselves at all times. He felt a shadow over himself and the whole room. When the song was over and the piano player lifted her hands from the keys, everyone sat down and a man walked up to the front of the room. He was one of the men they'd thrown out. George recognized him instantly. He looked over at Danny and could see in the whites of his eyes that he realized it as well and that he was having a hard time not getting angry.

"It is the day the Lord has made," the man began speaking. His voice boomed in the filled room. "Let us rejoice."

While the man spoke, giving a sermon that George only half paid attention to about the words of the apostle Paul and circumcision, George and Danny scanned the room as well as they could without making those around them suspicious. It was hard to see with all the hats and tall men in the room, but George spotted something out of the ordinary in a pew a few rows up and across the aisle from him. There was a girl slumped down low with a veil over her face. He watched her for the rest of the service. She barely moved and did not clap her hands when everyone else did. After the sermon was over and another hymn was sung, George tried to act along while he watched her. She stood but did not sing, her shoulders under a thick dress that he thought he recognized were as still as a statue.

Filing out of the room, they lost her for a moment. George felt a hand on his shoulder and he whipped around. The pastor was standing there. He could feel his poker face slipping. Danny turned around with him.

"Fellers," he said. "What brings you to the house of God today?"

"House of God," Danny mumbled. George didn't think the man heard him.

"Just wanted to check things out," George replied.

"Check it out, huh? Very well. I'm glad you could join us. I hope that Christ has been pressing on your heart today. I can only imagine if you spread the good news throughout your whole—what do you call them? Your circus folk?"

"Family," Danny blurted out.

"Family, yes. Throughout your whole circus family."

"I don't know if we'll be doing that," Danny said.

"Well—" the man began to speak and George spotted Charlotte leaving the room with her head low. She got close enough that he could see through the veil and he was sure it was her.

"I'm sorry," George said, grabbing Danny's wrist. "But we have to be getting on."

They chased her down to the end of the driveway.

"Charlotte," George half-shouted and half-whispered in her ear. "What are you doing here?"

The girl looked around for a moment and saw that everyone was behind them then and she lifted the veil. Tears stained her cheeks.

"I just wanted to see," she said.

"See what?" George asked. Danny was silently watching, walking beside him.

"See if maybe I was wrong about them. See if maybe I was the problem. See if maybe their spirit would move in me instead."

"I'll kill them," Danny said.

George put his arm around her and they walked back in silence.

SHE WAS GONE again, the next morning.

"Come on," Danny said to George, shaking him out of his sleep. "We've got to go get her."

"What?" George asked, climbing out of unconsciousness.

"She's gone again."

A group of men were standing in the yard of the church and they were speaking in hushed tones in little groups and the door to the church was wide open with one man standing in front of it. As he and Danny stepped into the yard, the men quieted. George watched as the big man stopped for a moment, looking around at everyone there.

"She here?" he asked them.

None of them answered. Some of them hung their heads. Danny looked around at them all one more time before pushing his way through them and up the stairs of the church. George followed behind best he could and, when they reached the doorway, the man there stood in front of them and would not move. George was behind Danny and couldn't see past him or the man.

"Let me past," Danny said in a low tone, similar to a growl.

"Let us take care of it," the man said.

"Take care of what?" George asked. The two men ignored him, and he felt like a small child again.

"I don't want to hurt you," Danny said, still in that cool voice of fake calm like how someone had once told George the wind gets just before a tornado hits you. But George didn't really believe them then. Still, he remembered it. "But I will."

And then, the man had seemingly stepped out of the way and Danny was stepping forward into that church. He stopped, just past the doorframe, and George tried to look past him but his broad shoulders took up all the space available. He heard the man make a guttural sound, like he'd been shot or stabbed, but there was no other noise with it.

"Danny, what is it?" he asked.

There was no response from the big man.

"Danny. Danny, what is it?" he pleaded.

And then, he dropped to his knees in front of George and George looked before him and Charlotte was there in the room but there was something wrong with her that he couldn't quite figure out at first. She was floating, that was it. He blinked hard, thinking he must be seeing it wrong. Danny moaned on the ground in front of him and he wondered why he was doing that and he blinked hard again and he saw the rope up there tied to a board on the low ceiling of that little one-room church and he followed the rope down and it ended at Charlotte's neck and he saw how she was swaying ever so slightly and how her face was pale, paler than he'd ever seen it, and how her eyelids were down over her eyes in a way that made it seem as if she didn't close them herself and how her mouth hung open and she was still in the old dress she wore to sleep in, the one he told her he'd like to replace with something nicer.

"Charlotte?" he said. "Charlotte?"

Danny slammed a fist to the ground and a well of tears exploded from his giant face and he threw his head down to the ground and his body shook violently. George jumped over him and ran to the front of the room where she hung. He reached out his right hand and touched her dress and it felt as real as anything. Suddenly, it all welled up inside of him, the weight of it and the pressure of it and everything about her that he loved came up from his stomach and he vomited there on the floor and onto one of the pews to his right. He wiped his mouth and hung his head for a moment and he heard one of the men, the leader, yelling at him for defiling their sanctuary even more with his bile and asking if they hadn't already done enough and George turned around to say something but Danny was already standing up and he seemed larger than ever, larger than any person had ever been, and he threw one of his big arms back and made a fist and coldcocked the man across the face. The man crumpled instantly on the floor and the rest of them gasped and started to run up there and do something about it but Danny began screaming like a lunatic, growling like Benjy had just a few nights before.

George ran up behind him and put his arms around the man and began to cry.

"Danny, calm down, Danny," he cried out. He could feel the man's heart beating like it might explode out of his chest.

"I'll kill you," the man screamed at those Christians on the lawn. "You did this. I'll kill you."

He kept screaming this and George squeezed him as hard as he could, whispering that it was okay, until he stopped shouting eventually and George told him to go on home.

"I can't leave her here," he said.

"I got it, Danny. That ain't, that ain't her no more. Go on home."

Danny looked at him and his face went from red to white again and his eyes lost all of their rage and their light with it and he asked George if he was sure and he said yes. George watched as the man walked out through that crowd of awful men with his head down to the ground and he watched him until he got out to the road and then George got his knife out and went to cutting his lover down from her place up there. While he cut, he looked down at the ground, for when his eyes were on the walls they seemed to sink in on him and her body and the room felt as if it might become just enough space for him to stand and hold her and it might never let them out.

"I'm sorry," he whispered to her over and over again. "I'm so sorry. I'm so sorry. I'm so sorry. I'm so sorry, Charlotte. I'm so sorry."

When she was down, he picked her up and carried her out of that building and all the way back home.

"I love you, I love you, I love you, I love you, I love you," he whispered to her as he walked.

She didn't speak, but he thought he could hear her saying thank you.

His arms were tired from carrying her but he didn't stop until he was in front of the tent and the whole crew was standing there waiting for him and Danny was there on his knees in front of them too. George walked up to him and told him to put out his arms and he placed Charlotte's body into them and walked off to his tent, not daring to look anyone else in the eyes.

"I didn't know," he heard Jack say. George knew that the boy didn't know. Nobody could've known but her. But he didn't have it in him to tell the boy. He walked into the tent he shared with Danny and laid down in his cot. His heart was a mess of scars, so thick he wondered how it kept pumping. He went back to sleep for two days.

21

ACROSS THE RIVER FROM HIM, George saw lights that looked like fire. At first there was one, then two, and then, finally, three. He stared hard, trying to discern what they were. Nothing was out of the question by then; they might be any sort of ghost or creature from storybooks. But then they began to fly in the air, in a circular pattern, and he recognized them.

The fires kept spinning and in their blaze, he could make out her hands and arms. Her face stayed shrouded in shadow and she performed her act for him. He didn't say anything or move until she was finished. He felt fine for a moment. He clapped and stuck his fingers in his mouth to whistle, but he hadn't done it in so long that nothing escaped his lips but air.

"Charlotte," he yelled out. "Charlotte."

He giggled like a boy, the light of the flames twirling. He remembered something Chito and Koi's father had told them, about fire being the people's direct source of communication with a higher power. Some things became clearer with this memory, his laid-bare soul briefly illuminated, and made sense to him for a moment. But then the lights went out and she was gone. It was dark around him. His pain returned.

"Charlotte," he shouted, one last time. "I don't think I was supposed to survive. I don't think I was supposed to keep on going. You should've taken me with you. You should have told me. You should have let me go instead. You should have—"

His voice trailed off.

"She's not coming back," Colt said. George had nearly forgotten the boy was there.

"How the hell do you know?"

"I don't. But you do."

"Can't you just leave me alone?"

"I wish."

He decided to get up off his haunches and try to walk. He pressed himself up and the ankle hurt so bad he fell back down. He thought to himself that he had to stop forgetting about it, but then he thought that a little self-grace might not hurt anything. He walked down the bank of the river, in no particular direction, clasping onto every tree he passed for balance.

22

ON THE THIRD DAY, George rose from the cot and his whole body creaked and ached as he stood up. His joints popped like he was an old man. He looked over at the other cot and Danny still lay there, snoring lightly. For a moment, in his mind's blurriness, he nearly forgot that it wasn't a normal day. But, he thought to himself then, maybe it was a normal day, maybe this is how things always would be. He felt himself hardening from the inside out.

He decided he had to leave the camp. This was no place for him to be. He rubbed his eyes one last time and stepped outside to grab a mug full of coffee. A few folks stood around the coffee pot over the fire. One of them was Jack. He had his hands in his pockets and he was looking solemn in the dramatic way a young boy does. His eyes met George's as he walked up and the boy looked at him with pity.

"Don't look at me that way," George said, grabbing one of the mugs left out on a table by the fire. He noticed that there was something different about his voice. Like he'd aged a few years in the time he'd been asleep.

"Okay, sorry," Jack replied.

"No need to apologize to me either."

"I didn't know she was gonna do that. I would've done something if I'd known."

"That's alright."

"I'm serious. I would've done something. I swear to it."

"Buddy, I know. It's alright."

"It ain't alright, George. It ain't."

George nodded.

"You're right. Maybe it will be though. Sometime soon."

He poured himself some of the black sludge and walked back to his tent without saying goodbye to the boy. Back inside, he gathered his things and remembered that there were burlap sacks they'd used for Benjy's feed still sitting in a stack out there by the old cage, so he went out for it and brought it back. As he stuffed it with his belongings away, Danny rustled behind him and woke. He didn't turn around to look at him but kept throwing the few things he had or had been given recently into the sack.

"Where you going?" Danny said, his words jumbling together in his grogginess.

"Leaving," George replied.

"Leaving?" Danny threw himself up and swung his feet on the ground. "You're leaving?"

"I can't stay."

"The hell you can't. You're gonna leave us now? She's not even in the ground yet."

"She's not?" George said this and turned around.

"You've been asleep for two days, George. I started to figure you were in a coma and might never wake up. But you were just sleeping the time away. We wanted you to be there so we waited."

"You didn't have to wait for me." He turned back around to his sack and began to tie a piece of twine around the opening of it.

"Why's that?"

"Huh?"

"Why's that?"

"I don't have to be there."

"Something wrong with you?"

"Everything."

"You don't want to see her?"

"I carried her the whole way home, Danny." He felt tears welling up in his eyes. "I carried her the whole way home."

George finished tying it and he stood up and started to just leave then and there but he knew it wasn't right so he turned back around and offered his hand to the big man. Danny stared at the hand and stood up, towering over George even with his neck bent to not hit his head on the tent roof. They both stood this way for a bit, looking at each other, unblinking and unshaking. There was no consciousness about George, no fear of the man left in him or worry about what he might think of him. He felt like a body just moving about, if he even could feel that. Every movement felt predestined, his mind unnecessary to keep him on the path he was going to take. After a while of this standing in silence, Danny turned around and grabbed a small box from underneath his cot and opened it to a roll of bills inside. He plucked a handful of bills out and stuck them out to George. George shook his head at the offer.

"I'm not asking," Danny said.

"I don't need it, Danny," George said.

"Everybody needs it, you little fool." Danny's face got red and his nostrils flared and George reached out and slid the money out of his hand and stuck it in his pocket.

"Thank you, thank you. I appreciate it."

"I'll give your regards to the crew. Got anything you want me to tell them?"

"Tell 'em I'll be off somewhere else, I don't know where. But if they run into me, I've got some of your money they can spend."

Danny's lips curled up just a hair into a smile and he stuck his hand back out and George did the same and the big man's hand enveloped his. He shook it and let it go and walked out of the tent, leaving out through the back of the camp so no one would spot him. Dew was still on the ground and he could feel the wet through his thin shoes. Clouds marked the sky. He got to the road there and turned the opposite direction of the church.

In his pack was enough food to last him a week or two. And that was about the extent that he thought through. He walked all day down the road through whatever part of Georgia he was in. He'd never paid much attention to the path the circus caravan had taken from Alabama to there and he was starting to regret that. There wasn't much around him, save some houses with barns behind them and otherwise just open fields. It was still too early and cold to plant anything and the fields were just miles and miles of set dirt. The wind blew over them without impedance. Sometimes a gust would come along that nearly knocked him over. Few cars passed and when he saw or heard them coming from far off, he would hide off somewhere in the woods or in the ditch. He didn't want any trouble and he knew that a young man that looked like he did and only carried a burlap sack as he walked down a road in the middle of nowhere in this country might as well have been stamping a sign to his forehead that said "TROUBLE" in big bright letters.

At nightfall, he was tired from walking, but he didn't feel like sleeping. He'd done enough of it for a month, it felt like. He eventually found a thicket just off the road and he couldn't spy any houses nearby where a man might come out and run him off or do something worse, so he stopped there for the night and dug in behind a tree.

He propped his back up on the thickest pine he could find and brushed leaves over himself for whatever warmth they might offer and lowered his hat over his eyes. He held the sack in his lap while he nodded off in case anyone or anything got any bright ideas. But the only consequence of the night was the cold. He only had two boxes of matches and he didn't want to go wasting them on the first night of however long this journey might be, especially since he'd need one box just for his asthma medication, and the cold that settled in with the darkness got deep in his bones and he woke up shivering at some point. He rustled more leaves over his legs and wrapped his jacket around him tighter but it did no good. Eventually he dozed off for another hour. He did this dance on and off until the sun began to rise and he decided that moving on down the road would probably do better for him than lying there any longer.

After walking for most of the morning, George came to a fork. A creek ran beside the road to the right and he went over to it and filled his hands with the cold water and it was a little murky but he didn't care too much and he drank it by the handful until he couldn't stand anymore. He decided to continue on down this road to the right because it made perfect sense. He couldn't have explained it, but he didn't have to. He walked all day and then night came, and it was the same as the night before. The next days were the same, an endless monotony of his legs hurting all day and his body shivering all night. He started to talk to himself to pass the time as he was so far out in the country then that there seemed to be just a road and nothing else. Some fields that weren't in use. Plots of trees that seemed to span on forever or only make up a half-acre. Everything was the same and yet nothing was. He sang songs from his childhood, nursery rhymes his mammy sang to him or the bits and pieces of old hymnals that he could recall while he hummed the parts he couldn't.

On what he figured to be the sixth day of his walking, he ran out of the food he'd stuffed away in his pack. He walked into a field in the middle of the day and looked around. He wondered if rabbits or deer hung around these parts. He'd never been to Georgia but he figured it couldn't be too much different than back home. The trees all looked the same anyway. He took the knife out of his pocket and looked it over. He figured it would do. So, he went and laid down on his stomach on the tree line of this field and he waited.

He didn't make a move or a sound for hours. No other nearby living form did either. The wind blew every once in a while, as if to remind him that it was still there, if nothing else. He'd just started to doze off when he heard the crunching of feet on leaves behind him. He startled a bit but tried not to move. Whatever it was kept moving, maybe ten yards away. George waited and waited and it eventually circled around into his view. It was a small doe, seemingly alone and totally unaware of his presence. She was pretty, like a good dog is pretty. She sniffed around. She chewed on something he couldn't see. He considered his options, the knife feeling heavier in his hand all the sudden. He reckoned killing her would be hard, if not damn near impossible. But he also reckoned that he wouldn't get any less hungry if he didn't kill her. As he thought it through, he realized that she was coming right up to him. She hadn't noticed him yet either. Within a minute or so, the seconds ticking in his head like a clock had lodged itself in his ear, she was on his right side, maybe a foot or two away. He could smell the musk of her never-cleaned fur. She started pissing there on the ground beside him. *Here goes nothin'*, he thought.

George jumped up and grabbed her by the leg. She bleated and kicked at him. He nearly lost grip of her but was able to keep his hand around her hoof until he could tear her to the ground. He jumped on top of the little deer, pinning her down, and realized he'd dropped the knife in the struggle. Without thinking about it any harder, he grabbed her by the neck. He didn't want to look down at her but he had to with her squirming. She kicked her legs around him and they landed hard stabs into his back and sides. Her eyes asked why he was doing this. Her eyes asked what kind of animal he was. Her eyes asked why she had never been taught that this was something to worry about. He wanted to tell her to shut up, but she wasn't speaking, she couldn't speak. He tried to squeeze the life out of her but he quickly found it to be harder than he'd imagined. He laid down on top of her, chest to chest, and kept his left hand on her throat and searched around with his other hand for the knife amidst kicking and bleats that occasionally sounded like screams. He felt metal and grabbed but it was by the blade and he sliced his hand clean open. He yelped and the deer kicked him with one of her front legs directly in the shin and he growled down at it that he wished it would just go ahead and fucking die and he reached back down and grabbed the knife again, this time by the handle.

In a swift motion, he lifted his chest off her and brought the blade up to her neck. She looked him in the eyes one last time. She pleaded with him to stop. He swung the blade across her throat and sliced it open. Blood started gushing and he held her down while she squirmed until she'd stopped moving altogether. He couldn't feel her breathing anymore. He smelled piss and shit and blood and he rolled over from atop her onto the ground and took a deep breath in. But he couldn't lay there for long. His stomach forced him up and onto his knees and he vomited beside the dead little deer. He looked over at her. She was already getting stale. He began to cry, too. How fast a life could end. He beat his fists into the ground. How fast you could take a life, and why? He beat his fists onto and into the side of his head. A pool of tears and snot fell from his face to the dirt and leaves on the forest floor.

He tired of this and stopped. He said out loud for only his ears and the wind and the now deaf ears of the deer to hear that he had to toughen up. He had to figure this out. By this time, it was the early evening and cold had started to settle in. He got up and grabbed the deer by a hoof and dragged it to the very back of the field, where he skinned her to the best of his little knowledge and started up a fire with whatever branches and sticks he could find. He put a slab of her backstrap on a stick and roasted it over the fire there until it was a dark enough color by his standards and ate it straight off the stick. Mid-eating, he realized the poor, little deer's head still sat there looking at him and he nearly threw up again so he put the food down for a moment and carried the carcass off in the woods a distance until it was far enough away that he hoped he could forget about it. He cooked another big piece of her for the next day's eating and covered it in some of Danny's salt he'd grabbed without the man noticing and wrapped it in some loose paper and stuffed it in his pack. By the time this was all done, it was dark. He slept that night by the dwindling little fire he'd created and held the pack in his lap and he was full and warmer than he'd been in days and he slept well. He woke in the early hours of the following day to the fire gone and the chill just beginning to settle in him so he decided to go ahead and get out on the road again.

IT WAS EARLY EVENING and George passed a house. He'd passed no less than twenty houses since he'd started walking and he'd gotten relaxed. There was rarely ever anyone outside these places and if there was, it was usually a child playing who would either look at him and resume playing make-believe or not notice him at all. But on this evening and on the porch of this house, there was a man sitting in a rocking chair. He had on overalls and a stained white shirt and no shoes. He rocked back and forth slowly. A rifle sat to his right, leaning against the clapboard wall of the home. George saw him sitting there and tried not to look at him again, not wanting any attention drawn to him and his walking.

"Hey, you," the man shouted at him from the porch.

George kept his head forward and tried to act like he didn't hear the man.

"Hey," the man shouted louder. His voice was old and angry. "I know you can hear me. Hold on over thar'."

George winced and thought about running but decided the gun at the man's side was good enough reason to hear him out, at least to start with. He turned towards the house and made his face out like he couldn't really hear the man and pulled his hat down to block the sun that was setting behind the old house and looked for a moment like he couldn't really see either and then faked spotting the man and gave a short, friendly wave.

"Where you headed to?" the man shouted out. George knew he didn't have an answer. He couldn't name four Georgia towns or cities and the three that he knew were all from Danny. He bought himself time by acting like he hadn't heard and the man repeated himself.

"Athens," he responded in kind.

"You got a ways to walk."

"Yessir."

"What you got in that sack?" the man was leaned forward in his chair then, a cigarette in his left hand, and he was squinting like it'd help him see closer in on George.

"Just some stuff to help me get by."

"You ain't goin' around here stealing are you?"

"No sir. I'm just trying to get to Athens."

"You white?"

George paused and looked around and he recognized that pausing didn't do him any good but that man's gun was sitting there looking menacing and like a goldmine all the same. He thought a lie couldn't hurt.

"Yessir," George shouted back. The man leaned back in his chair and it was like the world loosened its grip a bit.

"Come on up here then. I got some dinner cookin' up." The man said this and then walked inside the screen door there without giving George another look.

His body followed the man up the yard and into the house without his mind's permission. He even walked right past the gun, still sitting in its place on the porch. Inside was what you would expect from an old man with no woman around. Beer bottles and liquor bottles and plates with half-eaten meals were strewn on every open inch of every counter and table. There were two more rocking chairs in there, just like the one on the porch. The old man was in the kitchen stirring a pot of beans over a woodstove. When he'd finished up with the beans, he reached over and set a dirty pan on the flame and it looked to have strips of bacon on it.

"No vegetables, I'm afraid," he said with a chuckle. His back was still turned to George.

The man went like this for a bit and shouted over his shoulder for George to take a seat in whichever chair he liked better. George turned one towards the kitchen and sat.

"What's your name, pal?" the old man asked him.

"George."

"George. Alright. Mine's Elroy. Whereabouts you from, George?"

"Mississippi, sir."

"What the hell's got you up here in the middle of nowhere?"

"That's a long story, mister," George replied.

"Let me guess, a woman." The old man said this and turned around and chuckled. He came over and set the pot of beans on the table along with two seemingly clean tin plates. George wondered how many plates the man could have. He turned and went back over to the cooking bacon.

"That's not a bad guess."

"I might be old but that don't mean I can't remember what it was rightly like to be a young man. Hell, I've chased women all across this land and another'n too."

"Is that right?"

"Fought a war in Cuba just because a buddy told me he'd heard the women down there were good-lookin'. Swear to it."

George laughed, partly to be kind to the somewhat good-hearted nature of this man, and he then brought the bacon over still sizzling and set it down between them. The smell was intoxicating and George had to give it a hard sniff that made the man give him a funny look before doing his own bit of chuckling. He gave George a fork and they both piled food on their plates. George tried to eat as slow as he could but he hadn't had anything but that deer and some old jerky in more than a week.

"Yessir, I fought the Spanish down there in Cuba. You heard of President Teddy Roosevelt, I'm assuming?"

It rung a bell at least and George nodded.

"I fought with him. Sure did. Up on Kettle Hill. Heard them Gatling guns firing with mine own ears, what a sweet sound it was. Just a drumming and thumping them Spaniards and tearing them to bits. You think you've seen something bad, wait till you see what one of them guns can do to a man. And then, we go on over to Santiago and I get shot in the leg. Thought I was going to lose it. Was told I was going to lose it, but I got lucky and that infection passed after just a week of feeling rough. Hardly even a memory anymore. I was just a lad. Maybe your age."

"And did you meet any women down there?"

"Oh, a few. Wild ones. They just wanted to sleep with an American and have a baby so they could come back over with us. I made sure to pull out, yessiree."

George grunted and kept shoveling food in his mouth to hide any sort of disdain or any other kind of sentiment from seeping out of his stomach and onto his face. He ate until there was nothing left on his plate and the man motioned with his fork for George to take what was left, so he did and he kept eating.

"I was just hearing we're going to end up in another war."

"You were?" George's head shot up.

"Yep. Heard it on the radio. Germany is doing something over there in Europe. I don't know nothing about it. Might be a while. Hell, who knows."

They finished eating the bacon and beans in silence and when George was done he leaned back in the chair and let himself relax for a moment. The old man was chewing his last bite and started looking at him curious-like. After he swallowed, he still looked at George, moving his tongue around his teeth behind his gums, picking out bits of food. He put a wad of tobacco in and grabbed a mug from a table to spit in.

"Say, what kind of white are you?" he asked.

"What's that?" George said.

"I'm not trying to accuse you of nothing, but you don't quite look right. Maybe it's the light. Y'all got a different shade of white down there in Mississippi?" He said this in a joking manner but George's face started to get red. He couldn't help it. The old man saw this and cocked his head to the side.

"You ain't one of them natives, are you?"

George didn't answer.

"Now that I look at you, I could swear you was one of them. Maybe a little whiter than your average one. Anybody ever tell you that?"

"Yessir, sometimes," George said.

The man's face got serious and he stood up, adjusting his pants. He started to step towards the door and George shot up in front of him and beelined to the door, beating the man there by a step. He stood there for a second. The man stared at him and didn't move.

"You're acting a little wild, pal," the man finally said after a while.

"Elroy, no need to do anything crazy here," George said, thinking of anything at all to say.

"I'm in my own house. I can do whatever I'd like, thank you." He tried to walk past George as he said this, but George didn't budge. George snuck a look at the gun. It still sat there.

"Mister Elroy, please go sit down." His heart raced. A daily occurrence by then.

"What are you gonna do? Kill me?"

"I'd rather not."

"You know how many Spanish sons of bitches I killed down there? Three or four, at least. I stabbed one right in the gut before he could kill me his self."

George pulled out the knife that he'd forgotten he had and the old man paused.

"Sir, I'm going to take that gun of yours and leave. I'll even pay you for it. I don't want no trouble."

"You're not taking my gun."

"Go get the ammo for it. Every bullet you got. I'll make it worth your while."

"You're not taking my gun. I won't give it to you."

"I'm not asking, mister." George lifted the knife so that it was at eye level for Elroy and the old man thought for a moment and backed off, stepping over to a cabinet and opening one of the drawers. "What are you doing?"

Before the old man could turn around, George leapt across the space in between them and stuck the knife in the shoulder that was grabbing something out of the cabinet. Elroy howled like a dog and crumpled to the floor as George yanked the knife back out and blood began to pool out of the hole in his shirt immediately. He glanced in the cabinet. There was money in there.

"I was just going to give you some money. Take the damned money. Leave my gun. I need my gun."

George felt something welling up inside him. A shame deeper than he'd ever known. But something else there too, alongside of it, pulling him forward in time. He couldn't apologize or stick around. He couldn't trust this man to forgive him. He couldn't trust anyone.

"Mister, give me the god damned ammo you have for that gun outside or I'll kill you," he felt himself say. He went along with it. "I've already killed a man and I wrestled with a deer in the woods with that knife just yesterday and cut its throat. Look at the blood on the bottom of my coat for yourself. I just want the gun and the ammo and I'll get out of here. I thank you for the food and I don't want your money. You can buy another one with this cash after I'm gone. Where is the ammo?"

The man licked his lips and nodded. He leaned over to the bottom of the cabinet and pulled open a drawer. In it was a box of bullets. He stopped there and motioned for George to take them himself. As George pulled them out, a few fell out and he had to stoop down to pick them up with the box. The man grabbed his hand, lightly, and looked George in the eye.

"This ain't the way you want to live your life, son," he said.

He shook his arm free and nodded at the man without saying anything else and he almost told him to keep the knife but he'd been an idiot enough already so he walked over and grabbed it off the floor where it'd bounced between them and he slipped out the door and grabbed the rifle. He'd made it a hundred or so yards down the road when a shot rang out. He turned and saw by the light of the furnace in the man's house that he was standing in his doorway with a revolver. George took off running and he ran and ran and ran for as long as he could. His lungs hurt. The road became surrounded by woods and he couldn't see any silhouettes in the shadow of the path behind him so he slowed down and stopped off in the ditch to rest.

He'd fallen asleep for no more than an hour when he was aroused by a rumbling in the dirt from a car. It stopped a bit down the road from him and he laid there still and listened as hard as he could. Eventually the wind carried their voices down to him. One was Elroy's and the other was a man's he didn't recognize.

"He ran this way," he heard Elroy saying.

"Well let's search for him some and then I'm going to call it a night, Elroy. It's getting late." George heard this and when he stared a little harder at the car under the light of the moon he recognized it as a police car and the urgency of the moment hit him like a freight train and he was wide awake. He decided to crawl into the woods for as long as he could to make less sound. He did this for a while, some hundred yards, and he could no longer hear the men talking or walking in the trees so he got up and began to run with his sack and the gun. He ran and ran and ran and his calves cried out for a rest and then his knees began to cry out with them and he could no longer keep going on and he fell on the ground there. He waited to hear sounds from the two men but there was nothing but wind through the trees and the occasional bird's call. He dozed off there from exhaustion and when he awoke again it was daylight.

He figured he had two options then. He could go back to the road and risk getting caught for a petty crime in a state that did not want him there in the first place or he could keep walking in those woods until they dumped him out someplace else. The forest around him looked older than the ones he'd seen before on this journey. He decided on trusting the woods to take him somewhere.

He walked for an entire day and saw nothing but thickets that he had to circumvent and some wildlife that seemed so unafraid of his presence that he wondered if they'd ever come across a man before this deep in the woods. He stopped for the evening to eat and he didn't make a fire because he felt it was warmer than it had been a few nights before. He ate on that piece of the deer he killed and sat in silence. But he wasn't tired, so he stood back up and kept walking. The trees let enough moonlight in that he could walk alright and he wasn't too worried about snakes since it hadn't yet warmed up too much. He came across another bramble and decided to push his way through it and after a struggle with it he came on the other side and realized he was in a clearing. In front of him was a cabin.

He rubbed his eyes and it was still there and he blinked hard and wondered if he was truly going crazy but when he opened them again, it stood there as real as the fingers on his hands. No lights came from the windows of it and he heard nothing but the sounds of natural life around him that he'd grown accustomed to. Still, he stopped there on the edge of the clearing and waited for night to become day before he approached it. He slept for a couple of hours and woke to sunlight on his face. The cabin stood there like it had been and so he walked up and climbed the porch, boards creaking under his feet like they hadn't been touched in some time, and he wiggled the door handle and it was unlocked. He swung it open slowly.

23

HE WALKED ALONG THE RIVERBANK holding his side and limping and grabbing onto those cypress and pine trees and he thought about all the mistakes he'd made and all the shitty luck he'd had. And yet, like a mother does for her child or a good God with abounding kindness does for His people, he was reminded by his memory of the lucky breaks he'd gotten.

He almost wanted to stop and get on his knees and pray and give thanks for what he'd been given. But he was in no shape to do so. And there was the apparition of the dead boy still with him. He felt like if he stopped, he might join Colt in death, if he wasn't already there and just didn't know it yet.

The house in the woods, shining in the sun under so many cloudless skies, came into his view like a prophetic vision then.

"Ain't that something," Colt said. "You ever think maybe you were lucky?"

"Why would I think that?"

"If you haven't figured it out yet, I'm not the best for answering your questions."

"No, I don't think I was lucky. Not a damn bit."

"You know you pushed me first," the boy said.

"What?"

"You pushed me first. I bet you don't remember that. I bet you've made me into even more of a monster in your head."

"I haven't made you into anything you weren't already."

"That ain't how the mind works. My daddy used to say it plays tricks on you."

"No, that was Chito and Koi's pa who said that. That's my memory."

"Maybe it is."

"I pushed you first? Really?"

"As real as it gets."

George thought about this, trying to recall the memory that he'd done his best to push away and make invisible.

"I can't remember if I did or not."

"What does it matter if you can? I can. And I know that you've moved on, kept living, like everything bad has just happened to you. Like you didn't have anything to do with it. But you pushed first. I know it. That don't fit with your story very well, does it?"

"I don't think that way about myself."

"I bet you think you're washed white as snow, don't you? Like the bible says."

"No, I don't," George said, quietly growing angrier.

"You ever regret it?"

"Regret what?"

"Killing me."

"No."

In his ears, through his anger, a different memory rang. That boy, a different one than who stood beside him then, whispering in his ear that names meant more to some sorts of people than they did to others, especially depending on the color of your skin, and that a name meant a hell of a lot to him. George kept walking and his foot slipped and he realized the river was forking and he was about to walk slam into it. He held onto the tree beside him and listened to it run and he followed it down the right side of the fork.

24

HE'D BEEN THERE FOR THREE YEARS. The home had grown with him into adulthood. He hadn't seen another person in so long that he'd grown accustomed to talking to himself from daybreak to day's end.

That day, then years past, where he'd stepped into the cabin in the middle of the woods felt like a million years and multiple iterations of George ago. The memory of his time in it pressed tightly in his mind until it was but a moment in time. But he would always remember the home well. It was a simple structure, a kitchen, a sitting area, and a bedroom. There was a feather mattress in the bedroom if you would have believed it. George had never even slept on one of these before and he had to take it out and beat any bugs off and out of it and he found some lightly moth-eaten quilt covers in a cabinet to spread over himself. Cleaning the house enough to make it livable had taken him the better part of the first year. He had no supplies save what was left there and he could deduce that it had been abandoned no less than a decade prior. He fashioned a branch and some larger dead leaves into the best broom he could make from memory and it did alright at cleaning the dust and dirt off the floors. But all things considered, he marveled often at how the sealed house had been a time capsule, waiting for someone else to come along and make it a home again.

Outside the house there was a small shed. The first time he'd opened it, a raccoon had busted out of the door and run over his foot and both of them had squealed. George laughed so hard when he realized what it was that he doubled over and it felt good to do this. The little shed had been overrun by pests and the wood boards were so waterlogged that it might as well have been torn down, but inside George found a shovel and an axe that he quickly grabbed and couldn't help but smile at. And as he stepped in and reached for them, his foot hit something hard on the ground. He looked down and saw three metal tins that had the seal of the US Army on the side. He picked one up and it was heavy, so he carried the shovel and axe up to the house and then came back for the tins. It took him the better part of ten minutes to get them up on the porch but when he cracked them open he couldn't believe what kind of day he was having.

Inside all three were boxes upon boxes of .22 bullets, the same he needed for that gun he'd taken. He sat down on the porch there and cried over the bullets and over the axe and over the shovel and Charlotte and Danny and Chito and Colt and his mammy and he carried it all inside the house for safekeeping, still crying like he'd never done before because he couldn't stop it. His head began to pound hard and he collapsed on the floor of the living room. He woke the next morning as thirsty as a man could be and he took the last swig from his leather bladder that Danny had given him when he'd first started working at the circus.

That second day, he'd gone back into the shed when the light was better to see what else he had, if anything, and he found a whetstone and he remembered Koi teaching him about using these to sharpen axes, so he pulled it out onto the grass where there weren't a million spiders lurking in the shed and he worked all morning on trying to learn how to use it. Eventually he figured he had a sharper axe and he went out into the trees to chop down firewood until he was spent. Just as he'd gotten his last load of wood, he'd stopped for a moment to listen to the forest around him and he'd heard what sounded to be a stream. He threw the wood down like a madman and ran towards where the noise came from and there it was, a small cold stream running over delicately placed rocks like he was Moses, only without the rod. He leaned down and lifted handfuls out to his mouth and it tasted like pure life and he came back that evening with two buckets and filled them up for his house. Later on, he'd follow that stream as far as he could and he found a waterfall as clear as day and he would bask in it and nearly drown in the pool and come out laughing and it was too far to bring buckets to carry the water back so he considered it a day of pleasure every month or two to go to this waterfall.

He was hungry on the third day, so he loaded that gun and took it out to the woods. He saw a rabbit quicker than he'd expected and took fire at it and missed. He'd never shot a gun and he wasn't sure what he'd expected but he found that it wasn't as easy as he'd hoped. He missed four animals that day and the next day he missed two more deer and on the fifth morning he began to wonder if he'd have to take that knife back out and hope that he could get lucky. But that day he saw a doe as fat as a tick and it was no more than ten yards from him and he aimed down the bead on that old rifle and shot and its front right leg jumped up and it stood there like a statue for a moment before falling and kicking around for no longer than ten seconds and George immediately felt so horrible about it that he ran up to the old girl and placed the bore of the gun to her temple and fired once more and she was silent and still. He learned that the bullets weren't strong enough to kill them as quick as he liked, so he remembered to bolt the gun as soon as he'd shot the first time in the future, so he could put them out of their suffering quickly and not feel so damn bad about it.

Otherwise, life was simple like this, eating what he could kill and keeping the fire up when he needed it and searching through the woods for anything else that might be helpful.

IN THE SECOND YEAR, George was looking for his knife and he couldn't find it so he pulled apart every cupboard and drawer in the house. He'd almost given up when he reckoned that he should look under the bed frame and he stuck his hand under there and hit a piece of paper on the floor. He slid it out and found a half-finished letter in front of his eyes and he forgot about the knife and sat down in the one chair he had by the light of a window and read slowly, as he hadn't practiced this part of his mind in so long.

Dear Rachel,

I hope you are well. I miss you dearly. I am doing fine, although I believe I may be going crazy out here in the woods. I built this place with the last of the money I had after the collapse and I insulated myself from everyone and everything, thinking that this was the only way to live. You know that I'd always visited this clearing as a child on my pa's land and I think it was a bit romantic of me to imagine myself enjoying coming back here and putting a home on it where the only folks who'd know I was here would be the poor men who helped put it together. But what I did not imagine was how hard it would be. You probably presumed that I wouldn't be able to make it out here. From banks back to the holler. I'm surviving alright but I've had to do a lot of learning on the job, you might say.

I hope that your family is making it alright. I pray that your father made it and if he didn't then I send my love.

The letter stopped after this. There was no signature. George read it over again three more times before he set it down on the floor and looked out the window for a while, thinking. He wondered where that man had gone and if he was still alive. All this time, George had been so alone in this clearing that he had grown accustomed to the idea that the owner of the home was not coming back. But the possibility of his death troubled George and he felt awful for a few minutes sitting there in this man's chair. He wished he at least knew the man's name so that he could thank him, say it out loud in case he'd hear it from somewhere. That this man's decision to come back to his family's land had saved George, some decade or two later.

He returned to the floor under the bed and found multiple pencils and some empty paper there. He brought them out to the table in the kitchen and made his food and then practiced his writing while he ate dinner. He wrote every name he could remember and in the best spelling he could imagine. He wrote the Choctaw words he could remember. He felt as if they were growing fewer by the day. It brought them to life, each one of those people, momentarily. His hand cramped after a while and he resigned to practice more the next day, before heading off to bed and dreaming of biscuits on the table in his childhood home. He woke in general comfort and solitude and he felt himself becoming a monk like the bible characters he'd been taught but he had never felt farther from God and wherever He might be. He wondered if just doing enough to survive on His green earth could be considered a prayer. He thought his mammy wouldn't be happy that he wasn't praying but he had nothing to pray for any longer. One day he figured he would die, after a long struggle he could only assume, and that would be okay, for if death was an awful thing then he'd have to feel bad all the time about those he'd loved and he just didn't have the time to be doing that.

To clear his mind of death, he went for a walk. He found what looked like a wild blueberry plant and made the mistake of popping a few in his mouth. They tasted of chocolate. He hadn't had it in so long that he ate a few more. And then a handful more until some sort of premonition came over him to stop.

By mid-afternoon, as George sat on the porch, he was hit with a sudden headache. What followed was hours of vomiting and asthma attacks and pain in his stomach that might as well have been gunshots that didn't leave any holes.

His mind began to play tricks on him. He saw people, people that had no business being anywhere near his spot in the woods. Outside, a trick of the afternoon sun, there stood Chito near the shed. He blinked and the boy was gone. He shook his head but he could only do it for a moment as it hurt too much to move around so fast. He blinked hard again and when his eyes readjusted to the room he was in, Chito was standing there with Nehemiah. They were as real as trees are real. They stood with their backs to him.

"What are you doing here?" he called out to him, his voice hoarse from puking.

Neither of them turned around. He shouted at them again.

"Hey, you assholes, what are you doing here?"

He tried to get up off the floor. By the time he'd done so, they were gone. He stood there and turned back and forth like a wild man.

"Where did you go?"

He realized he was screaming. His stomach pain hit him again and he crumpled to the floor once more. He closed his eyes. He wanted to cry. He felt a hand touch his shoulder, a gentle caress. He smelled Charlotte's perfume. When he whipped his head around, he was still alone. He laid down on his side and held his legs. He felt as if he were becoming a child again.

After a while, George gave into the pain and passed out. He woke in the morning on the living room floor. He was so thirsty he thought he might die, but he knew he wouldn't. He could feel that he had survived whatever it was. He drank cupfuls of water until it made him nauseated. When he'd worked up the strength, he grabbed his knife and went back to where that plant was. He went to cut its roots up out of the ground and smash the berries. But he thought about seeing Chito standing there on his crutch. How he was right there in front of him again. He stepped back and stared at the berries. He picked them off each into his hand and gently carried them back home, leaving them on the table by the living room chair.

THE ONLY ANIMALS he'd seen roaming the area were deer and rabbits and a sparse pack of coyotes that would wake him up with their howling in unison, crying out at the moon once or twice a year. Otherwise, he ate a strict diet of lean, red meat, with the occasional bird that might have sat on a branch for too long at too close a vicinity and given him the opportunity to pop it with one of those bullets, but he usually found that his aim was still shit and he'd ruin the meat with the lead ripping through the ill-fated bird's breast.

Once, and only once in his time in the cabin that he'd named *haiaka chukka* after the Choctaw words for forest and home, a few more of the only words he could remember, he encountered an animal, a beast. He'd been out in the forest a ways from the house one evening, maybe a half-mile away, lying on the ground under a bed of leaves with the rifle lying on top of a log where he could jump up quickly and have an easy shooting rest. It was a silent afternoon and clouds were beginning to come in over his head and he was considering heading back in for the day. The birds had even stopped chirping and he'd learned to listen to their sound, or lack thereof, as cues for when he shouldn't be somewhere.

As he lay there and thought about getting back to the cabin, suddenly a sound so awful and bloodcurdling broke the sky and made him jump like a ghost had appeared before him. It was as if a chorus of women had screamed bloody murder to the heavens. George felt like his heart might beat out of his chest but he tried to stay still. There was nothing else for a little while and he decided the time to get home had never been better so he did.

He walked the whole way back looking over his shoulder but nothing appeared. While he cooked dinner, he stared out the window looking for what could've done it and while he slept he was tense, his muscles braced for that scream to wake him again but it never came.

A few days later, he washed his shirt in a bucket of creek water and he whistled a tune that the old circus band used to play and he was merry. But a tingling came across his spine and he darted up from the bucket and turned around. Standing across the yard was a cat the likes he'd never seen. It was bigger than any dog he'd laid eyes on and it was golden brown and its ears were short like a bulldog's and it stood broad-chested like a fighter and it stared at him with eyes evil and black. It was a demon from hell, come to take him for his sins, he could only assume.

Without thinking, he ripped his shirt out of the water and ran as fast as he could to the door of the cabin. He didn't look behind him but he could sense that the big cat gained on him at a pace triple his footspeed or faster. He flung the door open and jumped inside and yanked it closed and pulled down the bolt on the door and latched the hook and still held onto the handle, holding it tightly shut. He leaned his head over to the window and peered out and it was standing there on his porch staring at the door.

Gun, gun, he thought. *Where the hell is the gun?*

He peered around the room, his hand still locked onto the old brass handle on the door and he couldn't see the gun anywhere in the sitting room or the kitchen. And then it hit him and he looked back out the window at the cat still there and he saw that the gun was leaning up on the wall of the house right beside the animal on the porch. He sighed with great intensity and found himself completely without a clue. So, he waited.

Come evening, the cat decided to check out his yard a bit more. It roamed around just off the porch, searching its surroundings for what George assumed to be a bite to eat. He stayed silent as he watched it. If only it would walk another ten steps away from the porch, e might reach out and grab that gun. Three more hours passed and it was dark outside and George's stomach was grumbling but he refused to move from the door. He leaned over and looked out the window once more and he couldn't find the thing. His eyes darted back and forth and it was nowhere to be found. He thought this was his only chance so he slowly and carefully unlatched the door and swung it open and leaned out with his feet still in the house and wrapped his hand around the barrel of the gun and pulled it in close. As he did this, he felt the porch rumble and he yanked the door shut again and looked at the cat, standing there again in front of him. It had been lying right in front of him just to the right on the porch and he'd failed to notice. His heart raced again like it had their first encounter and he wanted to vomit he was so afraid.

He had to wait until the next morning, late, near noon, before the cat ventured into the yard again. When it did, he made his mind up to get it all over with and he creaked the door open just enough to get the nose of the gun out and point it at the beast and he fired and he watched it jump back with the bullet lodged in its shoulder. He bolted another bullet in the gun and the big cat turned and looked at him and it acted like it was going to take a run at him so he fired again. He swore he hit it square in the head but it ran as if that was no matter and he threw himself back in the house and he felt pain in his right arm and he latched the door once more. After he'd shut himself in again, he looked down and saw that the animal had taken its claws to his forearm and he had three cuts running down it, a few inches long but thankfully not deep. They bled, still, and he reached over and grabbed a piece of window curtain and ripped it and tied it around the cuts. He looked out the window and the cat was standing there with blood pouring out its side and it had a hole in the base of its right ear. It did its best to lick the wound on its shoulder.

"Why won't you die?" he screamed at it through the glass and it stopped licking and stared at him, showing its great teeth.

George grew so angry at this that he raised the window enough for the gun and fired right at the animal just a couple of feet away. It fell with a hit to the stomach and started to get back up but he bolted once more and shot again and it laid there still alive and he repeated the action again, pointing the barrel at its head and firing. He realized he'd been screaming the entire time and he stopped as his throat hurt.

He waited the rest of the evening for the thing to get up and start pacing back and forth on the porch again but he'd killed it. At nightfall he went out and picked it up, still warm in his arms, and he carried it into the woods. The next morning, he dug a hole and threw it in. He wanted nothing to do with the meat of the beast. He wanted nothing more to do with anything of the sort.

He grew a beard. He forgot how to speak, like his throat had frozen over. He grunted sometimes. He grew lean, leaner than he thought possible. He grew to love the smell of rain. He grew lonely. He grew out of his loneliness. He grew livelier and he grew tired. He grew until he grew no longer. He calloused. He thought he might live there until he died. Until his luck dried up. He grew closer to God. He prayed. He grew further from God. He grew lonely again.

"Chito?" he asked. He'd eaten a berry again. They'd had the same effect on his body, nearly paralyzing him and making him vomit everything he had eaten that day. But there he was again, his best friend in the world, in this empty and lonely place, standing in front of him by the stove. His back was still turned.

George watched as his friend reached in his pocket and took his knife out. He began to whittle on something, it seemed to George from behind.

"Chito, I brought you back," he said. "I need you here, so, so, so I brought you back."

He kept whittling, silently, wood carvings dropping to the floor.

"Buddy, I missed you. I, I'm sorry for leaving. Can you hear me out? I'm sorry for leaving."

His friend, still a boy in the same way he'd been when George left, stopped moving altogether. His feet moved. He turned around. His face was there, but blurry. George wiped at his eyes but he grew no more in focus.

"Chito, it's so good to see you here. Will you forgive me? Will you stay?"

A pain punched him in the gut and he let out a whimper and shut his eyes. He suddenly worried that when he opened them again, the boy might not be there. He spoke without opening them yet.

"Please don't leave without just saying something to me at least," he said. A gust of evening wind whistled by the window, the sun was setting low behind the trees. He whimpered again, he hurt so bad. He thought that he couldn't do this anymore. He was killing himself for nothing more than a vision of the past, a glimpse into a memory. He could just close his eyes and see his friend in this way without the need to put himself through this torture. But then.

"Thank you," Chito said. He heard it, with his very own ears. He lifted his eyelids and he smiled. His friend's voice was so sweet. Any voice at all. He wanted to jump up and hug his neck and tell him that he'd never leave again, that he would come home, that he was a fool, that he had gotten ahead of himself, that he was selfish and had grown since then. But when he looked, the space in front of the stove was empty. The wind had stopped.

He lay on his side and his chest convulsed. Vomit pooled out of his mouth. He passed out on the floor again, waking up the next evening.

The berries lasted two months. He tried to use them no more than every two weeks. The last two spoiled. He saw and heard nothing else from his friend. After a while, he figured that what he'd gotten was enough. He'd lost weight and strength and sometimes he considered if he wasn't doing it for some other reason.

A SIDE EFFECT of drugging himself. Dreams.

First, his mammy came to him. He was not surprised by this. He felt that she was general warmth and it made him happy when he woke up to know that she'd visited him. But the dreams grew in intensity and he began to worry.

Nighttime, out in the woods, George wrote down on the paper he'd found. It had gotten bad enough that he had to take notes of what he'd seen. If only to recall the details in an attempt at verifying that he'd seen it at all.

A cry echoes around me. I brace, thinking the cat is back or a new one has appeared. I do not know if they live in packs. I've been assuming not. The cry sounds like a barn owl or a woman in distress. I recognize that it does not sound like the lion. I wonder if a woman is near me. She sounds afraid. But I secretly hope that there is a woman. I desire to see a woman again.

I hear footsteps behind me. They are hard, like that of an animal with hooves. They punch leaves, making more noise than most animals take care to make. I turn around and scan. It's dark, the moon is small and the light from it is dim at its best.

I see movement. I follow it, with my feet as well as my eyes. I do not know why I decide to do this. I feel danger around me but I am not afraid. It is still walking, away from me it sounds like. I speed up to chase it. The crunching of leaves ceases. It is right in front of me. Its body is a shadow. It is a deer, I think. Tall though. But I see its hooves. It is standing above me, on an incline. It is turned with its back to me. I feel myself relax. I step towards it.

I see it more clearly. I gasp. It is the legs and hooves of a deer, yes, but where the rest of the deer should be is something else. It is a man, he is wearing no shirt. I can see his back clearly. His hair is long. He is native. I don't know how I can tell. I can sense it, I guess. He hears me gasp and he lets out the same cry I heard earlier. Birds fly out from the resting places above us. I feel the urge to run.

"What are you? Who are you?" I shout from ten yards below him.

He lets out a cry again. He looks as if he may turn around. A word appears in my head. A word from my mammy. Kashehotapalo. That is what he is. He cries again. My mammy told me about these beasts. That they cry like a woman when you enter their territory and that they warn the forest of hunters. That they can see murderers of animals.

"I am no killer," I say.

The beast lets out a cry again and kicks a hoof behind him. He runs, darting away from me. I do not follow. I wake with sweat on my forehead, despite the cold.

He read these words over again and put the paper under the bed.

Shortly after what he figured was near the third anniversary of his living there came and passed, a great storm came. It was an early fall day and he remarked to himself that the leaves were turning so beautifully this time around as he went to chopping some more wood down for the stove. By early evening, however, the sky had turned from cloudless to as dark as night and a light sprinkling had begun and the wind was starting to pick up, sliding down over the trees and into his small Eden.

He ate that night and went to bed to the sound of whistling gusts and rain pattering on the window and he didn't think much of it. By morning, he recognized that it was awful outside and in his drowsiness he heard the front door banging on its hinges and he found it to be open and swinging violently in the wind so he ran over and latched it. The porch was barely visible in the wind and rain and he wondered what had happened to the world.

George waited all day for it to subside and it never did, only picking up in its violence. He ate the last of some rabbit meat he'd cooked that night and sat by the burning stove watching it rain. He remembered then that he'd been taught about hurricanes as a child but they hadn't had one in his part of the country in years. He wondered if that's what this was. When he went to bed, he watched the great oak tree in the back yard of the house and its old branches swayed back and forth and every so often it would snap hard as a gust hit it. He wished there was something he could do about it but he couldn't and he generally liked sleeping to the sound of rain so he dozed off easily again that night.

He'd only been out for a short amount of time when the world became explosion. A great boom unloaded in the house atop him and the house creaked like it'd been hit with a mortar and he wondered if he was dreaming. Rain touched his face, lightly at first and increasing in quantity, and he wiped it off in the darkness.

"What the hell?" he said out loud to the house as if it would answer back.

His eyes adjusted to the ceiling and he saw a crack of open sky and a branch leaning down through it. The oak tree had fallen into the house, right above him. He jumped out of bed and looked around for something that might help him but there was no such thing. The ceiling above him groaned again and a board fell down. He backed up into the doorway and the roof collapsed in front of his very eyes. He darted his feet back into the hallway just as wood crashed down on his featherbed. He didn't know what to do, so he shut the door on the room so no more water could enter the house. He stood there for a moment and then ran into the sitting room. All was quiet there as if nothing had happened.

Outside, cracks of lightning lit up the yard in dangerous brilliance and illuminated the tree line bending and some of the younger pines snapping and their branches flying in the wind and George was scared like a child again. He sat in the chair, stunned out of his mind, and watched through the window as it all unfolded. Behind him, he heard and felt that massive tree fall further into the house and he could feel the wind coming through the back of the cabin and he ignored it because there was nothing left to do but hope that he would survive. He waited there in that stupor until morning broke, his eyes never closing for longer than a blink.

By daylight, the wind and rain had subsided and it was sunny and warm outside and he made a pot of coffee over the stove and took it out on the porch and sat there on the stairs and sipped, looking out on his little yard. It was practically a pond, water standing so high that small fish could have survived just fine in it. Trees were downed all over the line of the forest and branches were strewn about in such abundance that it seemed not a random act but an act of God.

He didn't check the back of the house until it was already early afternoon. He took his shoes off and rolled his pants up and walked around in the muck to survey the damage. It was devastating. Half the house lay in wreckage under the downed wood behemoth.

"Why?" he screamed out and it echoed off the tree line.

He screamed it again, rage and pain so clearly in his voice to anything that might've heard and his throat hurt from the growl of it.

He got no answer to his plea, so he walked back up onto the porch and in the house. He sat down in the rocking chair and considered his options. He figured he had but one, but he had not the strength to leave on that evening and so he went back out on the porch and tried to enjoy what was left of the day in solitude. He watched the yard and the trees and the few birds that had hung around during that mess of a storm and he hummed songs for a while until it was dark.

He went back in and sat in the chair. He couldn't help but feel that the walls of the house were starting to tighten. The wood boards began to close in on him and he searched around for help or a solitary moment but couldn't find nary and his heartbeat pounded in his ears and he started to breathe fast and he pulled one of those cigarettes out and lit it and he saw that he only had one left in the pack but he smoked this one anyway and tried to calm himself. The walls returned to where they had always stood and he leaned back in the chair, dozing off into a deep sleep that took him captive for the late evening and the night and a good portion of the morning. When he woke, he packed a few things in the same sack he'd come there with and tied the axe to his waist and grabbed the rifle in his open hand and he set off in the direction he'd been going that day three years prior.

He was thankful that the ground was sloped upwards for the better part of the first day of walking, enough so that the ground was mostly only waterlogged and not a great pool. The bottom half of his shoes, worn down enough to not do very much and nearly too small to wear on his now-grown feet, were soaked by the end of the day and there were still woods around him everywhere he looked but he figured things could be worse. They just had been. Yet, he was hungry and he hadn't killed anything since before the storm and it bothered him, so he decided to lay down for the evening earlier than he would have liked to have stopped walking so that he could try and stake out an animal for dinner. Nothing came and he slept there on the ground with the rifle in his hands until early morning the next day.

Halfway through the next day of walking, he wondered if ought to just turn around and go back to that house and try his hand at fixing it. He began to beat himself up for not thinking of that sooner. He'd just walked away from it like he'd done Danny. He stopped in the middle of the forest and started to turn around but instead he just continued on the path he'd been on. He didn't know why, but turning around hadn't seemed like an option before and it didn't seem like one then either. He was thirsty then and he took a swig from the canteen and realized there was only a bit left, he hadn't considered how much more he'd drink when he had to make this kind of trek and it was warm outside, so he shook it and shrugged and gulped down what was remaining and it tasted so wonderful then, taking his mind off of everything and sliding cooly down his throat, it tasted like music.

He walked for two more days like this. He was so hungry he felt himself on the brink of collapse at nearly all times. It itched out of the center of his stomach and grew like a cancer into all parts of his body, his chest and his groin and his shoulders and his knees and his forehead and down to his feet, everything crying out for some sort of sustenance, but it was as if the hurricane had killed all the animals, like a great pestilence had come over the land and he was the sole survivor.

"Don't quit, don't quit," George whispered to himself. He didn't really know why.

At first he thought the sound that he heard in the early afternoon was a great gust of wind and he felt fear rise up with the hunger at the prospect of yet another great flood. He knew he couldn't survive it and it gave him great pause to hear this. He stopped and tried to open his ears to listen hard. He heard it again and it wasn't wind, he knew, but something else that seemed familiar to a version of him from long ago that he couldn't quite place. He walked faster towards it and in front of him the woods began to thin out until what he saw in front of him was not more trees but another clearing of some sort. He stepped out onto it and saw that it was a road and a car had just passed by, a black car riding on by to a civilized world. He stood there and stared at it and rubbed his eyes to make sure he wasn't imagining it in his starvation. Then, he began to jump up and down and wave his arms like a mad man. The car was a couple hundred yards away from him then and it seemed absurd to dance around like this but he'd lost all care for what someone else might think of him in his time alone.

And then the car stopped, dead in his tracks. He quit jumping and looked at it. It turned around in the road and started back to him and he realized that he hadn't planned for the possibility of it actually happening and he laid the gun down behind him in the thick grass that lined the road and then he did the same with the axe before they could get too close so that he was only carrying his pack. The car pulled up in front of him and a man of some indiscernible age with a long beard sat behind the wheel of it.

"Hey, fella, you alright?" the man asked. George became suddenly so conscious of how he might look to another human that he wanted to crawl inside of himself. His beard and hair, long like the mountain folk of legend, unruly like forest brush. He hadn't bathed, a real bath, in so long that he must've stank like the dickens.

"Yessir," was all he could think to reply.

"You sure?"

"I've been worse."

"Haven't we all. You need a ride?" the man asked, leaning his head forward out of the window, looking around at George and the surrounding area.

"Where you headed?"

"Athens. Gotta get some supplies, storm emptied us out and every store in our town. Figured the city might have it."

"Athens. Is there a train station there?"

"Sure is."

"I'd greatly appreciate that ride, sir," George said, and the man just nodded in return and so George walked around the car and hopped into the seat, leaving the gun and axe there for someone else who needed them more to find.

In the car, George held his sack in silence for a few minutes, watching the trees zip by them.

"How'd you make it out in that storm? Never seen a hurricane so bad around these parts," the man eventually said.

"Hurricane, it was a hurricane?"

"Yeah, hell, it miss where you were staying or something?"

"No. Tree fell on my house," George replied, matter-of-fact-like. He reckoned he'd forgotten how to really converse with someone. The man turned his face to him with his eyes off the road and his eyebrows raised in concern.

"Damn, anybody get hurt?"

"No, sir. I just didn't have a house no more, I guess. So I'm out here walking."

"Mm. Well, that'll do it, won't it?"

George nodded. The man moved his eyes back to the road.

25

The man, who told George his name was Casey, dropped him off in the heart of downtown Athens and said to check by the general store or in that area if he needed anything else that day, he'd be glad to help him out. George told him thank you and didn't plan on requiring anything else, he'd learned from his mammy to only take what you need from a person, whether it be butter or sugar or a ride to a new metropolis.

The city was much like Jackson and he felt out of place immediately. But he remembered the hundred dollars Danny had given him and fished it out of his pack. He decided it couldn't hurt to get clean and buy some new clothes, so he first went to a hotel that seemed like it wasn't too fancy and white to not take him and the lady at the desk only asked him what sort of bed he wanted and he told her whatever bed came with a bath and she handed him a room key and took some of his money. She was pretty and blond and had small lips and he smiled at her as he walked off and she returned it. The room was small but the bed was soft and it had a window that looked out on the busy street below and he opened the blinds to let the light in and watch the people. It was odd but he felt that he missed seeing folks walking around, even if the quantity of them and the size of this city made him nervous. Down the street he could see a big government building with huge pillars holding it up in the front and it looked like a group of white people were standing at the doors yelling and holding signs. It only held his curiosity for long enough for him to strip down naked and wait for the bath water to heat up.

After his bath, which could only be described as required by the amount of dirt that came off him and glorious by the feeling the warm water and soap gave his tired body and longer than was necessitated but shorter than he could've made it, he called back down to the front desk and asked if he could have some clothes delivered. The desk clerk sounded surprised by the ask but said she was sure they could arrange for it and he told her to send someone down and buy some decent clothes, a full set from undergarments out and a new pair of shoes and she asked him sizes and he told her he wasn't sure so he could just ballpark it and they could figure it out from there once the clothes arrived. But he got lucky and everything fit alright except for the pants being loose in the waist but he cinched a piece of cord around them and moved on from it.

He called once more and asked for dinner to be brought up and the lady started to ask him what he wanted but he just told her to bring whatever they had, no need to make it complicated, and she said okay, suit yourself but he could tell that she was mostly happy to have less work to do and he guessed that she might've even had a little grin on her face and he liked that he might've done that to a woman again after so long. The food came and it was fried pork chops with white gravy on top of them and a bed of mashed potatoes and he ate it so fast he felt sick.

He called down again and it was a man this time that answered the phone and this man surely heard the disappointment in George's voice when he asked him if there was any way they could send some ice cream up. The man paused for a moment and said yessir and twenty minutes later he had a bowl of vanilla ice cream sitting on his lap in bed and he ate it far too fast as well and his head hurt from the freeze and he nodded off a few minutes later with it still sitting there.

In the morning, he rose early and put on his new suit and went out for a stroll. The lady at the front desk had returned and when he passed her, she whistled at him.

"The clothes fit," she said.

"Yes, ma'am, they do," he replied, knowing he was blushing.

"Now all you need is a haircut."

He realized he hadn't even thought about his hair and he could suddenly feel its heavy weight on his shoulders. He'd shaved with his knife while he lived in the woods but had only chopped his hair off at the shoulders once when it got too long to manage.

"Do you know where I can get that done?"

She smiled at him like he was a child and he felt like one.

"You never been to Athens before?" she asked.

"No, ma'am. First time."

"Two storefronts down, there's a barbershop. His name is Mike, he's my uncle. Tell him Annie sent you from the hotel and to not charge you nothing."

The air outside was crisp despite cars coming by and kicking up dust and spilling out fumes. It was only a short walk to Mike's Barbershop, as it said on the big red and white sign above the door. He walked in and there was a child getting his hair cut by a short man with a long mustache that stuck out at least two inches past his face on either side and the boy's father sat in a metal chair behind them reading the newspaper.

"Just go sit down over there a minute and I'll get to you next," Mike said without looking up, so George did.

After the boy was done getting buzzed, Mike motioned him over while he swept the floor clean around the chair and got his table of instruments reorganized. Once George had sat down, he finally looked up at him and he looked startled for a moment.

"Well, I'll be, I haven't seen that much hair on a man come in my shop in a decade. That thing a wig?" he asked. George watched his eyes and winced, waiting for the man to recognize him for who he was and tell him to leave.

George grinned and told him, "No, sir."

"Well then how about you take that hat off and show me."

George realized it was still sitting atop his head and he grabbed it and chucked it over to the seat he'd been in. The man stared at his head for a little while longer.

"Um," George started to talk and his tongue fumbled. "I'm comin' over from the hotel and Annie—"

"Annie sent you, told you to tell me it was a free one, is that it?"

"Yessir," George said, feeling bad about having asked for anything.

"She's a sweet one, ain't she? Alright, I'll deduct it from her birthday gifts," he chuckled. "What you want done to this mess?"

"I guess just lop it off."

"You sure about that?"

"Yessir. I have no need for it. Just couldn't get it cut for a while."

"A while sounds about right, alright."

When he was done his hair was buzzed short just like the boy's had been before and he felt lighter, like he could fly away then if he breathed in hard enough and the man spun him out of the chair and told him to enjoy his day and send his regards over to Annie when he got back to the hotel and George told him thank you. He walked straight back over to the hotel and Annie was there and she told him to take his hat off so she could see what Mike had done and so he did.

"Wow, you might as well be a totally different man," she said.

"Might as well be. Hey, um, is there any way I could get lunch brought over here?"

"Well there's a lunch spot just down the street, sandwiches and such. Why don't you just walk on down there. I can probably go with you on my break."

"I can't," he said.

"Why not?"

"You can't tell?" He said it and immediately regretted it. He knew he was going to be out on the street. She might even call all the other hotels in the area and tell them an injun was trying to sleep in white folks' beds.

"What?" she squinted at him.

"I'm, I ain't white. I'm Choctaw."

"Choctaw?" Her eyes got big but she still smiled. "Well, I've never met a Choctaw man. Or woman. Okay, I get it." She started to whisper. "Your secret's safe and sound with me."

"Thank you," he said.

"You like fried bologna?"

"Yes, ma'am."

"Me too. Two fried bologna sandwiches coming right up, just meet me back here. We'll take it over in the parlor."

He went upstairs and took a nap until it was lunchtime and he met her back down there and they took their sandwiches together and talked and laughed and he had the best time he'd had in a long time. Eventually, when they had a lull in conversation, he asked her where the train station was in town.

"Oh, you're not leaving me, are you?" she asked.

"I wish I had the kind of money to stay in a hotel forever, but I've got to get going."

"Why?"

"Why what?"

"Why do you have to get going?" she asked.

He stared back at her and he didn't have an answer to that question. In fact, he didn't even have an answer to where he would go, if she decided to ask that as well. He didn't know where the train went. He'd only been on one. He didn't want to go back; if he had he would have walked that way then. He just couldn't stay in Athens, he knew. He felt like a car driving along a road and there was someone else behind the wheel and he only had to follow their directions and he'd eventually be where he was supposed to be.

"I just can't stop moving," he finally said. Even he wasn't satisfied with it when it came out of his mouth.

"That's a poor excuse, a poor, poor excuse," she said, her distaste visible.

"We've only known each other for a day."

"And that's all it'll be, won't it?"

He shrugged and she balled up all the sandwich papers they had and went back to her desk and he watched her from his seat still. She was pretty, even in anger. After a couple of minutes, he got up and started to walk back up to his room to pack for the train. She put her hand out to stop him as he passed by.

"If you need somewhere to go, go on to Wilmington. It's in North Carolina, one of the last stops. I've got some family up there. They'll put you up for a few days. I'll send them a telegram."

"Okay," he said, and she furiously wrote down an address on a piece of paper and handed it to him and he started to say thank you but she'd already looked back down at the other papers on her desk. When he'd packed and was leaving an hour later, she was no longer there and he yelled out goodbye to anyone that might have heard him in the place.

The train station was a mile's walk and he was so full from eating that he took it slowly. He passed by the government building and there were still white people out there protesting and he saw their signs. He read them slowly and he pieced together that it was about black folk apparently being allowed to work government jobs. Those white folk seemed angrier than a mound of ants that got stepped on so he kept on moving past them. He heard the big engines before he saw them, great loud things that pushed steam into the air like he'd heard whales did with water in the ocean. He booked a ticket to Wilmington and nearly forgot himself before the conductor told him he had to ride in the back on the negro car and he said he was not negro.

"You ain't white," the man said. So he said that was true and he hopped onto the back car and sat in the only seat available and it smelled of smoke and women and children and men sat there in silence and it was as hot as the devil even with the windows open. He looked at the window at the passing landscapes the entire ride and it was all pine trees, save for a few rivers and lakes, and then the big black train came to a new city and it stopped and the conductor yelled out into the car that they were in Wilmington.

PART THREE

26

He didn't go to the address Annie had given him first. He wanted to see what this city was like, even if he held presuppositions that it would be no different from Athens or Jackson. The air in Wilmington was different at least. The wind was light and thin and the sun beat down and most folks walked around in short sleeves. He noticed that the white folks and the black folks walked in completely different directions when they each got off the train and he found it curious. He decided to follow the group of white folks as far as it would get him into the city.

He hadn't walked two blocks before he saw the water. It was a river, a great, gigantic, fast-moving river that cut right by what seemed to George to be the downtown area. He sped up his gait until he was practically running and had to come to a quick stop at the railing by the water. The wind there was stronger and it nearly blew his hat off. He stood and watched the water go by and boats ride atop it, steam engines and one-seat jon boats with old fishermen paddling along and every size of boat in between. Behind the river sat a green and lush marsh and he could just barely spot tall white birds that he remembered to be cranes from his childhood education.

Behind him, a man hummed a tune loudly and his voice was deep and rich and George turned around to look at him. He was an elderly black man waiting to shine the shoes of a passerby. He saw George looking at him and stopped humming and shouted out to ask if George would like a shoeshine. George walked over to him.

"You ever seen something as beautiful as that?" George asked the man.

"Now what's that?"

"The river, right up here on the city. I've never seen anything quite as pretty."

"You not from 'round here?" the old man asked.

"No, sir, I'm from Mississippi."

"Mm, got some family from 'round there. Well, yessir, that river is beautiful the first time you see it and every other time too. I guess you just stop noticing it after a while, don't you."

"You didn't give me your name?" George asked.

"Oh, nobody ever asks me mine, do they? Lot, my mammy named me Lot. Still waiting on my two angels and never seen nobody turn to a pillar of salt though," he said and chuckled, slapping his knee a little. "My ol' lady is meaner than a snake and wants to beat me with a frying pan most days but she still ain't turn into no salt."

George didn't get the reference and didn't try to understand it and the man kept talking.

"I'm guessing you don't know what the name of that river is then."

"No, sir."

"The Cape Fear. Now won't that make your heart shiver?"

George continued to stare out at it and he wondered why anybody would name anything so beautiful after such an awful feeling. But he had some assumptions that maybe he wasn't seeing the whole picture.

"And what brings you into town, mister?" Lot asked. "If I may so ask."

"I'm not so sure yet."

"What are ye'? A businessman?"

"No, sir, never had a business."

"So what then, you one of them boys went over there to Europe and got hurt and they sent ye' back with a nail in your knee or a missing finger, tell you to get better?"

"What's that?"

"The war, the war. You go over in the war?"

"What war?"

"Well I'll be," the old man said and before he could say anything else a tall white man in a pressed suit approached them and looked back and forth between George and Lot.

"Say, you gonna get him to shine your shoes or you just talking to him?" he asked George.

"Just talkin'," George replied. The man slid past him and sat down in the chair there beside Lot and didn't say anything else.

Lot gave George a nod that said the conversation was over and so he walked on back towards the intersection there where he'd started running to the water. He found a little diner that was packed to the brim with folks and he took his chances, getting a sandwich to go with most of what was left of the money he'd gotten from Danny all those years ago and leaving as quick as he could to eat it in a park he'd spotted. He sat down on a bench and enjoyed the ham and cheese. Folks passed by him, men who could've done all sorts of high-paying and important jobs and women who wore colorful dresses and had their hair done in ways he'd never seen before, some with it sitting high atop their heads and not a strand down to their shoulders, and children with little dogs trotting around on leashes or off-leash chasing after a ball. He could've cried at the happiness all around him.

He spent the better part of the afternoon roaming around the city. He walked all the way down to one end of the downtown area and doubled back. A couple folks who saw him go one direction gave him an odd look when he reappeared going back from where he'd come but he ignored them. He found a bar at the other end and it was beginning to be early evening and he could hardly remember what alcohol tasted like so he decided to stop in. It was a dingy place, the lights real low. There were no windows. Two men sat in a booth near the back with little bowl-shaped glasses atop tall skinny stems in front of them. Clear liquid rested inside the glasses and every once in a while they'd take a long, drawn-out sip from them. At the bartop, a man sat with a few shot glasses in front of him. He wore a cowboy hat.

George took the seat beside him and the bartender turned around and asked what he'd be having. He asked in return what was the best kind of drink for someone that hadn't had a drop in a while and the man nodded and opened up an ice chest and pulled out a cold bottle of brown liquid.

"Beer's on me for veterans," the bartender said.

George tried to keep the confusion off his face as much as he could and the man beside him in the wide-brimmed hat turned and asked him a question that he didn't hear at first.

"Where'd they put you?" the man repeated. "Over in Europe?"

"Oh, yeah," the lie came out of his mouth like it had been living in there and waiting to float right out.

"France? My cousin got sent to France."

"Yessir, France."

"Mm. His name was Conrad; you ever meet a Conrad? Conrad Wolfe."

"No, no Conrad." George took a big gulp of the beer and it tasted a lot like wet bread but it was cold and refreshing and he took another.

"Well, there's a bunch of boys out there. Damn shame."

George shook his head and didn't reply. He wasn't sure what to say.

"You know, sure is good a place like this will still serve you a beer on Palm Sunday."

"It's Palm Sunday?" George asked. He hadn't heard those words in years. It made him think about his mama.

"You must not be a Christian man. I should've guessed."

"I was raised it. My mama was as religious as it gets. Just haven't been to church in a while. A long while, really."

"They don't have churches over there?"

"No, the reservation has them."

"I meant France," the man said, cocking an eye.

"Oh, sorry," George said, racking his brain for more lies. "I was, was just thinking about my mama again. Got sidetracked. They have churches over there. But we weren't spending a lot of time in them."

"I hear ya. Well, it sure is. Palm Sunday. Ride into town on a donkey, would you believe it. But our good barkeep Fletch here will keep 'em pouring," he said, and lifted his drink to the man. Fletch was lighting a cigarette and gave a quick nod back. "Not everybody is all religious about drinking a beer or two. Ain't right to not let a man wet his whistle on any day he wants to, if he ain't doing no harm. No different than taking a dip in the pool, just cooling off."

George didn't say anything else for a while, sipping on the beer slowly, and eventually the bartender turned on the radio and turned the volume knob loud enough for them to hear. The broadcaster's voice spoke of total war and destruction in some islands he'd never heard of and some good news of German defeats. He listened intently, trying to pull context clues out of the words the man spoke but most of it just sounded like gibberish and he gave up after a while. When he finished the beer, the bartender set another down without asking and winked at him.

He finished it quickly and gave his thanks to the man and walked out into the cold air. He was about to walk off when he heard someone call for him back where the bar was.

"Hey, where you headed to?" George turned and it was the cowboy calling out to him.

"I'm not sure," he replied.

"I've got a little roadster. You hop in and tell me where you want to go."

"You sure, mister?"

"I ain't heard from my cousin Conrad in forever. You can put the gas money on his tab."

When they got in the car, George was completely out of ideas of where to tell the man he should go and it was too late to try his luck at booking a room in one of the white hotels in the downtown area. He remembered the slip of paper from Annie and pulled it out of his jacket. He showed it to the man, who told him his name was Randall, and he just nodded and made a left turn at the next intersection.

"What's your full name, George? In case I see Conrad again, I can ask him if he might've met you over there. Maybe your memory is just fuzzy. Heard that a lot of you fellers came back with fuzzy memories."

"Norris," George said. The lies were floating out of him even easier with the beer in him. "George Norris."

"Is that right? I knew a couple of Norris boys when I was growing up. Sure did. They might stay around here still. Hell, you might be cousins, huh?"

George smiled and nodded and they spoke no more until the man pulled the car in front of a big white house. It looked like one of those government buildings he'd seen in Georgia with its pillars on the front porch. He could see light in the front windows and so he decided the time to go knock on the door wasn't getting any better. He shook Randall's hand and grabbed his sack.

"Hey, you need a job you head down to the marina, okay? My other cousin Cindy, her husband Carl owns it and they're alright people. Well, he's a sumbitch but she's a good girl, always has been. Tell 'em Randall sent you. If they turn you away, you head on back to the bar and find me or John, the bartender, and let one of us know. I'll kick Carl's ass. He owes me one."

George told him thank you and started to step away and Randall added one more thing.

"But maybe don't wear that suit. It'll be working on boats, you don't want to appear too fancy," the man said, laughing and pulling away with a lead foot.

George stepped down the small stone path they had to the front door and by the time he was there, Randall was long gone down the street. He knocked three times and stepped back off the porch as to not give off an air that might be taken wrong in the late hours. The white door on the house had a small, foggy glass window at the top and he saw a shadow appear behind it and then the door creaked open and a man stepped out. He was in his boxers, that was the first thing George noticed, flannel boxers, and he still had on a nice, button-down shirt like he'd been wearing a suit that day. He was a tall man, towering over George, and he wore bifocals with thick lenses. Behind him there was a short, skinny hallway and it was illuminated with electric lights and George had never seen a private residence with electric lights, or at least hadn't been in one. The man looked him over and his eyes looked huge behind his glasses.

"What is it?" the man asked, his voice suggesting a lifetime of smoking cigarettes the way George remembered his pawpaw spoke just before he died. George wasn't expecting this question and he stood there for a beat.

"Hello, sir, is this," he pulled the sheet of paper out again and read it aloud. "21 Sand Hills Drive?"

"Yes, it is," the man replied dryly.

George looked from the paper to the man and back to the paper and then he shoved it back into his pocket. "And are you the head of the family?"

"I like to think so."

George nearly gave up then. He had no clue what to say or think or do and he thought about giving up and walking his way back to the riverfront even though he couldn't half remember where he was on account of the beer and his lack of attention to the turns Randall had made. Then the man spoke again.

"What's your name, boy?"

"George Norris, sir."

"George. You the boy little Annie sent that telegram about? And I think she called Mary Beth about you too."

"Yessir, I met Annie—"

Before he could finish his sentence the man turned around and said "follow me" and walked back into that well-lit hallway and George did as he was told. They walked down to the end of the hallway and there were doors on either side and the man took the one to the right and it opened up into a room with more couches than George had ever seen in one space, three or four of them, and a couple reading chairs by a large window. In one of the reading chairs sat a small woman, thin as a rail with dark hair, and she was reading a book by candlelight with her feet up on the second chair, a pillow under her heels. As they entered the room, she turned her head and George saw that she was quite pretty for her age and figured she must have been this man's wife and she cocked her head to the side.

"Who's this, John?" she asked the tall man. Her voice was frail.

"He says his name is George."

"The one that Annie sent about?"

"The very same."

Then the little lady got up and she stood at least a foot and a half shorter than her husband but she walked with an air about her that made George want to close up on himself. She came right up to him and stuck her hand out and he took it and she shook harder than any woman he'd ever met.

"It is nice to meet you, George. My name is Lily and my husband's name is John, but you probably already guessed that. Are you hungry?" A warmth took over her face.

"I don't want to put you out of any food," he replied.

"Honey, I've got plenty of food to go around. Especially if you're going to be staying here."

"I am?" He could hardly hide the surprise on his face.

"Well, that's what Annie told us. Do you not want to? Find somewhere else to stay?"

"No, ma'am."

"Then that settles it. Let me heat up some of that ham and potatoes we had for dinner. John, will you please show our new guest to his room? George, there are more of us here, two daughters, but they are in their beds fast asleep. You'll meet them tomorrow. Go drop that bag off and come on back here. And wait, is that just a burlap sack?"

George nodded.

"You poor thing. Alright, go ahead."

She walked over to a door at the front of the room they were in and pushed it open and it looked like the kitchen. He saw a big beautiful stove and nice cabinets in there and then the door swung shut behind her. John walked him across the hallway to the other side of the house where there was what seemed to be an office, the door not fully shut, that had a giant desk in it with papers all over it, and they passed a few other rooms that he couldn't see in before heading up a staircase to the second floor of the home. Most of the doors were shut up there and John led him to the end of this hallway where he opened a door to a bedroom and stepped to the side and motioned George in.

"It's small but I hope it'll do alright for you. Was supposed to be for a third kid but we just never got around to it."

The room was almost twice the size of the one he'd grown up in where he had to share the bed with his mammy until he was too big and they bought a cot for him to lay on. In front of him was a bed that looked to be just as nice as the one he'd had at the cabin. Beside it was a small nightstand with a lamp atop it. A chest of drawers sat against one wall and a window with curtains drawn was on the other wall.

"It's perfect," George said. The man left him to getting comfortable and he laid out all the items left in his pack. He had three dollar bills, one solitary asthma cigarette, a handful of .22 bullets, the knife in its sheath, a tin mug and plate, and a nearly empty box of matches. He dug around in the sack some more and couldn't believe that's all he had left of his belongings. For a moment he just stared at his life there laying on the strangers' bed. He stuck the bullets back in the sack, along with the knife and mug and plate, and shoved them under the bedframe to not raise any suspicions, and he shoved the rest in his pockets.

When he went downstairs, a plate of ham and mashed potatoes sat on one of the small tables and it had all been pulled in front of a couch. Miss Lily sat in her chair again but she'd turned it around to face him. He sat down and stared at the food and she told him to go ahead, don't be shy, and so he did. While he ate, she asked him questions about himself and he tried to not answer with his mouth full but it was hard because the food was delicious and he was shoveling it down his gullet as fast as he could.

"I almost forgot," she said, getting back up and walking to the kitchen. She returned a moment later with a glass of milk and told him to have it and he took a gulp so large he almost choked. He could've cried at how filling it all was and how rich it all tasted and when he was done he said thank you.

"You're welcome, George, but if you're going to be staying here for a while you don't have to say thank you every time. From here on out I'll just know you're thinking it. That alright?"

"Yes, ma'am," he said.

"So, where's your family, George?" she asked.

"I don't have any, ma'am."

"Not a single one?"

"No, ma'am, my ma died nearly a decade ago now, I guess. And I only knew my pa in, in passing."

"Mm. Ain't that evil, a father not knowing his son. Or any child of his at all."

George nodded. "I do have some friends that I lived with after she died, my ma that is. But I haven't seen them in so long that I don't know where they are or if they're even alive anymore."

"How long have you been away from them?"

"I haven't been back home in four years, I believe," he said. "But time is starting to run together on me a bit."

She stared at him dead in the eyes until he felt uncomfortable with it and so he looked at the floor. He was rightly amazed at the power this woman held and how she had already made him feel warm and small, all in a matter of an hour or so.

"You have a lot of pain behind your eyes, don't you, honey?" she asked him eventually.

He didn't know what to say and so he didn't answer. But he didn't really know what he had behind his eyes anymore. Or in his heart. He was like that big cat, just roaming around looking for food and a place to sleep and surviving as best as he could on luck and a little bit of school and, lately, a whole lot of hospitality from others. If pain was really behind his eyes so evidently, it was only on the surface. After he'd been beaten up and scratched and bit and shot at so many times, he felt like the only pain that could get him would be the sting of death and then he would be no more and would probably feel not much different than he felt in that moment. Would he meet his mammy in the afterlife? Or Charlotte? Would God take her even after what she did? Was there a heaven at all? These questions floated around in his mind but they were the only questions he had about dying. He'd made up his mind about the rest. He heard footsteps then from behind him and mister John eventually came into his sideview.

"Lily, I'm going off to bed," he said.

"It's getting late, isn't it. Alright. George, I can talk your ear off another day, you go on to bed and we'll see you in the morning. Get some rest."

And with that he went to bed and the house was silent and he laid on his back and stared up at the dark ceiling and a vision of laying on the front yard at Chito and Koi's house popped into his head.

What do you want to be when you grow up? Koi had asked him and Chito.

A carpenter, Chito answered.

I don't know, George said.

You don't know? Koi asked.

Yeah. Anything, I guess. Something good, George said.

Something good, Chito chortled.

That ain't so bad, Koi said. *Hell, I hope I'm something good too.*

You already are, Koi, you've got it all, George said.

I do? Koi asked.

I think so, George said. Chito nodded beside him in concurrence.

Something good, Koi chuckled again.

And then the memory stopped like a record when the song is over and George was back in the room and the ceiling was dark and blank but the projector of his mind was turned off for good for the night and he closed his eyes and dozed off to no dreams. When he woke, it was well into the morning and the sun was shining down through a crack in the curtains onto his face. He threw his clothes back on and rushed downstairs. The parlor they'd sat in the night before was empty but he heard voices coming from the kitchen. He quietly made his way over to the door and pushed it open with care and standing in front of him was Lily at the sink cleaning a pan and she had her back to him. When he took another step in so that he could see the full room, he saw two other people in the room. They were both girls, or women—he was still relearning how to discern anything about anyone.

They were talking to Miss Lily, but they got quiet when he walked in the room and all three of them turned to look at him. Before he could get a good look at the two girls, Miss Lily dropped the pan in the sink and walked over to him.

"Morning, George, I hope that bed treated you okay last night?" she asked, getting close to him.

"Yes, ma'am, best sleep I've had in weeks."

"Good. Now, are those the only clothes you own?" She asked this while she grabbed his shoulders and looked him up and down. "We need to get you some new clothes, huh? You need more than one pair of pants to wear."

Behind her, he heard the two girls start laughing under their breaths and he felt his face get warm and red in embarrassment. Miss Lilly looked up at him and realized what she'd done to him and she turned around and gave what George could assume was a motherly leer to her daughters and they stopped laughing. George looked at both of them for the first good time and he could not believe what he saw. The first was a younger girl, still a child, small and wearing a thick nightgown and with a face that held no sign of blemishes. Her face was fuzzy and sticking out every which way and she was holding some kind of pastry filled with jam, nibbling on it every minute or two and getting a little of the jelly on her face. But beside her was the most beautiful thing he'd ever seen in his whole life.

She was just a bit shorter than him and she had long, black hair and she had tied a blue handkerchief on top of it and she blushed when he looked at her. She wore an apron and there was flour still on the front of it. She had freckles on her nose and dimples that were shaped like crescents and were made clear in the small grin she put on then. Her nose was straight and long and barely lifted off her face and her eyes were green. He felt like he could look at her all day.

"Oh, I forget myself these days, don't I?" Miss Lily said. "George, these are my two daughters. Francis is our baby and then this tall girl with flour all over her is Mary Beth. Girls, please say hello to our guest."

Mary Beth and Francis waved at him and he stared at Mary Beth a little while longer and he felt a flurry in his stomach.

"George, how old are you?" Miss Lily asked.

He thought about it for a moment, attempting mental math as fast as he could. "Twenty-one, I believe."

"You believe? Hm. Mary Beth here is nineteen and we've been working on her getting a nice-paying job and getting her out of the house on her own. But here we are with a twenty-one-year-old in the house. We'll never get her out," she said with a laugh and Mary Beth blushed even harder than she already had been.

Miss Lily took him out shopping and invited Mary Beth along and they walked a few blocks until they were at a row of stores. One was for menswear and she told him to pick a couple of outfits out and made him try them on for her and Mary Beth before he was allowed to leave with them and she purchased it with her own money. She asked him if he needed anything else and he said that he could not think of anything.

"The man wants for nothing," she said out loud to the sky, as a joke he'd figure out later. She did these kinds of jokes all the time, as if she were performing for an audience that was not visible to the eye.

"Mom, MaryBeth would say with more than a trace of aggravation in her voice at her mother's antics.

Miss Lily asked to stop in the butcher's market before they returned to the house and George waited outside with Mary Beth while she did so. At first they stood in silence and he tried to not look at her in case she might be uncomfortable with his presence. But he glanced over once and saw that she was looking at him.

"Annie told me you were very kind," she said. Her voice was soft, and she spoke slowly like George had seen syrup do, running out of a tree when he and the boys would stick a Bowie knife deep in the trunk and yank it out after a minute or two, licking off the sap.

"She was very nice," he said. "I'm very lucky to have met her."

"Did you think she was pretty?" Mary Beth asked him. He blushed. It seemed that all the two of them had been doing all day was blushing.

"I, I—"

"That's alright," she laughed. "You don't have to answer that."

"Okay," he said.

"She also said you were very handsome, if that's any consolation."

"I appreciate that." He stared at the window on the butcher's market to see if her mother was coming out any time soon to save him from his heart stopping right then and there.

"Do you think I'm pretty?" she asked him. He looked over at her and she had her hand over his face to block the sun and she was squinting to see him but she still stared hard into his eyes and down past them. "And you have to answer that one."

"Yes," he said, with less hesitation than he'd hoped. None at all, really.

"That was a quick answer."

"Yes."

"What's it like?"

"What's what like?" he asked, looking around for Miss Lily to appear again.

"Being Indian. And what kind are you anyway?"

"I'm Choctaw."

"Choctaw," she said, expressing the consonants with extra emphasis, the front and back of her tongue pressing off the roof of her mouth with clicks. "You didn't answer the first question."

"I don't know what it's like being Indian."

"How so?"

"I haven't really been it in years."

She laughed until she realized that he wasn't messing with her.

"I don't think it's something you have to be. You just are it."

"Mm," he grunted, squinting and seeing that Miss Lily had emerged from the store with two big bundles of wrapped meat in her arms. "You might be right about that."

George got up and rushed over to grab the packages from her arms. She smiled at him and he turned around and Mary Beth was looking off down the street at nothing in particular.

"What were you two talking about?" Miss Lily asked.

"Nothing," George replied.

"I asked him what being Indian was like," Mary Beth said.

"I don't think that's very polite of you, Mary Beth."

"It's alright, ma'am," George said. "I've seen worse. Much worse."

He tried to act normal for the rest of the walk home. The weight of the meat helped considerably as he was out of breath within a hundred yards of walking and he could no longer speak. Miss Lily asked him, in a concerned tone, about his breathing when they got home and he could finally set the meat down somewhere. He informed her about his asthma and she took out a notepad and wrote something down. She said they'd go out the next day and make sure he was stocked up on what he needed for it and he did not understand what he had done to deserve the treatment he was receiving but he was not so much a fool as to try to mess it up just yet.

27

"I HAD TO DO IT," George said. He closed his eyes then. He hurt so bad.

"Probably you're right. But that don't change it."

"How would you know anyway?" he asked, looking at the boy again. He was as real as ever still.

"Good question for somebody else."

George nodded his head from his dirt perch. His eyes were still closed.

"What were you like before?" George asked.

"Before what?"

"Before I met you. What were you like outside of that night?"

"Why do you want to know?"

"I wish I could tell you. Maybe I'm just becoming kinder in my dying."

"You won't get salvation from being kind to me. I'm already gone."

"I know that. You were never going to be my salvation."

"Unfortunately, I can't offer you anything more than you already know. You can make up the rest. I was an evil kid, bound for destruction of self or someone else eventually. If it wasn't you and me, it would have been me and someone else, wouldn't it? Whatever makes you feel better at night. Whatever makes it work for you."

"Nothing makes me feel better at night."

"Some things have."

"What would you know?"

"I'm inside your head, friend. I am as much you as you are yourself. Think about it."

"Don't call me friend."

"Think about what you're saying. Really think about it. I'm being serious, really, think about it."

"I've gone crazy."

"Long before now."

"Where will you go after this?"

"Hell or heaven. Purgatory, maybe. Your choice."

"I don't want to make that choice. That's not why I'm asking."

"Then why are you?"

"I don't know."

"Well you already made the choice. A long, long time ago. You killed me, man. Listen to yourself. You're a grown man now. Have the decency to listen to me at least once and tune into what's going on here. You killed me, not the other way around. You're the one got to keep on living. Got to marry, have children. Got to live a life. You buried me in the trees. You don't even know if anyone found my body. My own family couldn't bury me. Not that it would have mattered either way."

He opened his eyes and looked at the boy and a bat flew right through the top of his shimmering skull and a bullfrog croaked somewhere nearby.

28

After three days of living in their home, he learned that their last name was Powers and Miss Lily made a joke about "the Powers that be" and mister John laughed like he'd never heard it before but you could only assume he had. Then he had taken George into his study and asked him if he'd thought about what he might do for work in Wilmington. George told him about his chance encounter with Randall and about his offer for ensured work at the marina. Mister John nodded and said that he'd only heard good things about the family that ran it, although he'd only heard a couple of things, and that he'd be happy to drive him there that day. George figured the time wasn't getting any better so he obliged.

The marina was about a quarter mile from one end of the downtown area, the end that was closest to where the river dumped out into the ocean. They pulled into a parking lot that overlooked a number of boats tied to the dock. George had never seen so many boats all at one place, and so many of them were the biggest boat that he'd ever been near. Men scuttled about them, some looking like they were getting them ready to go out for a ride and some seeming as if they had just come back. The water off in the distance was choppy but the marina was placed in a cove and it lightly lapped against the edge of the dock that ran around the perimeter of the entire marina. On one end was a shack where a big woman was coming out. She looked angry as she walked towards the parking lot and they got closer to her.

"Carl in there?" Mister John asked as they passed her. She stopped and huffed from walking.

"He's there. I don't know why anyone would want to be around his sorry ass but he's in there," she replied before she walked past them.

"Mm," Mister John grunted. "I'm not gonna tell you what to do or discourage you from working here, but that's not the best sign of a sound work environment, buddy."

Inside the shack was dingy and barely lit and a bald man with wrinkles up and down his face sat at a desk in the middle of the room smoking cigarettes and writing on so many papers that George wondered how he could keep track. The bald man didn't look up at them when they entered and mister John cleared his throat after a while to announce their presence.

"Oh, hey there, fellers. What can I do you for?" he asked. Mister John looked over at George and nodded for him to start talking.

"I met Randall and—"

"Aw hell, he met Randall," he said, throwing his pencil down dramatically and looking around for someone to commiserate on the joke with but they were the only three people in the place. "Buddy, what did my brother-in-law tell you?"

"That you could get me a job."

"I bet he did. What did you do for him?"

"Nothing."

"Not a thing?"

"I met him when I got into town. We talked for a while and he told me about Conrad. Drove me to where I'm staying and told me about you."

"Mm, Conrad. Good boy. Hurts the whole family waiting to hear if he's even alive over there. Alright, well, you ever worked on a boat?"

"No, sir."

Carl shook his head dramatically, like everything else he did apparently.

"Randall, Randall, Randall. You know how to scrub hard, son?"

"Yessir," George answered.

"Tomorrow morning. Six a.m. sharp. You hear?"

And that was that, no other questions asked. George thought it funny how the man talked about Randall but appeased the man's wishes so quickly, even when he was not there. He figured Randall wasn't lying about Carl owing him.

He thought about the concept of it for a while on the ride home. Owing someone something. He thought that maybe everybody owed somebody something. And they'd call collecting it eventually. But he shook his head for thinking crazy. It was just a job and a favor.

THE NEXT MORNING he was there ten minutes early and there was no one there. Carl showed up at 6:01 and the rest of the crew showed up a few minutes later and no one paid George any mind. A few minutes later, Carl met him outside with a mop and a sponge and a bucket and told him to find a boat and clean it, nothing else to it. He worked in silence all morning until lunch and he'd washed the hulls of two boats pretty well, he thought, and his arms were growing tired so he stopped for lunch. Outside the shack, three other young men that comprised the rest of the cleaning crew sat on the concrete eating sandwiches and he joined them.

"What's your name, bucko?" one of them asked. He had a crooked smile and crooked teeth.

"George."

"George what?" he asked with a large dose of sarcasm on his face.

"Norris."

One of the other boys perked up as he answered.

"Norris? You say Norris?" the boy asked. His voice was higher than George had expected and he had a large black grease stain across the front of his shirt and a cowlick on the top of his blond head of hair.

"Yep," George answered.

"Where you from?" the same blond boy asked.

"Mississippi."

"Well I'll be, I got some family down there and they're Norris's, true as true can be."

George grunted and took a bite out of the sandwich he'd found on the table by the front door that morning with his name written on it. It was turkey and lettuce and mayo and it cooled him down as soon as he'd swallowed the first mouthful.

"Damn tough story though. My cousin Colt was killed at the fair in the state capitol down there. Yep, killed at the fair of all places. And they never found the sumbitch. Beats me. I told my ma it sounded like Mississippi was no place I wanted to be. His older brother called one time and we got to talkin' and he told me that if he ever found the cold-hearted feller who did it, he'd kill him. I told him I'd do the same. Who kills somebody at the fair? You ever hear about that down there, George? I reckon it had to have made the radio news."

George took bites out of his sandwich while the boy talked so that he wouldn't show any signs of recognition on his face or blurt something out that would get him stomped to death right then and there.

"No, I don't think so," he said once he'd gotten another mouthful down and collected himself. "Can't say I heard about that happening. Sorry to hear that though. I know people been killed too."

"Yeah, like who?" the third boy asked. George thought that he was so plain and unpeculiar that he could just fade away. In fact, he'd forgotten the boy was even there with them for most of the conversation.

"My mama," George said.

He took another bite to stave off the tears in case they thought about coming and it was his last bite. None of the boys spoke anymore and they finished out the rest of the day cleaning in silence, or at least not talking to George any longer. Mister John picked him up at 4:00 and asked how his day was and George had already fallen asleep in the passenger seat of the automobile.

"Hey, you awake?" called a voice in the middle of the night in his second week of staying at the Powers' house. George shot up in bed and looked around like a madman. The door to his room was shut and it was dark and he thought he was imagining things until he saw a shadow move by the chest of drawers. "Don't freak out. Relax."

The voice was Mary Beth's and he started to calm down from the idea he was about to be killed before he remembered who Mary Beth was and his heart began racing again.

"What are you doing in here?" he tried to whisper without his voice shaking but it was for naught.

"Move over," she said.

"Move over where?"

"In the bed. Move over in the bed, idiot," she said and then suddenly she was slowly rolling her tight frame onto the mattress beside him and he scooched over so that she would have space and he wouldn't be touching her.

"What are you doing in here?" he asked again and now that she was so close, not only was his voice shaking but his shoulders and chest too.

"I wanted to see you when it could be just us," she said.

"Why?"

"Do you really think I'm pretty?" she asked.

"Yes, Mary Beth, but I—"

"You mean it?" she interrupted him and then her hand was on his chest and she was leaning up on her stomach looking at him from above. She smelled like rose petals and he wondered if she always smelled that way or if she had just put perfume on before coming in and he came to the conclusion that it didn't matter either way. His eyes were still adjusting to the dark of the room instead of the dark of the back of his eyelids but he could see her more clearly now and she was in a purple, silk nightgown that hung tightly to her and her hair was up in a ponytail.

"Yes," he replied.

"I like it when you say my name, it sounds pretty when you say it."

"Okay," he said.

"Well, say it." She leaned down then and whispered this into his ear and he felt himself tense up and the blood rushed from his heart to his groin.

"Mary Beth," he said.

"One more time," she said.

She climbed on top of him and straddled him then and leaned down to where her face was right in front of his and he said her name once more and she kissed him. She still tasted like the cherry pie they'd enjoyed after dinner and he got an extra helping of the flavor when she lightly lowered her tongue into his mouth while they kissed and ran it along the top of his tongue and put a hand in his hair and moved it around and he wondered if he'd died and gone to heaven.

"Have you ever had sex?" she stopped kissing him and asked.

"Yes," he replied.

"Good," she said, resuming to where she was on his lips. He was glad she didn't ask any other questions. He thought then that she had the same powerful air about her that her mom had. He didn't mind it. In fact, he liked it a good deal in that moment and the moments to come.

When they were finished, she stood up and pressed her nightgown down and kissed him on the cheek and put one finger up to her lips to ensure silence and then she snuck back out of the room and to her own. He didn't sleep that night. When her pa met him downstairs the next morning, he made note of the bags under George's eyes and George said indigestion kept him up all night. John told him that Miss Lily would fatten him up and give him the worst indigestion he'd ever had if he didn't stop her and chuckled and the conversation was over. George slept harder than he had in months that subsequent night, at least after he'd waited an hour or two in the dark to see if she'd come again. But she didn't and he knocked out quickly once he gave up, waking to drool covering the pillow in the spot that he hadn't moved from all night.

A few evenings later, he caught her at a rare time when the rest of the family was outside on the front porch. He walked into the kitchen to find a snack and she was standing over the oven reading a cookbook. He admired her when she wore her apron. There was something about it that he fancied.

"Hey, stranger," he said.

"Oh, hey," she said, absentmindedly giving him a short glance from the book. He poured himself a glass of milk and stood there for a beat or two, sipping from it and watching her.

"Are we going to talk about the other night?" he asked.

"Keep your voice down," she said.

"Alright," he lowered his volume. "Why have you been avoiding me? We live in the same house for god's sake."

"Because I wanted to leave you alone and see if I missed you. See how much I liked you," she said, walking over to him and grabbing his glass and taking a swig. It left a line of liquid around her upper lip that he reached over and wiped off.

"Oh, alright," he said. He stood there, looking at the tile floor, his brow displaying his mind was hard at work. "Maybe we should talk though."

"About what?"

"I'm not so sure this is a good idea."

"Well I can think of a million reasons sneaking around with you in my parents' house is not a good idea, George. You don't think I'm smart enough to see that?"

"No, no, it's not that. I'm just not sure that I'm right for, well, that I'm right at all."

"Right? What do you mean right?"

"Right in the head. Right for a girl like you. Hell, right for a house like this. I've seen things, I've done things. Stuff that was wrong and mean and maybe even evil."

"You aren't evil."

"You don't know that."

"I can look at you right now and tell you that there is nothing evil in you. The world around us might be, but you aren't."

"You're very smart. Too smart for me too," he said. He felt that she was so young and naive to the world and its ways. But she was beautiful and she was kind. And she was smart, he wasn't a liar, even if she hadn't experienced a quarter of the things he'd seen. But he couldn't help but be pulled to her and her smile and the intimacy she gave him.

"I'm not too nothing," she said, grinning.

He laughed and felt his heart pump a little harder.

"So you don't want to know what's come of it then? My experiment?"

"No, I do. If it's good."

"It is," she said, planting a wet kiss on his nose. "See you tonight, don't act so frightened this time. And enough of that worrisome talk."

This arrangement went on for long enough that he stopped counting the days and George grew ever paranoid that they would be caught eventually, by her parents or Francis, who sometimes fell victim to bouts of sleepwalking. But it never happened and they enjoyed the pleasures of each other night in and night out and he felt his heart warming in ways that he didn't imagine were possible anymore. After a handful of meetings, she called them scheduled meetings as a joke, she came in and took her gown off before getting in bed and he realized that he hadn't seen her naked yet. She even walked over and opened the blinds and stood there for a moment when she saw him ogling her from his supine position.

"Take a good look," she whispered before crawling on him. He'd gone at her so rabidly that he had to cover her mouth when she moaned. She apologized for making noise after the fact, but she did so with a big grin on her face and he knew she wasn't really sorry.

AFTER NEARLY FOUR MONTHS of George staying there, he came downstairs one morning and the family was sitting in the reading room together on the couches. He could feel the tension in the thickness of the air. They all turned and looked at him. He started to say hello but Mary Beth got up and grabbed him by the arm and sat him down beside her on a couch.

"What's going on?" he asked.

"Mary Beth was just telling us that she's in love with you, George," Miss Lily said. He watched her face for shock and horror but it was mostly blank save for the same small smile that she held most times she talked to him. He looked over at mister John and the man nodded before speaking up.

"George, what do you think about this?" mister John asked.

"I, uh, I think—"

"And you can be honest, honey," Miss Lily added.

"Well," he paused. "I think I love her too," he said.

Mister John nodded and got up and walked over to the window. They all sat in silence and waited on him to make some kind of movement or decision or something. Mary Beth looked over at George and smiled and mouthed "thank you" to him and he just shrugged. He felt his heart beating out of his chest and the longer the man stood there, the more concerned he became for his life. When he finally turned around and faced them again, he had a look of discernment on his face, a face that George then thought was wise like he remembered his pawpaw's being.

"George, do you have any interest in learning under me with my business?" he asked. The family business, and the sole reason they lived in a house as grandiose as they did, was that the man owned a small gun manufacturer and owned several businesses in the southeastern area of the state where they both sold and fixed firearms. Mister John himself always kept a shiny Colt revolver on his side. He'd told George once that it was the inspiration for him getting in the business he was in and that it had saved his ass a time or two so he took care of it. The man continued with his line of questioning. "I ask because I want my daughter to have a good life. Not a hard life. And I think you're a hard-working young man and a stand-up man. I've even gone by to ask Carl about you because, well, I had my suspicions and he said you cleaned boats faster than anybody he'd ever seen. But washing boats is not the life I want for my Mary Beth. Does that make sense?"

"Yessir," George said, because he'd forgotten the original question.

"Well?" the tall man leaned in and asked.

"Oh, yessir, sorry, I would greatly appreciate you teaching me anything you'd like to teach me. Especially if it means spending more time with your daughter."

The words spilled out of him like he was predestined to say them and the matter was settled and Mary Beth leaned over and hugged him tightly.

"This is a good thing, George," Miss Lily said.

"It might be the only good thing happened to me in a long time," he said.

In early summer, they were to be married. The Powers were Baptists and so George was going to have a Baptist wedding. As the days crept closer to their wedding day, he became more and more conscious of the fact that he'd have no one there for him except for her family. With a week remaining, he got the nerve up to ask Miss Lily if he could use their phone to call home. In reality, he was more so asking if she could show him how to make a phone call, as he'd never done it. He called back to the operator in Mississippi and after a little while of what sounded like she was flipping through pages on the other end of the line, he was connected to a home number for Koi and Susanna.

"Hello?" a voice said into his ear. He nearly fell down when he recognized it as Susanna's. He wasn't sure what he was expecting but he wasn't prepared for it and he didn't answer her at first.

"Hello?" she repeated.

"Susanna?" he asked.

"Who is this?" she said.

"Is Koi there?"

"Who is this?"

"Is Koi there with you?"

"George, is that you?"

He paused before answering. "Yes."

She did the same. "George. Oh, George," she said. He heard soft sobs in the telephone receiver.

"Is Koi there? Or Chito? Are you okay, Susanna?"

"Koi is dead, George."

"What?" He fell back into the wall and gripped the receiver like it was the only thing keeping him in this world.

"Where have you been, George? Where have you been?" Her sobs got louder.

"How did he die?"

"What does it matter to you? You weren't here. Why do you care?"

"I care, Susanna. I never stopped caring."

"They made him go to war. You weren't here."

"And Chito?" he said. The world began to fade around him.

"What does it matter?"

"What?"

"What does it matter either way? Why should I tell you anything else?"

"Susanna."

"Where did you go?"

"I had to leave. I had to," he said, the strength in his voice slipping. "There was nowhere for me to go. I had to."

She didn't reply for some amount of time. The silence between them, the sound of the phone line fuzz. It could have been measured in distance better than seconds.

"Just come back home, George," she said, her voice measured and slow, breaking the silence. "I'll forgive you. You can come back."

"I can't," he said and it took everything out of him to say it aloud. "I don't have a home there."

He heard a muffled "okay" and then the click of her line cutting off and he hung the receiver back on top of the stand with the microphone and he sunk to the floor with his head in his hands. He forgot to mention the wedding at all and he couldn't call her back then. He heard footsteps in the room and he looked up and Miss Lily was there, standing over him.

"I'm sorry," he said, starting to stand. "I hope you didn't hear that. Let me get myself together."

She leaned down and placed a hand on his shoulder and he sat back down on the hardwood floor and she slowly sat down beside him there, cross-legged.

"George," she said. "I think you have a burden on you that you need to share with someone. At least by telling what has happened to you."

"I don't know, ma'am," he said.

"I'll sit here and wait until you're ready," she said.

He worked up the courage slowly and started from the murder of his mammy and worked his way all the way up to Athens and the moment he met Annie. She listened intently and did not say a word until he was finished.

"I'm sorry for leaving all of this out," he said. "I understand if you would like me to leave. I've done horrible things."

"Horrible things have been done to you," she said. "Horrible, horrible things. Don't worry about what I think. I cannot imagine. You poor thing."

They sat in silence on the floor for a while and then he realized that she was giggling a little and he turned to look at her and tears were streaming lightly down her face while she smiled and laughed a silent laugh.

"I'm sorry," she said. "I just can't believe that after all that, you fought a mountain lion and won."

"Is that what they're called?" he asked.

"Yes," she said. "Mountain lions. My pawpaw called them panthers."

He rolled up the sleeve on his shirt and showed her the scar of three slices down his forearm, once bloody and now a simple drawing of white lines down his skin. No hair grew where they stood slightly raised. She looked at them intently for a moment and shook her head.

"A lion tamer, indeed," she said, with one last chuckle.

29

THEIR WEDDING WAS SMALL and moved faster than anything in his life ever had and she was beautiful in her wedding dress and when he lifted her veil he was hit with a reassurance in his gut about it. The preacher gave a short sermon on the apostle Paul's letters but George hardly paid attention. Annie was in the crowd and he thought he saw her shed a tear at one point. His thoughts swam to what his mammy would think and he knew that she would think this girl was beautiful and that she would call Mary Beth her daughter the same way Miss Lily called him her son. They kissed in that Baptist chapel on the waterfront and it was the singular kiss of his life after hundreds of them already shared between them and George finally felt like his constant movement for what felt like his whole life had come to a head and proved itself to be worthwhile and then, in that moment, was when he could stop. He was at a finish line, he just knew it. He felt a weight off his shoulders. He told her he loved her as they walked down the aisle and then three more times as they ate dinner with the family afterwards. They moved back into her parents house after. They were still working on the particulars of buying a home down the street. But they were allowed to sleep in the same room without a need for secrecy for the first time and he felt warm and secure and he told her this before she fell asleep that night, that he felt safe, and she told him that was good but he knew she didn't really understand what he meant and that she only cared for him deeply and that was enough for him. Instead of dozing off like he thought she would then, she climbed on top of him and they consummated their marriage and she moaned aloud once and then giggled.

"Why me?" she asked him when they finished.

"What?"

"Why did you want to marry me?"

He thought for a moment. His head was clear in the way he'd found it could be after sex.

"Peace. You might be the only peace I've ever had. For a long time at least."

"Really?"

"Really."

Neither of them said anything for a while. They breathed softly.

"Have you ever been on a Ferris wheel?" he asked her.

"Of course. Have you not?"

"Once, a long time ago."

"What about it?"

"You remind me of how I felt up there, I think. I don't know if that makes sense."

She soon fell asleep, her light body on top of his and her heartbeat a light drumming on his abdomen and her toes intertwined with his out the end of the covers and the whisper of her breaths in his ear. The beat of her blood pumping lightly on his chest loosened something in him. A scar healed, a grip loosened, a weight removed. He moved the ring around on his finger with his thumb and felt its coolness and pressed it to his cheek to feel it better. He laid there awake for a while, just listening to her be alive.

30

HE GOT TO WORK at the same time as usual that day and there were sparse clouds in the sky. The sun was beating down on him and everyone else around and through those clouds. It was windy and the air pushed sound from the downtown area towards them and he could make out the reverberations of a band playing a show on the waterfront every minute or so closer to lunch time. He walked to the shack when his internal clock ticked and made his stomach grumble at the same time it did every day and joined the other cleaners there on the ground. They were talking when he walked up and stopped as soon as they saw him and he thought it odd, as if it was his first day all over again.

"Hey fellas," he said as he sat down.

No one replied and eventually most of them had eaten their food and gotten up to return to work and it was just him and the blond boy named Nolan who he'd tried to befriend from a short distance as best as he could, and who was a cousin of George's bloody namesake. When George took the last bite of his food, he looked up and saw that the boy was staring at him.

"What is it, Nolan?" George asked, chewing down on the white bread and turkey.

"Nothin', just thinkin'," the boy replied.

"About what?"

"Well, if you wanna know, I was speaking with my aunt the other day. She came to town to visit from Jackson. And I told her I'd met a Norris from Mississippi and she couldn't believe it. Said she'd never met another Norris in all of Mississippi that wasn't kin."

"Ain't that something," George said. "I was from up north though, we probably just would've never crossed paths."

"Mm, right. Well so she asked me what you looked like." The boy stopped to work a piece of food out from a top row tooth with his tongue. "And so I told her and you know, a crazy thing happened."

"What's that?"

"Her face got white as snow. Or at least what I've heard snow looks like. Doesn't come our way much. And you know what she told me? With her face white like that? Like she'd seen a ghost?"

"What?"

"That your description sounded a hell of a lot like the description my dead cousin Colt's buddy gave to the police. Of the murderer. A hell of a lot like it. What's that expression? Eerily similar, that's it."

"Huh," George said and he felt his internal temperature rising to a boil and he stuck his hands in his pockets so that they wouldn't visibly shake. "You said he was killed at the fair, didn't you?"

"Mmhmm, state fair. In Jackson."

"I've never even been down that way. I must have a twin. An evil twin," George said, squeezing out a laugh with it. Nolan laughed a sarcastic guffaw back.

"But ain't it funny, George? Somebody who looks just like you and, by God, you have the same last name as the dead boy. Ain't that funny?"

"A whole lot of coincidences," George said. "That's for sure."

"George, do you think I'm stupid?" the boy asked him and his face had taken a turn to serious and darker than George knew was possible under his blond hair. "Do you remember what I said I'd do if I ever found the killer?"

George didn't answer.

"I said I'd kill him. I may be too young yet to join that war over there and kill somebody, but I can damn sure still do it over here if I have to. I ain't afraid, George. I ain't afraid of it."

George stood up and wiped the crumbs off of him and tried to act as if everything was alright and that he just had to get back to work but when he turned he saw that two of the other boys were standing behind him and they looked like sharks who'd smelled blood in the water and he asked them what was going on and Nolan spoke up from behind him and he turned back around.

"George, did you kill my cousin?" he asked.

"No, Nolan, I did not. That's an awful thing to accuse someone of."

Then, the two other boys came up on him and grabbed him by the arms and he tried to writhe himself out of their grasp but they were strong and he could do nothing. Nolan walked right up to him and punched him in the gut and George bent over, the sandwich immediately pushing back up in his throat.

"George, did you kill my cousin?"

"No," he replied with what was left of his voice.

The boy stepped up and punched him harder in the gut this time and then gave him an uppercut to the chin, just as his head had dropped again and George's world was spinning on its axis. The two boys holding him laughed and cheered on Nolan. Through a ringing in his ears, he heard Nolan tell the boys to lay him on his back on the concrete and they did and he was looking up at that bright sky with its few clouds and the boy stood over him and blocked his view.

"George, this is the last time I will ask you. Did you kill my cousin? Did you take his name?"

"Yes," George exhaled.

Nolan's face grew bright red and he laughed a high-pitched, squealing laugh and the two other boys stepped back as he brandished a knife from his boot. It was a switchblade. George had only seen one once as a child when a boy on the farm pulled one out and said he'd nicked it from a store to kill worms with. He leaned down over George and spit in his eye and it burned with the remnants of tobacco juice and he tried to blink it away but he couldn't so he kept only his good eye open to watch the boy.

"I'll fucking kill you," the boy yelled.

George saw the knife come down to where he couldn't see at his stomach and he felt a hot pain jump and he screamed out to the river and the birds above it and he lifted his head to see Nolan pull the blade out of him and it was covered in blood and he saw it start to flow out of him and then the two other boys were lifting him up and they carried him out to the road a good ways until they were tired and threw him on the asphalt and the world dimmed and became quiet and the light of the sun was the last thing he saw, a tunnel of yellow light closing in on itself.

He woke to bright light, blinding white light that made him close his eyes as soon as they'd been opened and he heard the sounds of metal on metal clanking and voices speaking back and forth to each other in hushed and determined tones and he felt as tired as he'd ever been. He wondered why he'd woken up at all. The room around him smelled clean like soap and then he heard someone say, "He's waking up." He opened his eyes and lifted his head a little but the strain it put on his stomach nearly made him faint and then he saw a face appear before him and it was an older man with a beard and glasses.

"Hey son, stay with me for a moment," the man with glasses said before he retreated from George's vision and the overhead light blinded him again.

"Where am I?" George asked and his lips were dry and his tongue was dry and his throat was dry and it hurt to speak.

"You're in the hospital. You're alright, we've just about got you sewed back up," the man said from out of view. "You're a lucky man with a good father-in-law, I'll tell you that."

"What happened?"

"You tell me, buddy. I only know that he went to pick you up from work early, said he had some good news, and he found you lying on the street bleeding out of your stomach. You remember any of it?"

"I was stabbed," George said, the memories flooding back to him as if they'd been severed from his mind by a dam and it was just opened.

"I could tell you that. You remember why?"

He did but he wouldn't say. "I got jumped. Three boys."

"Why?"

George didn't answer the question and after a few minutes the doctor told him that they'd fixed him up and would give him some medications and he could go home in an hour or so after they'd watched him to make sure nothing else happened. Mary Beth came in then and her family followed and she grabbed him by the face gently and kissed his cheeks and nose and forehead and told him that she loved him.

"Why did they do this to you?" she asked, pulling her head back to show tears down her red face. Before she could speak, Miss Lily came up behind her and placed her hand on Mary Beth's shoulder, lightly pulling her up.

"George, how are you feeling?" she asked.

"I'm okay," he said. "I just don't remember hardly anything."

"Well I'm just glad that John here was coming with good news and found you before it was too late."

"I haven't seen anyone in the shape you were in since I was over there in the first war," Mister John said. "Glad you're alright, buddy."

"George," Miss Lily spoke with a cool tone as she said this. "If you start to remember what happened you tell us, okay? This crime will not go unpunished. Somebody will pay for this."

He asked if he could tell them when they got home, that he didn't want to draw any ears of passersby or doctors or nurses in the hospital and Miss Lily nodded her head and they took him home that evening. He was only allowed to drink water and eat a slice of bread that night for fear of complications with his intestines but even white bread tasted like heaven to him as they sat in the parlor and waited for him to speak.

"Miss Lily, all of this will have to do with what I've told you," he said. "And that's why I didn't want to say it aloud in the hospital."

He went on to tell the story of killing that boy at the state fair, from seeing the man who had sired him to being accosted by the two boys and taking that dead boy's name and having to run away with the circus. While he spoke, he saw that Mary

Beth's eyes grew wider and wider and her mouth dropped in awe and then she'd close it when she realized what she was doing but it would just fall back open a moment later. He told them an abbreviated version of living in the cabin in the woods and the hurricane that had made the pieces of his life tumble over once again and that led him to Annie in Athens and then to Wilmington and their family. He told them that the boy had figured him out by total chance. That he'd been unlucky so often and when he'd met this family he thought his run of just barely scraping by through punch after punch was over but then this boy beat him and stabbed him and left him out to die in the same way he'd done that awful boy years past. He was sobbing hysterically and had to calm himself, pulling out an asthma cigarette and drawing on it slowly until he could breathe well again.

"The boy thinks I'm dead now, I guess," he said. "Which might be the only blessing."

"You can't stay here," Mister John said. "You'll have to go somewhere."

"Daddy, what do you mean?" Mary Beth asked.

"The boy thinks he's dead. He'll try it again if he finds out George is still hanging around." The wise-faced man that George had grown to love like a father turned and began addressing him then. "You'll have to keep moving, son. I know that's not what you want to hear. But you'll have to."

"Where to?" Mary Beth. "Oh, I hope not too far."

Mister John had to think about it and he walked off to his study. The rest of them sat in silence for a while, George drinking water as fast as he could to ease the dryness of his throat that just would not subside. Francis spoke up then.

"Can I come with you?" she asked.

"No, honey, you've got to stay with us," Miss Lily said.

"I'll miss George," the little girl said.

"He's not dead, Francis," Mary Beth said. A loud pop came from her throat then and she threw her face in her hands and cried so hard that her shoulders convulsed and you could've thought she was seizing. George wrapped his arms around her and she did not stop for a while until her body was simply too tired to carry on in this way. Mister John came back in the room with brisk steps.

"I've got it," he said. "I've got it."

"What is it, John?" Miss Lily asked.

"Sandy Creek. I just bought that storefront down there. It's an hour or two drive away, out in the sticks a bit but it sits on a river and oh, the stores there are beautiful and the people are country and always in need of a gun. Let's buy you a house and get you set up running that store. How does that sound, George? Mary Beth? Oh, you can get a house twice the size there as you can in Wilmington for the same price. It's perfect, isn't it?"

A WEEK LATER they were taking multiple cars down the road to Sandy Creek. The night before, Mary Beth had come to him and said she wasn't feeling well and they took her to the doctor and discovered that she was pregnant. The family exuded happiness, in the face of everything, and George felt insulated in it. Mary Beth found a new energy in this and sprung back to the girl she was before. The ride to their new home was bumpy and long and they passed through several towns that Francis commented they might as well just stop and live at instead of keeping on going down that road. Eventually they came to an intersection where their only options were turning left or right and Miss Lily turned left and they passed those storefronts and she pointed out the one that would become George's place of business. It was a red brick building, at the end of a row of five or six buildings and there was a blank, faded spot where a sign used to be above the front window of it. It sat beside a hardware store, which sat beside a furniture store and a hot dog shop and so on down the line until the brick buildings ended and there sat a big white church.

"Oh, isn't that wonderful?" Miss Lily commented and George smiled and nodded because appeasing his new family was something that he enjoyed doing.

They drove on for another three miles and made a left and then a right and they were on a dirt road surrounded by fields of densely planted pine trees for only a couple hundred yards before the forest opened up to a yard and a little white house sat on it. The house had a small porch hanging on the front of it with a swing on one side and chairs on the other and the yard seemed to go on forever behind it, sloping down a little until it hit the tree line. When they got out of their two cars, mister John came over, beaming with pride at the place.

"Don't you love it?" he said. "And an offshoot of that river runs right down there. A lovely little creek, I was told. Big ol' yard, bigger than I ever dreamed of at your age. Don't you love it?"

George and Mary Beth made love on the floor that night, after the family had left and they had yet to put the bed frame together in their new room because they were so tired. She laid a blanket down on the parlor floor and threw pillows on top of it and laid down there and he laid down on top of her and the old wood that made up the floor creaked under them as he was inside of her. They ate a dinner of ham and cheese after and sat out on the swing, watching the stars go by in the country. Mary Beth noted that she'd never seen so many stars and George said he had but it had been a while and that he'd missed them.

"But they've never looked so pretty as they do right now with your eyes on them," he said and she blushed. They went inside and made love again and he fell asleep rubbing her belly where his offspring lay, growing slowly.

THEY LIVED LIKE THIS for a week before their honeymoon was over and they finally put the bed together. George went to work for the first time and the sign had been placed and there was already another man standing behind a counter in the store, cleaning a shotgun. His name was Bill and he said he'd been hired to be the shop's firearm repairman and George figured that was alright. The shop had no customers for three days before a man came in and said that he was the owner of the furniture store down the street and that he'd heard about a new Winchester rifle he was interested in buying. George showed him a catalogue and they pieced together which one the man was looking for and George got it ordered. He was proud of himself and the work continued on like this.

Mary Beth had Chito Jack nine months later. When they learned it was a boy that she pushed out of her belly, she asked George to name him, and he did not hesitate. She said they could call him CJ for short and he said that was fine. He held that tiny creature of his own creation and he loved him so quickly and fully and he could not believe that he had been given such blessing. He wanted to squeeze the little boy so hard but he knew he couldn't so he just looked down at him and touched his fingers and his toes as gentle as he could. On the birth certificate they'd asked for a last name and George had just given Norris without thinking and Mary Beth, in her exhausted stupor, still was able to throw a look at him but it was too late and the woman had written it down on the paper.

Life was wonderful for them in nearly every way for a while and George forgot his troubles. He was no longer plagued with thinking about Charlotte's face, hanging there dead in the air, as he went to sleep or the remembering of the night he'd killed Colt and how his mind would play it back from start to finish in vivid detail the second he closed his eyes.

George had the storefront selling guns left and right after a few years and they were making enough money that they could build an addition onto the house for a third bedroom. Mary Beth was getting antsy for a second child and he figured it wasn't going to be a better time than right then. They started building it in September and Mary Beth moved with CJ back to her parents house for the week while the men hammered and sawed and yelled out to each other at all hours of the day.

But on the fourth day of construction, storm clouds appeared in the sky and George turned on the radio to learn that the tropical storm that had been weakening in its approach of the Carolinas had suddenly intensified into a hurricane and was now barreling down on them. The builders went home and he called Mary Beth who was frightened for him but he said he'd be alright.

"It can't be any worse than it's been on me before," he told her.

He had three days' worth of food in the fridge and two loaves of bread and he decided he'd stick out the storm. And it was three days of hell. The wind picked up quicker than he'd ever seen and he thought for a moment that a tornado had touched down directly on his land. Out the window on the second day, he watched a tree topple over in the same way he'd seen before. He was afraid then but he had nowhere to go. That evening it got the worst that it would and the back yard where it sloped down to the creek was filled with water so high that he could've fished in it and then a heavy gust blew the frame for the new addition off its platform, wood boards flying off into the woods where they smacked against their forebearers.

Outside, the wind howling around the house, he thought he heard the scream of a big cat. He shook his head, he thought it couldn't be.

The next morning, there was only heavy rain and he ate in peace. Mary Beth returned with CJ a couple of days later when the flooding subsided and she hugged him hard and she was distraught when she saw what had become of their third bedroom. He told her they could take it in the chin, that life got worse than this and that the builders would be back in a few days regardless.

"It's only a matter of money," he told her. "Not life."

A YEAR LATER, she was pregnant again.

"Do you ever wish your life wasn't so boring now," Mary Beth asked him one night after they'd eaten dinner and CJ had gone to bed.

"What do you mean?" he replied.

"You've done all this adventuring and moving and you fought a mountain lion for goodness' sake, and now you are running a shop and having children and coming home to the same wife every day."

"And?" he'd asked.

"Does that not bore you?"

"I used to dream of boredom," he'd said.

They named her Nora after Mary Beth's grandmother. Miss Lily was sickly when the contractions began and she wasn't able to come see the birth of their second child. Two days after, mister John called and asked that they make the drive to Wilmington, as his wife had died.

The funeral was reminiscent of his mother's, George thought. The preacher spoke of how God loved strong women and how, in the Bible, they were the ones who spread the news of Jesus' coming back from the dead and he told other stories of strong women and George couldn't help but think that even with a pastor that seemed to be more progressive, he would've still never understood the things that George's mammy had seen and the promises that she'd been told about how the world would be if only she would convert and the lies that they were and he could listen to the man no more. When Nora started crying near the end of the sermon, he told Mary Beth he'd handle it and he smoked a cigarette outside holding the baby and rejoicing new life.

He thought about Miss Lily and the conversation she'd had with him and he thought that the pastor should have been telling stories like that because that's where real people came out. Not in a book but in their actions to others. Not in the pages of history but in their kind ear and their loving words.

Nora and CJ grew up like twigs into trees in front of their very eyes and one day she was four and he was ten and life had happened. George had relearned how to throw a baseball and bought gloves after CJ asked to train for the school team. And he learned how to braid hair for a little girl with black, straight and long hair that ran down past her shoulders just as his mother's had.

One day he walked past a mirror in a hallway in their home and he looked over at himself and the boy that he had been before was no longer there. There was no sign of him, he was lost to time. There were wrinkles on this man's face and a short beard and his nose had sunken in some and when he lifted his hands he saw that they were calloused and every second passed by so fast that he wondered if time were speeding up for everyone, or just the folks that were getting to enjoy it. He saw that Ferris wheel again and he heard Chito screaming with pure joy and he thought that he couldn't bear to go anywhere else, that he had to be done, and maybe it wasn't a choice but something that just happened without his knowing or his deciding.

"Honey," he heard Mary Beth call out. "Chito would like you to take him out to the creek."

The name split him into two directions on his timeline and as he walked he remembered that boy with the snakebite on his leg and how he'd held George's hand the whole way home from the doctor that day. When he and CJ got down to the creek, they picked out the shiniest and smoothest pebbles and put them in their pockets for safekeeping.

31

HE'D DECIDED TO DROWN HIMSELF, not too long after following the river to the right. The river was right there, after all, and the pain was all over his body and he was so tired, so tired of living in this moment and every moment that had passed before him.

He got down on his hands and knees by the river and he thought that if somebody walked by they would've thought he was praying.

He stuck his head down in the water and sucked it in as best as he could and he instinctively started thrashing but he pushed on and wouldn't let himself up.

Then, he felt something take ahold of the back of his neck and pull him hard and his head was lifted out of the water. He spat it out and coughed and sneezed it out and he felt as if water was in every opening in his body and he lay there on his stomach on the bank expelling it until he felt it wasn't doing any more good.

He pushed himself up and looked behind him and Miss Lily stood there.

"What do you think you're doing?" she asked.

"Dying," he said, falling under another coughing fit.

"Why do you think you're allowed to do that to yourself?"

"I'm my own man, Miss Lily."

"You are the man that people made you to be," she said. The moon shined through her translucent body.

"I made choices," he said.

"Don't we all."

"I couldn't have made it this far without you."

"You made it much farther without me or anyone else. And you'll make it even farther, I think. I think you could go to the moon if you wanted to. But you don't get to kill yourself. That's the only choice I won't let you make."

She made him feel like a child again, but in the way that his mother had. Loved was the word.

"I'm going to die regardless."

"When God decides. Not you. You don't think he's been the one keeping you alive this whole time?"

"No, I don't. I don't think I do."

"Mm. Keep going, George," she said, and then she was gone.

He'd all but forgotten the apparition of the boy still standing there alongside him until he heard a grunt and a clearing of a throat.

"She seemed like a nice lady," the ghost of Colt said.

"One of the best," he said, coughing what felt like the last of the water up.

"Do you really think you're going to die?" Colt asked. It was then that George came to fully recognize that this was still a boy talking to him, only a child, with childlike innocence at his heart, even if it was cold, even if it hadn't drummed a beat in decades.

"I don't see any other way this ends. What did you think of it? Dying?"

"It was terrible, I'd have to guess."

"What?"

"Don't worry about it at this point. I do have one question though," the boy asked. George saw that he was beginning to shimmer and fade a bit.

"Go ahead."

"Would you still do it again? Same scenario. Nothing different. Would you kill me again?"

"I'd still do it again," George said, after a pause.

The boy started laughing.

"Of course you would. You can't change it no way."

"I wish I could ask for forgiveness."

"Deader'n hell, huh?"

"How does it feel?"

"Full of pain, like your whole body is pain. And then nothing at all. Blackness, abyss. Absence."

"Blackness?"

"What, you disagree?"

"I don't know."

"Maybe you do. Maybe it'll be different for you. Is that what you want? A different answer?"

"Why didn't you pull me out of the water?"

"Huh?"

"Miss Lily had to come save me. But you were right there."

"Why the hell would I save you? Buddy, I'm the part of yourself that doesn't want you to be saved. Open your eyes. I'm the hole in your heart. Me and you, we put you in that water. We put you on the ground with that deer, in the door with that lion, on the street with your bones broken, in the woods with holes all in you. It was me, I never wanted nothing good for you from the moment I met you to the moment you killed me. But it was you too. It's you right now."

"I'm sorry," George said.

"Do you see? Do you see why?"

"To be forgotten."

George felt his lungs begin to constrict and he tried to suck in a breath but it wouldn't go down. He placed his hand on a tree and bent over and wheezed and pulled at the air around him and begged for it to enter him. He heard the boy laugh again and then he heard silence. He finally drew in a single breath, his chest ballooning out. He stood up as straight as he could and looked around. Colt was gone. He walked on, because he had to, begging for each breath in to find its way to his lungs.

32

HE WAS AT THE BAR IN TOWN, a hole in the wall across the street from his storefront named Dave's after the proprietor, and it was getting late. He'd started going once a week with Bill on Friday nights after they closed shop late and he'd been doing this weekly ritual for months by then. They'd shoot billiards and shoot the shit with local men, who almost exclusively had bought their guns from him, and drink cold beer. He couldn't think of much better to do at six on a Friday.

They sat at the bar, him and Bill, talking with Dave about the local high school's baseball team and a boy they had that could throw a fastball faster than anyone had ever seen. George asked Bill about his wife and kids, who were the same age as CJ, and they laughed about how they were getting old already. How time had sped up on them the last few years. Or maybe how it had been speeding up the whole time.

Behind them, George heard the door to the bar swing open and a group of voices emerged into the room. The voices approached the bar and asked for four beers and George gave them a glance. In front of his very eyes was the boy who had caused him so much pain and strife in that hospital bed. He couldn't place his name and he looked away from them before the man would see him.

He began to question himself. He told himself that could not be that boy again, he had no business out there in the sticks. He told himself to calm down. Bill said something to him and he didn't hear him. His heart pounded through his ears. A familiar pang shot off in his abdomen where the scar still lay.

"What was that?" he asked.

"I just asked if you'd ever hunted any big animals, predators or something. Bigger than a deer," Bill said. George was looking at him to his right again but he couldn't help but hear every sound that the group of men made to his left. He tracked them with their voices. He thought he could tell that they sat down in a booth at the back of the room.

"Big animals? Like what?"

"Oh, I don't know. You said you're from all over. A wolf or something," Bill said.

"Well, I killed a mountain lion once."

"No shit," Bill said, his eyes wide.

"I was living out in the woods and it wanted me for food. Had to hole myself up in my cabin and shoot him through the door and a crack in the window."

"With what?"

"A .22, if you'd believe it. Took a handful of good shots to even make him sit."

"I'll be damned."

"I had never even heard of one of those things before. Imagine my surprise when it calls out at me while I'm hunting in the woods one day. About shit myself." George tried to laugh while he said this but his nervousness could not be abated.

"I heard they look like little lions without the mane and that they're twice as angry."

"Not a bad description."

"Got any more stories like that?"

"What? You don't have any?"

"I've never killed no mountain lion. You don't want to hear about me sitting up in a tree stand and shooting when something walks up. Ain't interesting."

"Killed a deer with a knife, once."

"You what?" Bill said, his voice climbing in volume and pitch.

"Didn't have a gun and was hungry. It walked up on me and I grabbed it."

"I'll be damned."

"It was awful. I threw up. Wouldn't do it again. That poor little thing," George said, taking a swig.

"Aren't you just a damn son of a gun, I swear."

"Excuse me." From behind him, George heard a man clear his throat and say this. He didn't turn around and Bill looked up at whoever it was.

"Yessir," Bill said.

"Heard y'all telling hunting stories, is that right?"

"Take a seat, hell," Bill said and put his hand up to order another beer from Dave. The man behind him took the seat to George's left and George turned around and was face to face with the devil himself. It was that same old boy, just aged. His face looked worn out but his blond hair hadn't yet left the top of his head, despite the years. The rest of his group were sitting over at a booth, giving glances their way every once in a while. He smiled at George and George took a sip of his beer and wondered if the boy recognized him after all that time.

"You a hunting man?" Bill asked once he had his refill.

"A little bit, but I grew up in the city. Mostly fished. Would like to get into it sometime."

"It can be fun, especially if you're putting food on the table."

The man stuck his hand out to Bill first and introduced himself as Nolan. Then he offered it to George. As he shook the boy's hand, George's mouth was still and his lips stayed glued together. Bill looked at him kind of funny but moved on.

"I've been in this area a long time. Grew up eating only what my mammy grew in the garden and what my pa could kill. Deer meat might not be on any of those city restaurant's menu but I'll be a liar the day I say it ain't delicious."

"No, no venison on a Wilmington menu. No, sir." When he said this, he looked over at George and smiled and an alarm rung in his head like the Baptist church in town's great bell would ring on Sunday mornings and he decided he had to get out of there then.

George finished his beer and stood up. "Fellas, I need to get on back to the missus," he said, lifting his belt and straightening himself up.

"I didn't get your name, buddy," Nolan said.

"It's, it's George," he said. He nodded to both of them and walked out before he could see the man's reaction to the name.

He sped home, watching the rear view mirror for anyone that might be following him, the tires squealing at every sharp turn he made, the engine roaring in his 1953 Chrysler. He walked in the door out of breath. Mary Beth was setting hamburger steaks on plates and CJ was getting ready to say grace. They all looked up at him as he slammed the door. Mary Beth scolded him with her eyes for interrupting the beginning of the boy's prayer. He nodded for CJ to go on and sat down beside him. He ate absentmindedly.

After the kids went to bed, he sat in his reading chair and looked over a manual for a new Remington shotgun they'd gotten in stock. He shifted uncomfortably in his seat for a while. Mary Beth sat on the couch beside him and he noticed her eyes on him.

"Did you drink too much or something?" she asked.

"What's that?"

"You're acting funny, George."

"Oh, oh, no, only had a beer."

"You don't think you're acting funny?"

"No, dear," he said, putting on his best look of faux concern. "I'm sorry if I did. Must be more tired than I thought."

After she went to bed, he stood at the front window and turned all the lights off in the house and opened the blinds and watched the road. He listened for car tires. He thought about being hit and hit over and over again and being laid down on that hot concrete and that boy shoving that knife in his side and then dragging it out. An owl flew across the yard and he startled. He decided to go to bed.

He fell asleep quickly but found himself in a vivid dream state.

He was back in the old cabin, sitting in the living room. He was hungry and picked up his rifle without thinking much more about it and headed out to the woods. He turned around once to look at the old house again and he saw that the tree was atop of it and it was crumbling and then he turned around and kept walking.

He laid down on the forest floor. A caterpillar walked across his left hand. He stuck the gun on the log in front of him. He slowed his breathing down and got still.

He heard a cry, the scream of the mountain lion. He jumped up. It was closer than it had been the first time. He looked around. It cried out once more and it sounded like Mary Beth and he shouted her name to the sky.

He heard footsteps and he looked all around and could not see anything.

He was thrown to the ground from behind. Something heavy jumped on top of him and stood on his back as he thudded to the dirt floor. The forest was silent around him again.

"Do you think you can get away from me?" He heard from behind him the voice of Colt, as recognizable as it was the day he killed the boy. He did not answer it.

"Do you think you can run far enough?" the boy asked again. The weight was suddenly off of George's shoulders and he pushed himself over. Standing in front of him was the mountain lion. It licked its lips and its sharp teeth and slowly stepped towards him. He reached for his gun but it wasn't there. The cat purred at him. George begged for it to stop, to turn around, to leave him be. The cat snarled at him. It was bleeding from its side and its ear had a hole in it. It slowly looked more and more like a creature of the undead.

George slid backwards on his haunches and tried to stand. The mountain lion jumped on him and clawed at his face and everything went dark and it tore at his abdomen and he screamed.

"George," Mary Beth said. "George, honey, wake up."

He opened his eyes and his wife was staring at him. He scanned the room. It was still dark and he was in his home again.

"George, it was just a dream," she said.

He nodded back to her and said he was alright and she rolled back over and dozed off again. He laid there with his eyes wide open until it was daybreak and he got up before she could wake, going outside to mow the lawn.

"DID YOU GET THE CHANCE to read that Remington manual I sent you home with?" Bill asked him, mid-morning that following Monday while they had a break in between customers.

"Yep, yep."

"Want to take a run at pulling this one apart and putting it back together?"

Bill had taken to attempting to teach George how to repair guns. He'd said it was to make him a better store proprietor but George knew that the man was starting to develop a shake in his hands and he wanted to be able to leave the store in good shape at some point. George walked over and tried to reassemble the gun but he got lost. It was simple work but he was tired from a weekend of recurring nightmares and his mind was on Nolan.

"You alright, buddy?" Bill asked. George thought about what the answer was.

"Bill, you remember that old boy we met Friday night? At the bar."

"Nolan, was that it?"

"Yep, Nolan." He started to continue with what he wanted to say but his words got stuck in his throat.

"What about it?"

"Bill, not too many people know this," he started.

"Alright, get on with it."

So, George shared the story of his chance encounter with the boy and how he'd been attacked by the boy's cousins so many years before and had to do what he could to survive.

"I'll be damned," Bill said.

"Yep."

"You sure it's the same boy?"

"Never been surer of something."

"You think he knows that you're the same boy?"

"I hope to God not."

The next morning, George was bent over the counter, still reading that Remington manual and trying to understand how to install a magazine plug, when he heard the door open. He looked up to see a group of men, Nolan in the front. The man from his past smiled at him and walked up to the counter. He looked over at Bill, who was cleaning a gun for an elderly man who lived in a shack down by the river and had gotten too old to work with the tiny parts anymore.

"Hey there, pal, I didn't know you owned this place," he said. "George, that's it, right?"

"That's it. Welcome. Y'all in need of something?"

"We're looking to do some good old-fashioned duck hunting. Never done it before. We're all down here for work." He said this and motioned to the other men in the shop who were looking at the stock on the walls and in the cabinets. "Working on the new railroad. Met an old boy who said he'd let us hunt at a pond down by his house for a small fee. But we don't have any guns."

"Railroad pays that much?"

Nolan laughed. "They're practically giving that money away with all them state subsidies."

George showed him what they had in stock and they pulled three shotguns down from the wall. Nolan asked if there were anymore they could look at. George asked Bill if he could go in the back and see what they had, but he thought he remembered a couple lying around that they didn't have space for out front. As soon as Bill was out of the room and while the other men were still looking at a row of pistols in a glass cabinet near the front of the store, Nolan leaned in close and whispered to George.

"I know who you are," he said, leaning back and smiling. He showed his teeth and George saw there were a couple missing.

"What do you mean?" George asked.

"Don't play dumb with me." Nolan said this and winked. Bill returned with two shotguns in his hands. The men bought four of them and left and Bill congratulated him on a big sale but George was as pale as snow.

"What is it?"

"He knows," George said.

33

George didn't get a good night's rest for two weeks, despite Nolan not showing back up in his life for the time being. He started drinking and drinking and drinking. He went to the bar three days a week. He went to the bar four days a week. He went to the bar at lunch. He bought liquor and brought it home, something Mary Beth had forbidden. He hid it in the toolshed he'd built out back. Mary Beth came out to where he was by the shed once, the bottle hidden behind a five-gallon bucket, and asked him if he was drunk. He slurred back at her.

"I can smell it on you."

"You can't smell shit."

In the screen door on the back of the house, they could see the kids were watching. She shouted for them to go to their rooms.

"What in the hell is wrong with you?"

"Nothing is wrong with me. Nothing at all. Just enjoying the evening, Mary Beth."

He stared at the road at all hours of day and night whenever he was home. He'd sit on the front porch all night, climbing into bed just before the crack of dawn so that Mary Beth wouldn't be suspicious. Once, he was sitting alone at night and CJ came out to get a glass of milk from the fridge and it startled him so bad he jumped up and yelled. The boy stared back at him in fear. Mary Beth found out about this and gave him a strong talking to.

"Just tell me what's going on," she told him after she'd calmed down.

"Nothing is wrong with me," he told her again.

He began drinking in the morning on the weekends. Mary Beth stopped kissing him. He didn't stop. He couldn't stop.

His hands started to shake nearly all the time. Whenever he did sleep, he woke up in screaming fits.

He began to nap at the counter during the workday. Bill didn't say anything about it for a while but when he was awoken by the doorbell one day and screamed "Who's there?" at the top of his lungs, scaring an old lady who'd come by to purchase a gun for her grandson's birthday, he finally had to bring it up with George.

"Is something going on, buddy?" he asked. "Things not well at home?"

"Nothing is wrong with me," he said.

"I didn't ask you that, George."

"Nothing is going on, Bill," he said.

He decided to go to bed at the same time as Mary Beth one night, to make it better somehow. He put his hand on her leg and caressed her gently and she slapped it away, not opening her eyes. He went to sleep angry. He dreamed of the mountain lion again. He dreamed that it was playing with him like a cat with a mouse. It would let him fight back and then slap him with its big claws across the chest and he would howl out in pain. It would let him get up and run and then jump on him once again and scratch at his back, tearing the flesh out from under his shirt. He woke up howling and Mary Beth was standing beside the bed staring at him with terror in her eyes.

"I'm sorry," he said. He began to cry. "I'm sorry."

She walked out of the room, it was still dark. He followed her out onto the porch and she pulled a cigarette out of a pocket in her nightgown and a box of matches with it and she began to smoke. She sat down in one of the rocking chairs. The stars were out in full force.

"Since when did you start smoking?" he asked.

"Since my husband turned crazy," she said.

"I'm sorry."

"I don't want an apology. I want to know what's wrong with you. I want to know what's the matter. I'm your wife." She said this with a calm demeanor that surprised him. Like she'd been angry for so long that the rage had cooled off into something else.

"I can't tell you," he said.

"You can't tell me? I'm your wife, George."

"I don't want to cause you worry."

"You've already done a world of that." She laughed a laugh of exhaustion and pain and weariness and pity. "You've already done it plenty of times."

She finished her cigarette and went inside without him. He stayed out on the porch, watching the road and scratching his arms anxiously and absentmindedly. A truck that he didn't recognize went by just before dawn. It went slowly and he couldn't see inside of it. It bumped along the dirt road and the suspension creaked as it went by. He reached for his gun on his hip but he'd left it on the nightstand. He sat there and watched it until the bumper was blocked by the trees along the road and heard it go on until the sound of the engine dissipated into the air a mile away.

He tried his best to calm himself but he was lost.

He began seeing Nolan's face around town. A man would turn around at the hardware store and he'd flinch, his vision attaching blond hair to a man with black hair. He'd hear a voice and turn around to spot the boy who'd try to kill him and it would be the old man who lived by the river.

He went fishing alone. He borrowed Bill's jon boat and paddled out a ways down the river early on a Saturday morning. He brought a cane pole and dropped worms in the water, looking for bream. He thought that it might have been what he needed.

He heard a rustling in the woods. He shot around and looked. There stood a deer in front of him in between pine and cypress trees. A young buck, four antlers atop its head. It was skinny and alone. It chewed off a leaf from a small tree and looked up at him.

He remembered what he'd done long ago to that little doe. He remembered the way it smelled.

"I'm sorry," he yelled out to it. Ripples followed his voice across the water. A fish near the surface shot away from him.

The deer stared at him for a moment and lifted its tail. It turned and ran, still chewing on the greens.

"I'm sorry," he said. He felt a tug on his line and yanked the fish out of the water. It had swallowed the hook. He had to rip it out of its throat and blood splattered on his hands. It was small but dying so he threw it in his catch bucket. It had nowhere else to go. He thought he should tell it that he was sorry too.

He thought that Mary Beth was right, he was out of his mind.

"How are you doing, George?" the doctor asked, walking into the exam room and extending a hand. He was a tall, gray-haired white man with a belly large and round enough to protrude out of his white overcoat. His last name was Barnhill. He owned multiple bolt-action rifles and a Colt revolver that were in need of regular repair and cleaning at George's shop and he was the only doctor for miles around.

"I'm doing alright," George lied.

He was there on his own volition, even if mostly due to the opinions of his wife that had spurred him into action. He worried that Barnhill wouldn't be the right kind of doctor to bring his problems to, but there were no other options and the man owed him a good deed. He liked to shoot his guns damn near three or four times a week, George had to figure, and the constant service on them often created a backlog for the other work he needed to get to.

"Hardly anybody is doing alright when they make it all the way to me in this office," he said, sitting down on a stool. "Otherwise, they'd be wasting their money. What brings you in here today?"

"Couple things, I guess."

"Fire away."

"Well, I need to get some more of my asthma cigarettes. Didn't realize until a few days ago that I'd plum run out of them. Don't need them as often as I used to but would hate to be caught somewhere without them."

"Mm. Tell you what, I'll do you one better. I'm going to write you a prescription for an inhaler. Just a small piece of plastic, you put your mouth on the hole at the end and press the button at the top and take a good breath in. Shoots a powder in that works a good deal better than the cigarettes, from what I understand."

"Alright. You sure it works?"

"I prescribed one to a boy a few months back, was having a real tough go of it. His mom hasn't been back to complain or get it changed. So I'm pretty confident."

"Alright, well then, thank you," George said.

"Now, I do need to ask you something, George. I've heard word that you've been acting a little off lately. I'm not trying to corner you in here. Your business is your business. But might you be in here to talk about that as well?"

"Well I didn't plan on it, but what have you heard I've been up to?"

"No specifics. George, have you been drinking?"

"A little."

"How much is a little?"

"I don't keep count. Not enough to kill me."

"You know, that stuff is mighty dangerous. Especially for someone like yourself."

"What's that supposed to mean?"

"Don't take offense, George, but the Indian people have had their share of problems with, um, fire water, I believe they call it."

"That what you're trying to say? I'm a drunk Indian?"

"I'm just looking out for you, as your doctor, George."

"Just give me the prescription for the goddamned inhaler," George said, standing up as tall as he could, feeling his blood rising to his head, and grabbing the door handle like he might tear it off. He turned back around to Barnhill. "I don't want to hear no more of that shit. And I better not hear any of it going past me to Mary Beth. It ain't right to talk about a man behind his back that way."

"Just be careful," Barnhill said.

"Same to you," George replied, swinging the door open and storming out of the office, his shoes pounding the tile floor.

BUT HE KNEW IT WAS TRUE. He decided to give himself one more shot to come down off that lonesome mountain of his mind. What could help that, he figured, would be to reach back into history and take what he could find and get his hands around and give it to his children. Find the good parts of his past. He sat them down one morning after breakfast and told them they'd be learning Choctaw that day.

"What's Choctaw, daddy?" Nora asked. George smiled at her and the genuine innocence on her pretty little face, but he couldn't help but feel the weight of his children's ignorance to the history of their forebearers.

"A language, sweetie. The language that my ma and my grandparents spoke and their parents and their grandparents, all the way back," he answered.

"All the way back to when?"

"Hundreds of years."

"Why are you teaching it to us now?" CJ asked.

"Good question," he answered, rubbing his chin in fake thought before chuckling. "Because I want to."

He taught the numbers and had them speak them back to him over and over again and it gave him a shot of joy, straight to the heart, as if you'd stuck a needle right in it and pushed in pure serotonin. He taught them the easy, fun words for dog and house and other things.

"What's the word for love?" CJ asked.

George couldn't remember. He tried his hardest to pull it off the shelves of his mind but it was gone. He could see Charlotte there across the table from him in the Alabama moonlight. He could see her smile. He could hear her asking him to teach her some of the words of his ancestors. He could see his mammy teaching him. But he couldn't remember the language.

"I don't remember, buddy," he said. "You know what? It's already been an hour of this. That's enough for one lesson. I'll try to remember some better stuff for next time."

The next day, on his lunch break, he went to the Sandy Creek library and he asked if they had any books on Choctaw culture or language. The old white woman who ran the library from her unmoving seat behind the front desk asked him what Choctaw was and when he stared back at her with a cocked-to-the-side head, she said, "Oh, is that one of them redskin tribes or something? Like the Apaches? They's a good number of cowboy and injun books but a lot of 'em is for kids."

"Alright, thank you, ma'am," he said and left with his head hung.

As he drove home, a memory of sitting in Koi and Susanna's home flooded over him. They had just eaten dinner, Susanna had cooked hominy after learning it from his mammy. They'd eaten it with pork and the three young men were sitting on the front porch smoking and talking while she cleaned up.

You hear about what's going on at the schoolhouse? Koi asked.

Naw, both boys replied.

They're not allowing anymore Choctaw to be spoken in the classrooms, not even names of people or words that might work better for what they mean. Nothing.

Why would they do that? George asked.

Because they're achukma kiyo. No good people, George. That's how we get Georges and not Holahta hopaii or Nitushi. No offense, buddy, but they're evil. They don't want us. They want white people.

That can't be true, George said. They're not killing us. They'd kill us if they wanted white people.

They'll kill us in any way they can. Hunt down what they want changed and chase it till they get their hands on it. They won't stop. Look around you sometime, George.

You are depressing, Koi, Chito interjected.

If Susanna and I have a child, they'll be white. Our kids will be white children. Everyone will make an exception for them because of her family but they will only do it if they are white and not Choctaw.

Way depressing, Koi said again.

Aboha holihta pʊt akʊmmi, Koi said.

What? George asked.

The walls have closed. They've closed in on us, boys.

As he said this, Susanna came outside and she gave them cold glasses of milk and she sat down beside them and they stopped talking about the school and the language and George couldn't remember another time someone spoke to him in Choctaw after it. The memory was gone then and he shook his head to make sure it left him and he drove home, realizing that any lost word was just lost and that maybe his friend had been right. There were no more Choctaw language hours to be had. CJ and Nora didn't ask about it again.

ONE NIGHT. It took one night to crumble. If he had the time to consider it, he might have thought to himself, *Isn't that funny? After all this time?* He might've tried to understand how things had gotten so far off course so quickly. How he'd become this way. How the kinder moments of his life could be remembered in segments in between periods of hate and loss and longing. But he never found the time.

He'd dozed off in the chair after watching the road for a while that night. He woke to a sound in the house. He didn't open his eyes but tried to listen. It was footsteps behind him, leading to the door. The door creaked open. He opened his eyes and grabbed the pistol from the holster on his hip and turned and pointed the gun at the noise. It was CJ. The boy put his hands up and looked frightened at his father.

"CJ, my God," George said, lowering the gun. "What are you doing?"

"I just, I just had to pee," the boy said, tears starting to fall from his face that was scrunched up into a wet ball of wrinkles.

"Why are you going outside?"

"I just like to pee outside, pa. You do it sometimes. I'm sorry. I'm sorry for doing that." The boy sobbed loudly and George walked over to try to hug him but he ran back to his room.

He sat back in his chair and he watched the full moon outside. He dozed off and dreamed of a great storm. He was no longer in his house but in that cabin in the woods alone again. He was sitting up late at night looking out the window. He saw clouds and heard rumbling and rain flooded the glass panes until he could see no more. And then a giant wave crashed into the side of the house and swept him up and washed him away until he could no longer fight it or breathe and he simply let it take him. But he knew, while he was in it, that it had to be a dream. He had never dreamed so much in his life.

He woke the next morning in the reading chair to a slap across the face. He opened his eyes to Mary Beth standing over him. Her face was as red as a tomato.

"You pulled a gun on my son?" she yelled.

George sunk into the chair and he wished that he could die an instant death instead of deal with his angry wife.

"What do you have to say for yourself?"

"Nothing," he said.

"Nothing," she laughed.

She and the children were packed up and gone by mid-morning. He tried to hug them and she stood in between him and his children and told him to get it together. She drove off in the car to Wilmington to stay with her aging father. George sat in the chair all afternoon and cried. The walls of the house felt like they were smaller than they'd ever been before and he stood up and went outside and he grabbed an axe from the toolshed and went back in the house and he swung the axe at every wall in sight. He swung it until he was tired and the interior walls had huge gashes in them and you could see sheetrock everywhere and he grabbed the bottle of whiskey he had and took a pull from it and he laid down on the floor and the ceiling caved in on him in his vision and he fell asleep there on the carpet. He called Bill that night after he woke and asked if he could pick him up for work the next day, doing his best not to slur his words.

"You alright?" Bill asked.

He didn't answer in case he might start crying again. It was Good Friday.

34

BILL TRIED to get him to move in with his family for a while to get himself straightened up. He harassed George on what was going on for long enough that he had to tell him. George thought that the man was good and that there weren't many like him. He told him that.

"So, you'll stay with us? I can even drive you back home to pick up some clothes. Got an extra bedroom, mother-in-law stayed in it for a while after she had hip surgery. Might just smell a little like an old woman still."

"I can't, Bill," he said.

"Yes, you can."

"It's not safe."

"Well, hell, why don't you just sleep here? Surrounded by guns. I'll go get the mattress and bring it here for you. Might be the safest place in a fifty-mile radius."

"I can't do that."

"You won't tell me why?"

"No. I can't. I don't know that I have a good enough answer for it to matter."

"You're worrying me, buddy."

"No need, no need," George said, grabbing a rag and wiping off the barrel of a shotgun on the wall.

HE LEFT WORK EARLY. He'd heard about a tribe in North Carolina not too far down the road, a group called the Lumbee.

"You one of them Lumbee?" a man, a new customer, come in to get his rifle cleaned, had asked him a week earlier.

"What's that?" George asked.

"Lumbee, the tribe. Hell, I guess not if that's your response."

"Never heard of them."

"Not too far down the road. Head on down to Lumberton, see 'em yourself. So what are you then? If you ain't Lumbee."

George looked over at Bill, who seemed as if he was reading the room for tension. He grinned a little at him.

"I'm Choctaw, from Mississippi."

"Choctaw? That Indian? Imagine it has to be with the way it sounds. Sure ain't Irish," he said, chuckling.

"Yes, we're Indian. Grew up on a reservation."

"How'd you end up all the way in this little watering hole of a town then? Don't know many Indians traveling across the country without the rest of their tribe. And usually they're being made to."

"You could say I was made to."

The man cocked an eyebrow and his smile dissipated slowly.

"Mm. Well, maybe you ought to go meet some of your Lumbee brethren then, since you ain't yet. Good for a man to be around people like him, I believe."

George let him leave without any further disagreement. He rolled the new knowledge over in his head again and again until this day when he was so bogged down in his sorrow and misfortune that he had to do something. Maybe the man was right, maybe he needed to be around other people that looked like him.

What he found in Lumberton was what he'd hoped he wouldn't find. Poor people, ramshackle cottages, the eyes of hungry children, their ribcages more defined on their shirtless stomachs than their noses were on their destitute faces. A group of teenage boys played basketball on a makeshift hoop, stopping to watch him as he drove by. He came upon a man and his wife, of some uncertain age, wrinkles over frowns, sitting in chairs in their front lawn, watching the road. He stopped the truck in front of them and got out.

"What you want?" the woman asked. She wore a loose white dress, stains on the bottom where it dragged in the mud.

"I came here to, well, are y'all Lumbees?" George asked. He didn't know what he wanted.

"What does it look like?" the man asked. Their faces were darker brown than the Indians he'd grown up around.

"What are you?" the woman asked along with him.

"I'm Choctaw."

"Choctaw? No Choctaws in North Carolina that I know of. Have we heard of Choctaw before?" the man asked his wife.

"Not that I know of."

"Well, there's at least one around here," George said, attempting a grin. He hadn't felt so nervous around people in years. Like he was a child around adults with authority.

"You look mighty white," the man said.

"Got a little of that in me too."

"What you want?" the woman asked again.

"I guess I just came here to talk to another Indian. Haven't done that in so long. Since I left home."

"We ain't much good for talking," the man said. "And I don't have another chair to spare. But we got some biscuits in there from lunch. Go grab you one."

George felt as if he had to accept the offer or get back in his truck and leave, so he went inside their one-room home and took a biscuit from the cast iron pan on the stovetop. It was still warm, but when he bit into it, he found it dry. He choked it down regardless and quickly went back outside, trying to ignore the rest of the home and the quality of it.

"Thank you for the biscuit," he said, holding it, a hard puck, with the one bite taken out.

"It's dry," the woman said. "But you're welcome."

"You have questions you wanted to ask?" the man asked.

"I'm not sure, to be honest with you," George said. His mouth was so dry he found it hard to talk. "I think, hell, I think I just wanted to know if there really were more Indians around here."

"They tried to kill us off, but they didn't get us all," the woman said.

"Always find a few of us when you round a corner. Hard to root us out," the man said.

"What's your name?" the woman asked.

"George Norris."

"Norris?"

George nodded, trying to hide the shame on his face. It slid down his body from his neck to his stomach.

"That your family's name?"

"No, family didn't have a last name."

"Mm," the man grunted. "Take a seat on the grass if you don't have anywhere to be."

George obliged and sat on the best patch of grass he could find. The moisture soaked the seat of his pants immediately.

"Where is home?"

"Mississippi."

"How did you end up here? Can't imagine it's much better," the woman motioned around to the yard when she asked this. It was true. George thought for a minute and then he began to talk. He told them everything. They listened without speaking. He choked up at all the death and they let the silence of his stifled cries be still until he was ready to speak again. When he finished, he took another bite of the biscuit and swallowed it down with the tears that had run into his mouth.

"That's a long way to come," the woman said. Her eyes were kinder than they had been before.

"And it still don't matter how far you go. It follows you. Ain't that a shame," the man said, shaking his head.

"Are you a Christian?" the woman asked.

"I don't know. Most of the time, no. My mammy was. But it didn't do her any favors."

"It didn't do Jesus any earthly favors, Paul or Stephen or none of the rest of them either. That ain't the point."

"What is?" George asked.

She looked at him and then looked off into the yard. She closed her eyes and took a deep breath. A child shouted somewhere near them, a cry of playful joy.

"To have somewhere to go where you don't have to suffer no more," she said. "Where there ain't any more poor folk or dry biscuits or people pushing you away from where you're from or death or anything bad. Just you and God and all the angels."

"You don't think it was pushed on us? You don't see a problem with all this suffering we have to go through just to get to it?"

"Every time I hear about a new place, whether it be Mississippi or Germany, all I hear about is some new evil and all that it's doing to people over there. Same story. What we have to go through ain't so special. Bible says God so loved the world he gave us the way to Heaven, not the way to make it easier around here."

Another cry of joy sounded off, a basketball making a thud off a metal hoop.

"I wish it felt that way for me, but it just doesn't," George said.

"Well I'll pray that it does," the woman said. George felt something well up in him and he stood.

"I'll leave y'all be and head on home. It was good to meet you," George said.

"Be safe," the woman called out as he turned around.

He drove out of the city until he came to a place where he could pull off in a field. He put the truck in park and he let his head hang into his hands and he cried.

THAT NIGHT, alone at home once more, he picked up the phone and called his father-in-law. It rang and rang until it rang no more. He called again immediately. It rang on and on and still no one answered. He got up and paced about the room. He walked back over to the phone and spun the dial until he'd reached the right number again. It rang three times and a voice picked up.

"George, stop calling," the old man said.

"Put Mary Beth on the phone, please."

"I can't do that."

"She's my wife, put her on the phone. Let me talk to her."

"I can't do that, George. Please, hang up, put the bottle down, and go to bed, son."

"Put my goddamned wife on the phone right now. I don't give a shit who you are," George spat into the receiver. "She's my wife. I can talk to her when I damned please."

"I should've known, I should've seen it coming," the old man mumbled. "Just like your people, that damned drinking. I should have known."

"Fuck you, fuck you, fuck you," George yelled into the phone before slamming it down.

He passed out on the floor again, and awoke to the sound of an engine outside. Rumbling through the floorboards. His head pounded from liquor. He tried to tell himself to ignore it, that he was just going crazy. Getting older and more insane by the minute. He listened for it again and it wasn't there and so he kept his eyes shut. He thought that he should stop drinking. He heard voices and he kept his eyes shut. He thought that he'd throw the bottle away right then and there if the voices would go away. He heard footsteps on his porch and he started to cry. He wondered if his mind was fully gone, after all this time. If this would be what did him in. He heard the door handle jiggle, and he kept his eyes shut.

"GO AWAY," he screamed, his hands over his ears.

A great bang. He opened his eyes. He shot up from the floor and turned around. A hole in the door where the doorknob once attached looked back at him.

35

His face was still dripping wet as he walked. The air oppressed him, taunting him with every failed take at breathing again. He heard the sound and he couldn't believe it. It called out across the sky so loud that the birds flew off from their resting perches and the tree branches shook with them as if the oaks and cypresses of old were afraid of the animal too. It called out over and over again, the same refrain that he'd known in life and in dream so well that he did not have to place it in his mind any longer. It was like the warm smell of a long-time lover or the voice of a friend.

The mountain lion sang to him, beckoning out danger into the world. He followed the sound step after step.

"Come and kill me," he shouted out to it. The words, hampered by the spasms in his chest, came out in the voice of a ghost or a whisper or as if from another person, far below him.

36

THE DOOR WAS KICKED OPEN and he wanted to shut his eyes again. He wanted to pray that God would wake him up. That this was just another one of his dreams and that big cat would walk through the door then and tear him to bits and eat his liver. That that mountain lion would call out his name in the voice of someone he loved and then it would bury him alive in the back yard before he could wake up.

When the door swung in, he did not see a cat or his wife but saw Nolan and the men he'd been with.

"Well looky here," Nolan proclaimed, smiling from ear to ear and holding the same shotgun George had sold him. Behind him, the other men were carrying theirs as well.

"What the hell is going on?" George shouted.

"You thought I was just gonna go away? Is that what you thought?"

"What are you doing in my house?"

"I told you not to play dumb at the store, weeks ago. Here you are still playing dumb. George Norris," he said this and laughed. "George fuckin' Norris. Norris. Norris, for god's sake. I heard you was still parading around with that name. Ain't that something. We couldn't beat it out of you all those years ago. Hell, we couldn't even bleed it out of you."

"Get out of my house," George said. He started to reach for the pistol on his hip and Nolan raised the shotgun barrel at him.

"Whoa there, buddy, let's not do anything rash just yet. Mike, go over there and take that gun off our friend George's hip, why don't you?"

Once he was disarmed, the man named Michael grabbed him by the arms and pinned them behind his back and George did not fight or try to get free. Then, as if he were thrown back into the past via a time machine from a bad film, he watched Nolan set his gun on his hardwood floor, the floor that he owned, and take careful steps across that floor and cock his fist back, the same fist that he'd met too many times in one afternoon, and punch him in the gut. He bowled over in pain and Michael picked him back up. Nolan punched him in the stomach and he wanted to fall to his knees but Michael held him up. Nolan picked his gun back up and turned it around and shoved the butt end of it into George's chest and they finally let him fall to the floor where he coughed and coughed and couldn't catch his breath. As he sat there on his knees, wheezing, Nolan got down to ground level with him.

"What do you think is going to happen next?" he whispered.

"Just kill me," George said. The man laughed at him when he said this.

"Just kill you. That what you want?" He stood up over George.

"Just fucking kill me."

"Y'all hear that boys? Just kill him, he said."

They all laughed and George knew then that he was not dealing with a single person of good character who might change his mind and then he really did wish that he could die right then, that his heart would stop and he would just fall over on the floor and not feel any pain and just be gone from this world that had treated him like a dog, like a mangy, good for nothing dog. Michael picked him up then and was handed some rope and they tied his hands together and drug him out onto the front yard and into the truck. It was the one he had seen a few nights before.

"Where's your family, George?" Nolan asked as they pulled him, his knees beating into the soft dirt.

"They're gone."

"Your buddy Bill said you had a family. Said you was a good family man. I had to keep a straight face while he said this. I thought to myself, a family man? The man who killed my cousin as dead as a man can be? With a fucking knife? A family man?"

"I told you they're gone."

"What if I don't believe you?"

"Don't worry about my family."

"I'll worry about whoever the fuck I want to worry about, you injun piece of shit," he spat. "Just be glad they aren't here too. All carrying around a family name that don't mean nothing to them. They haven't earned it either. I swear, the idea that a family of half-breeds could go around with a white name just offends me to my heart. Listen at me getting poetic," he laughed. "I ought to write about this, write me a book. The death of a mongrel, I'd call it. I think I'm pretty good at it, now that I think about it. I could write all about saving the world with the killing of a few choice folks. Ain't that right? Just like that book by that senator from down where you come from. Randall Knight is his name. Yessir. Maybe I could get him to write the introduction. Let me stop doing all this talking."

Nolan kicked him once more before they put him in the truck.

"I had to make some calls. Turns out you had a pretty rough time in the hospital back then, huh?"

"You can kill me or you can let me go."

"Hell, I know that."

"Pick one."

"How far did you run, George?" he asked as they threw him in the truck bed. "All the way up to North Carolina from Jackson, Mississippi. Or even further, you probably grew up on one of them reservations, they call them, huh? Injun land. Ain't that a story. Came all that way, hundreds of miles, and death followed you. And his name was Nolan. Shit luck, buddy. Shit luck."

THEY DROVE OFF to the river where he was meant to die. He laid there, the truck flying so fast on dirt roads and sharp turns that he was thrown back and forth across the bed. He tried to watch the stars as he laid there, but with a turn too sharp, he flew against the side of the truck and his head hit the wheel well and he was knocked unconscious. He woke to the truck stopped and them standing him up under a tree.

"We should've got a cross," one of them said, laughing a little.

"He ain't no damn Indian Jesus," Nolan growled back.

They stabbed him. They beat him. They talked uglier to him than anyone ever had.

"I'm sorry," George whispered to Nolan in their final moments together, just before they pulled away. The others were in the truck. One shouted that they needed to get going, the moon was too bright and somebody might catch them.

"You're sorry?" Nolan asked, looking him in the eyes, his voice breaking a little. "Fuck you." He spat in George's face and got in the driver's seat of the truck.

They left him to die.

37

THE CAT CRIED BACK TO HIM, a snarl across the sky that got closer with each step George took.

"Don't you hear me? Come and kill me," he cried.

The lion returned screams to his plea.

"Fuck you, you beast," he shouted. "You should've killed me. You should've just killed me out in those woods when you had the chance. You could've saved me from a world of torture. Is that what you wanted? For me to be tortured?"

The scream that called out to him in reply said that the choice was never either of theirs and he knew it and it said this in a voice that he knew well but couldn't place and it was just in front of his face, only a few steps away in the darkness. He saw a bush there and he pushed his way through it. He came out the other side tumbling onto the ground, glimpses of yellow painted lines and moonlit trees in between blinks. Under his head was something harder, like asphalt. The panther no longer cried out to him. He looked to his left and far off he saw a light coming towards him and he reached out to it. He wheezed and his lungs hurt one last time, clawing at his ribcage for oxygen, before subsiding into emptiness.

He felt himself begin to lift off the ground and he closed his eyes. For a moment, time came before him like an object that he could hold in his hand and inspect from all angles. He grabbed onto it and looked. He saw death, so much death. He saw breaths drawn in between pains and pangs and the pressing of lips together. He saw beautiful people. He saw vile, ugly-hearted people. He saw so many ugly hearts. He saw Mary Beth. He saw how close she was and how far away too. He saw that there were miles in between them but there had always been something else there too, inside of him.

He lifted and lifted, and he thought he heard a voice above him say something, exclaim something, and the voice was happy. He opened his eyes and he saw that he was flying above the world.

"What do you see?" a voice asked him, from both inside and out.

He saw the sun beginning to ascend over the horizon, just barely peaking out from behind trees miles away.

He saw the light on the road become two and as it continued its approach he saw that it was a car.

He saw his body on the ground. He saw the car stop beside him. He tried to yell out to the car but he no longer had a voice.

He saw a man get out of the car. He saw the top of his head, balding. He saw the man lean down over him and touch him. He could feel the touch in his body as he continued to rise over the land and he knew then that it was the old man who lived out there, somewhere out there in the woods, who could no longer clean his own gun, and he tried to tell the man to leave him be but he could not speak still and the man slowly, with great effort, lifted his body and placed him in the car and drove away.

But he did not descend into the car. He rose and rose until he was up so high that the wind roared around his ears. He saw Wilmington in the distance. He thought, if he could just fly a little closer, that he might see Mary Beth and Chito Jack and Nora and he wanted to tell them that they'd loved him more than he deserved.

He saw the whole of humanity, on the ground of a giant spinning ball. Running and lying down. Sitting and standing. Loving and hating, all the same.

He saw that he was one of them and all of them. He saw that he was what the world creates and that his world was what he had created all the same. He saw that he had nowhere else to go. He saw that no one chased him any longer. He saw that there were no lions up there. He saw that there was no pain. He saw that evil had no more memory of him.

He took in a deep breath. His chest filled with every bit of air that the world had to offer. He saw that there were no walls, too. He saw his mammy, her arms out, carrying him upward, there in front of him and everywhere around him in every piece of the sky.

He could almost laugh. He saw it then. One big great Ferris wheel. That's all it was. He wished everybody could see that.

"Is this what it feels like?" he asked the voice. The reply rang inside of him. He smiled.

Acknowledgements

Thank you to Alan Good and Malarkey Books, for taking a chance on this novel—literally, having not even finished reading it before sending the offer letter. I cried some big, wet tears when reading that and my dog had no clue what was going on.

To my writing pals—thank you for sticking it out with me. Richard Liese turned this from a colossal mess parading around as a book into a novel with a through line. To my writing group crew—Layne, Kassie, Trish, Elissa, Shannon— you read a lot of stories that were sometimes bad, decent at best, and you made me feel like I was a real writer when I disagreed—for all of that, I am grateful.

To my family—thank you for encouraging me to pursue art in whatever form I pleased and for pushing me to stick with it over and over again.

To Grace—thank you for letting me go manic for a while to get this done. This whole thing is impossible without you. You can read it now.

Thank you to the Choctaw Nation, for its unbelievably comprehensive language and historical resources. The book would have been impossible without these. I sought to tell an authentic story— if that is possible with fiction—and to do no harm along the way. I hope I have accomplished this.

Joshua Trent Brown is from a little North Carolina town you've never heard of. This is his first novel. He hopes you enjoyed it.